SECOND WORLD WAR SANDWICH

The son of a respected judge and the youngest of three children, Digonta Bordoloi grew up moving around Northeast India. This mobile, multicultural upbringing made him socially adaptable and fluent in six languages before the age of fifteen. As a young man, Digonta moved to Mumbai where he worked as a copywriter in advertising. Once the gloss of corporate life wore off, he set sail for Africa, spending time in Uganda, then Swaziland and Tanzania, reconnecting with a slower pace of life and wrote his first novel, *Slow...* It was while on a safari in a game park in Africa that he met the love of his life. Today, he and his wife, Susie, call India and Australia home.

SECOND WORLD WAR SANDWICH

DIGONTA BORDOLOI

PAN

First published 2021 by Pan
an imprint of Pan Macmillan Publishing India Private Limited
707, Kailash Building,
26 K. G. Marg, New Delhi – 110 001
www.panmacmillan.co.in

Pan Macmillan, 6 Briset St, Farringdon, London EC1M 5NR
Associated companies throughout the world
www.panmacmillan.com

ISBN 978-93-89109-52-8

1 3 5 7 9 8 6 4 2

Typeset in Dante MT Std by R. Ajith Kumar, New Delhi
Printed and bound in India by Replika Press Pvt. Ltd.

To

Lakshmi Dhar Bardalaye (1934–2019),

my Dauta (father), who never raised his voice or hand on me...

IN THE MIDDLE...

...RAAN'S HANDS SHOOK UNCONTROLLABLY AS HE MANAGED TO insert one bullet out of every three into the 303 magazine. Dropped bullets piled up on the ground, but there was no time to pick them up. Only reload and shoot. He was no soldier; he was a cook. Good at slotting firewood into a hearth, not bullets into a chamber. From the constant kick of the 303 rifle, Raan's shoulder threatened to come off its hinge. He longed for the sun to come out and the onslaught to end.

Like harsh waves lashing at the sandy shores of the garrison's defence, the Japanese were relentless. With defences eroding, wherever the cook-turned-soldier looked, they were closing in. The only thing protecting the scantily clad garrison was its advantageous position. Located on top of a mountain range, hills laid bare, ploughed clean by mortars and cannons, the garrison defenders easily spotted the Japanese approach. The Japanese infantry could see them too. Yet the defenders were not easy targets to pick from below. Entrenched in the bunkers, the garrison defenders were like turtles. They could snap at the invading Japanese and quickly withdraw into their shells.

The Japs charged and fired at vague targets that were scattered around. Though the Japanese were numerous, it was hard to mount an attack with no cover to hide or firm ground to step on. To make matters worst, their supply lines to Burma were cut, so they were left with very little food and limited ammunition. Their numbers were big, but they were weak with hunger and the repeated march up the tough terrain was exhausting for their body and spirit. With daylight the Japanese surge halted. Instead, they staggered down the steep incline towards their holding positions. To make sure they were retreating, the garrison defenders fired a few rounds in their general direction and the bullets found their mark amidst the plentiful targets. The Japanese advantage was in their numbers. Their disadvantage was also in their numbers...

PROLOGUE

ANGSEN'S ONLY MEMORY OF HIS GRANDFATHER WAS OF AN OLD shrivelled man who had a smile that transformed him into a child. That changed the day he received a phone call.

Angsen lived in Kohima, a hill station that grew along with him. When he was a child, Kohima was a small town of just forty thousand people. Now he was thirty-three and pot-bellied, and Kohima was a city exploding with half a million inhabitants; roads jammed with cars and hills packed with houses. His grandfather's village, Poilung, was a day's drive from Kohima and miles away from any 'development'.

Angsen's grandfather was a devout Nature worshipper, a man from the past. His parents were devout Christians from this age. They had no common ground. The only bridge between his grandfather and parents was his grandmother. When he was a child, mostly because of her, his parents used to make their annual trips to Poilung. As he grew older, first studies and then responsibilities towards his own parents, who were also advancing in age, never allowed him to travel the distance from Kohima to Poilung.

For over a decade, Angsen had been teaching the history of India and the world to his students at the Kohima Arts College. Yet, he had never realized that within a day's drive, a rich history lay hidden from him. So that day, during a break between classes, while he was reading the dark news from a glossy newspaper, he received the phone call in the lecturer's common room. A frail voice greeted him. It took a while for the cobwebs in his memory to clear and recognize his grandfather's voice – "Angsen, you have to meet me. I don't have much time left, child. I hear you teach about the past. Then you should also know our past. Come, son, come and see me."

Old borrowed apprehension made him wary. Yet his instinct knew better, "Okay, Grandpa, I will come this weekend." As he replaced the receiver, suddenly a heavy weight of guilt lifted. He knew he had made the right decision.

For twenty-one years, that smile had been waiting to greet Angsen. That smile which had bid a twelve-year-old boy goodbye. Bedridden, when Angsen arrived, his grandfather used his twiggy hands to create some space for him on the rickety bed. The bamboo walls of the hut were greased black from smoke. It would have been a very gloomy room had it not been for the evening sunlight piercing in streaks through the bamboo weavings. The bare few objects in the room were old artefacts fit for a museum. It was a room as ancient as the occupant lying there on the bed. He sat beside his grandfather as gently as he could. The ancient man held his grandson's arm and propped himself up on his elbow to examine the years in the young man's face. His frail, unsure fingers touched his grandson's sparse stubble as he shook his head in disbelief. Without words, he sighed and pointed to the bottom of the bed where Angsen found and pulled into the scattered sunlight, a rusty locked trunk.

Removing a multicoloured bead necklace made of

semiprecious stones from under his withered shirt, the old man took his grandson's hand and placed the string in his open palm. It held a single key. With a squeaking click the trunk opened to unlock a past he had shut away for seventy years. The first object that struck Angsen was a fading black-and-white photograph. It pictured a young Konyak man – a tribal warrior from one of the sixteen Naga clans, famed as headhunters. Along with the Konyak youth, an assembly of white men in shabby army uniforms stood in front of an M3 tank. All looked very pleased with themselves. On closer examination Angsen recognized the young Konyak as his grandfather. The tribal tattoos marking the face of the youth now hung on his grandfather like a wrinkled Salvador Dali painting.

Taking the photograph from Angsen, the old man looked intently, giving out a deep sigh. After all these years, suddenly propelled back into the thick of it. Surrounded by a sea of bullets, shrapnel flying around, ear-splitting explosions, blood-curdling cries. In his hand, a razor-sharp *dao*, his whole body bloodied, a string of gut dangling from the tip of his spear…

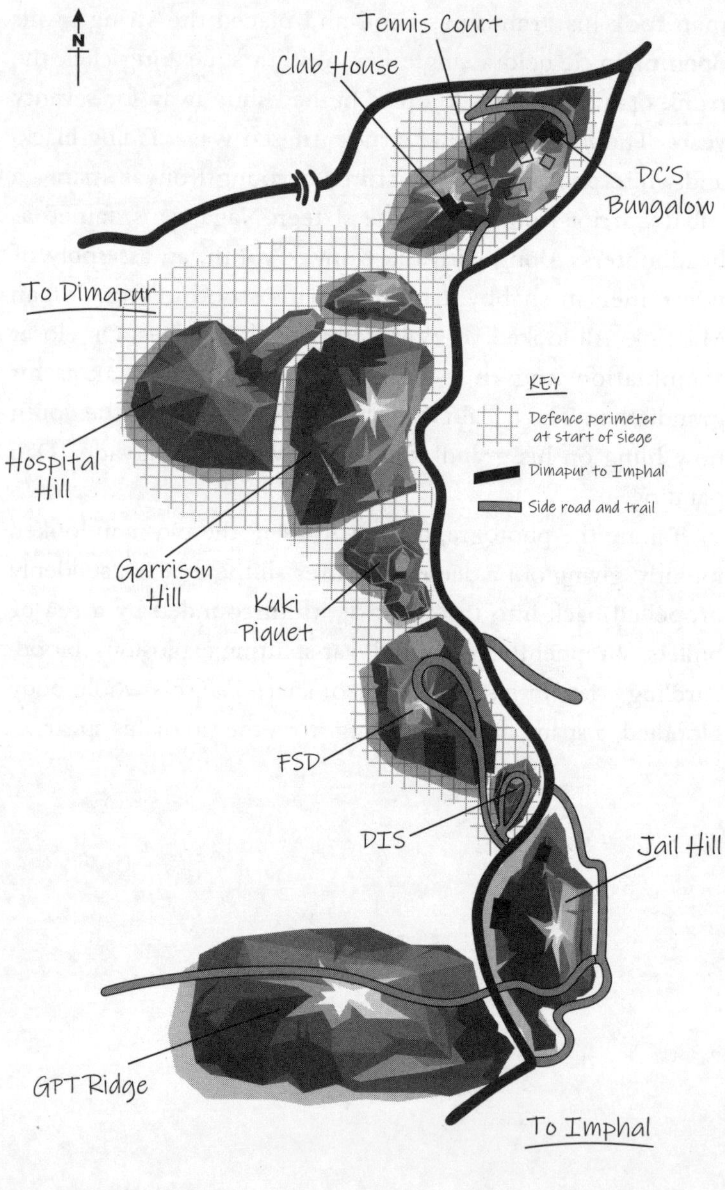
N
Tennis Court
Club House
DC'S Bungalow
To Dimapur
KEY
Defence perimeter at start of siege
Dimapur to Imphal
Side road and trail
Hospital Hill
Garrison Hill
Kuki Piquet
FSD
DIS
Jail Hill
GPT Ridge
To Imphal

ONE

THE LETHARGIC SUN, NEITHER ASLEEP NOR FULLY AWAKE, BEGAN sending weak rays, announcing its arrival to a portion of black earth that had turned grey. The rats seemed nervous inside their burrows. They weren't wary of the owls; in fact the owls themselves, sunbirds, jungle fowls, and squirrels, all looked on anxiously from their holes and thickets, kept awake through the night by unusual sounds and cries.

In the distance, marching footsteps sent ripples over the still, eerie morning. Breaking through the morning's gown of haze, Captain Timothy Hastings lead his section of men up the Aradura Spur. Where they trod, the face of the mountain was still under the spell of the night spirits, untouched by the sun.

The monsoon had come early that year, and was currently at its peak. Every tree, shrub, vine on the hill, loomed healthy, strong and full of vigour. With every step, the greenery clasped at Captain Hastings and his men, impeding their march. Thorns grabbed at their uniforms and pricked their skin. Vines threatened to trip them up, sending them hurtling down the mountain. At the ground level, a weeklong relentless downpour had added a thick layer of slime to the grasses, rocks and tree roots weaving in and out of the vertical landscape. On the slanting, slippery surfaces the hard leather soles of the soldiers' boots acted like steel blades on ice. In contrast, wherever the earth was exposed it swallowed their feet whole, much like stepping into a bucket of glue.

Suddenly a shot rang out. Captain Hastings, or Tom, as his men and fellow officers knew him, was a lanky man with long unwieldy limbs who found it difficult to duck. Diving flat onto the incline, Tom kept his face down for a few seconds, then turned around to see his *subedar,* the chief native officer of Tom's Indian men, Chetri, climbing up towards him. His second in command, *Subedar* Chetri, was plump and stout. In Chetri's village, such corpulence was considered a sign of prosperity, displaying to all that he ate well. Chetri's short, jet-black hair contrasted Tom's long flowing blond hair (as long as army discipline would allow), accompanied by a moustachio whose ends he lovingly twirled upwards. An addition he made after meeting the Maharaja of Koochbihar at a tea estate party. Chetri, on the other hand, had no facial hair worth shaving daily. Yet what he lacked in manly fuzz, he made up with courage. Being a Gorkha, courage was in his genes. Not so much could be said for Tom, whose manliness was perhaps most exemplified in his facial hair.

Scrambling to regain his foothold, Tom put all four appendages to work. Chetri offered him a hand.

"Sorry, *Saahab,* it was one of my men who mistakenly let off a shot."

"What?"

"*Saahab*, I just recruited him last night. He has only ever fired a shotgun. Didn't know how to put the safety lock on the rifle."

"What?!" Tom exclaimed in muffled surprise.

"What to do, *Saahab*? Last night you ordered me to have

twelve men ready for this raid. We only had five men, so I picked six more, who looked brave enough and said they had previously fired a gun."

"His mistake could cost us very dearly, you know that, Chetri. The enemy will know we are coming. What was the use of waking up so early?"

Shaking his blond locks, Tom resumed the climb.

It was the morning of the 3rd of April 1944 when Captain Tom and his men went up the Aradura Mountain. This story is from a time when the British had been the rulers of India for 118 years. Not a long period when you compare the British rule to the thousands of years for which this ancient Indian civilization had already been around. But, during those 118 years, four generations of Indians had grown up under the British rule. A third of that population accepted being ruled by the British as their destiny. Another third opposed it. The rest didn't know or care who ruled over them as long as the rulers didn't directly interfere in their day-to-day lives. To that latter group of Indians, belonged Angsen's Konyak Naga grandparents.

It would be three more years before India became free from the shackles of the British empire. Those very shackles had pulled India headlong into the Second World War – a war which India had otherwise no business to be part of. In 1942, Britain lost Burma to the Imperial Japanese forces. In defeat, the British General Slim's army, routed in Burma, crossed over the Chindwin River into India. From then on it was only a matter of time until either the British returned to claim lost territory or the Japanese sought again to claim more British territory. By

1943 there were confirmed reports that Japan was strengthening its army in Burma for an onward assault into India.

By the beginning of 1944 there were scattered rumours of Japanese advances from Burma into India through the far eastern borders of the Northeast of India, which then was the undivided state of Assam. But no one imagined the sleepy little garrison town of Kohima would be a target of the Japanese. Dimapur, a town to the northwest of Kohima, had a railhead and an airfield and seemed like a more worthwhile target. Before the posting of the army garrison, Kohima's claim to importance was its District Commissioner sporting the only motorized vehicle in town. The Commissioner loved the attention his car drew from the awestruck locals. This amazement, however, was broken with the arrival of the army vehicles. Instead of just one car to stare at, the local Nagas now looked on with awe at the army trucks and jeeps of the garrison.

By the end of March 1944, villagers travelling from afar into town to barter or sell their wares spread rumours about an approaching Japanese army. How big these invading forces were, was a question disputed among the ranks, officers and departments of the British Indian Army. For Angsen's grandparents and other fellow Nagas, the war didn't matter so much, as long as both foreign warring sides wrapped it up quickly and left them to carry on life as before.

Monsoon was early that year in Kohima, and so were the Japanese. Normal logistical calculations by the British intelligence suggested that the Japanese would take another month or a couple of weeks at the least to reach Kohima. An army, fuelled not by strong logistical support, but by raw determination arrived in Kohima long before British intelligence predictions. The evening prior to Tom leading his company on the patrol, Naga trackers had spotted a section of enemy soldiers taking position on a hill. They reported their findings to the Garrison headquarters and Tom was ordered to go on a scouting mission to investigate.

A Naga tracker led the way, with Tom and his troops scrambling behind, trying to keep up. Suddenly the tracker's gaze turned sharply towards his right and pointed to some bushes. In the still murky grey of morning, Tom saw only a shadow. Quickening his pace, Chetri moved past Tom towards the tracker and raised his rifle to take aim. But the shadow moved so quickly, so quietly, that before he could bolt a bullet into the chamber of his 303, the form vanished from the sights of his gun. Chetri lowered his gun and turned towards the tracker.

"Angami, *ke asile*?"

"*Najene* ho."

Unable to follow the conversation, Tom enquired, "Did you ask him what it was?"

"Yes, *Saahab*. But he doesn't know."

"Was it an animal?"

"Looked like it, *Saahab*."

"Well, we are not here to hunt animals." Tom whispered his stern reproach. "We must not fire another bullet until we are at the enemy position. Is that understood?"

"Yes, *Saahab*." Chetri reluctantly dangled his rifle back over his shoulder.

With every metre they hauled themselves up the unrelenting mountain, the six Gorkhas, Chetri and his five regular men, already pumped with adrenalin, were infused with more as the prospect of their Japanese encounter approached. They had heard about the fierce fighting qualities of the Japanese soldiers. Yet it was still hearsay without proof. They were thrilled that soon they would be able to put the rumours to test. Tom, on the other hand, left breathless by the climb was too exhausted to think of anything else. He was glad that Chetri and his regular soldiers overtook him the moment their guide indicated that they had almost reached their target. It was Gurkha protocol to never let the Captain comc in harm's way. Hence they formed a six-man wall in front of him.

Tom ordered the other six fresh soldiers in Chetri's section to cover the flanks. Those six were happy to be behind everyone else. Now that the prospect of firing a gun at another human seemed a reality, their collective thought was to question why they volunteered to be soldiers. The hands of two of those six men were accustomed to carrying files inside the garrison's administrative office. Another's hands were used to steering the wheel of a car. Another was used to wielding shoe polishes and brushes to shine the garrison officers' shoes. The hands of the remaining two soldiers, till the day before, had brandished whips to keep the garrison's beasts of burden in line.

Up above the thirteen men, behind the thicket, now well out of view, a form moved straight up the hill; effortlessly balanced on two legs. As it sensed the presence of life beyond the wild steamy mountain vegetation, it looked up and at once bent on all fours, merging with the thick undergrowth, moving quietly and as efficiently as a serpent gliding through luscious green grass. Through the rusty light of the morning sun, on the crest of the mountain the beast's eyes made out the unmistakable signs of a cave. It was too uniform to be natural. Silently, it climbed towards the cave, drowned in the undergrowth, and as it reached the clearing in front, slid to a side.

Inside the man-made bunker, ten Japanese soldiers lay in wait, ready for Tom and his men. Their eyes and gun barrels were fixed on the hill's incline rising to greet them. As expected, the misfired 303 bullet had alerted them to the enemy's approach. And yet none of them had any inkling of the form blending into the darkness of the bunker, as silent as a trailing shadow.

Soon Angami, the Naga tracker in Tom's patrol party, pointed their attention towards the peak of the mountain, a spot of fresh brown amid the green and grey – the unmistakable sign of a freshly dug bunker. His job done, Angami turned back, dissolving into the bushes. Expert guides were rare. He was much more valuable to guide soldiers through these unseen paths than join the fight and become a casualty of war. Chetri looked towards Tom who now gave the signal to break up. The six Gorkhas, the mountain lions of Tom's company, steadily climbed towards their target. Chetri was to encircle the enemy bunker along with his five men; two of them, along with him, would approach the trench from the right, the remaining three from the left. Tom and the six novice soldiers took positions to give the Gorkhas covering fire.

They fanned out and closed the distance; through the leafy vegetation Chetri spotted the ribbed barrel of a Type 96 light machine gun protruding like an arrow, marking the enemy's position amidst the wilderness. Instinctively ducking under the carpet of green, Chetri gestured to his men to do the same. Expecting bullets to zip over them like buzzing bees, Chetri and his men lay flat; anxious index fingers wrapped tightly around 303 rifle triggers. Consequence of reprisal and discipline prevented their index fingers from squeezing the triggers. The Gorkhas were so still that not a leaf moved unnecessarily because of their presence.

So as to avoid sounds reaching the Japanese ears, Chetri shifted his rifle to his right and kept his left hand free to communicate with his men through gestures. He kept his head to the ground and counted till ten. Once he was sure the Japanese intruders weren't aware of their presence, he gave the order to move. At the signal of their *subedar,* the five Gorkhas sprung to their feet, bodies bent low, and made their way up, trapping the bunker from both sides.

Tom ordered the remaining six soldiers to ready their rifles and checked his own Sten gun to provide whatever covering fire they could. Tom noticed a soldier didn't have his rifle on the ready. It was the same soldier who had earlier in the climb mistakenly fired his gun. It was still strung to his back. Tom gestured to him to take the rifle on to his hands and take aim. The soldier shook his head in refusal. Tom waved him over. The soldier came on all fours.

"What's the matter, soldier?" Tom whispered.

"Nothing, *Saahab.*"

"Then why don't you have your rifle ready?"

"But *Saahab*, *Subedarji* told me not to touch my gun."

"You fool!" Tom burst out, then immediately lowered his head and voice, "That was for then. Now you listen to me, Soldier."

The soldier returned to his position, rifle in hand, confusion in his head.

Tom gestured all six to inch forward with him. The moment he spotted the barrel of the enemy machine gun, he raised his arm for the freshers to stop. To say the least, the six with him, all from the plains of the heartland of India were no mountain lions; neither cats to move silently towards the enemy position. He didn't want the hard work of his Gorkhas, who had moved so stealthily, to go to waste. From his lopsided position, Tom aimed his Sten gun at the barrel of the Type 96 light machine gun. He reckoned, if nothing else, at least he could try and jitter the accuracy of the machine gun by hitting it with a few bursts from his semi-automatic. Under normal circumstances he wouldn't have believed his marksmanship capabilities to be that accurate. But now, with six truly novice soldiers at his disposal, desperate times called for desperate beliefs.

Through unblinking eyes he kept the sights of his gun fixed on the thin cylindrical target. As if by design, a lime green caterpillar floated down on a silky thread and hung mid-air, right between the sights of Tom's gun and his target. Gently, it twitched and curved, as if pole-dancing for the Captain. Irritated by the performance, Tom looked beyond the caterpillar to spot the three Gorkhas creeping towards the mouth of the bunker. Anticipating action at any moment, his grip tightened instinctively. With the Gorkhas just few feet from the protruding barrel of the Japanese machine gun, Tom's index finger rested gingerly on the Sten's trigger, while his thumb swiped the sweat mounting his brow.

Next, Chetri and his two men came into view, circling in from the left, moving in behind the first three, straining their necks to peep in. Then, to Tom's horror, the front line stood up right in line of the Japanese machine gun. Gesturing towards Chetri, they rushed into the bunker. Following suit, Chetri and his two men crawled up to the entrance. Chetri dove in, while the last two Gorkha soldiers stood up and strolled into the bunker as if stepping into a bar for some beer.

Unable to figure out what was going on, Tom glanced back at the novice soldiers. All six responded to the Captain with equally perplexed looks. Moments later, Chetri poked his head out and shouted, "*Saahab*, all Japanese dead!"

TWO

CAUTIOUSLY TOM CLIMBED UP TOWARDS THE BUNKER, FOLLOWED by the six novices. Coming face to face with the barrel of the machine gun, his instinct was to swerve away. But what he saw turned his reaction from fear to disgust. Bent over the machine gun was a Japanese soldier's corpse, its head missing. As Tom entered the cave-like bunker where the Japanese had hid, he was suddenly a boy of six, climbing the stairs of the *Bhairavi* Temple, the sound of a brass bell holding him in calming trance.

A city boy, freshly arrived from London, his father had taken him to the temple in the town of Tezpur, Assam. It was the day of Kali *puja* that his father had chosen to acquaint Tom with a different culture of India – a day when peace and violence coexisted. As he walked up the stairs of the temple, a thick red stream flowed down from the temple under his feet. It had a metallic smell and stuck to the leather soles of his shoes. As he climbed higher, the red flow increased, became fresher, warmer, more fluid. When the platform of the temple finally came into view, what he saw almost made him fall backwards.

Lying in a heap in the temple courtyard were the severed heads of five buffalos, ten goats (in shock, Tom counted each one), and innumerable ducks and pigeons. So many birds had been killed that the heap of sacrifices looked like a small hillock – alive and dead at the same time, the heap of headless bodies convulsed under rivulets of blood. A wooden block placed in the middle of the temple courtyard was the sacrificial alter. The size of the wooden block reminded Tom of a fully-grown ox sitting in the middle of a road, a scene he had witnessed often in the streets since his arrival in India. An eleventh freshly sacrificed buck lay on its back next to the log, legs still kicking the air as if to gallop away. Resting peacefully next to one end of the thick sacrificial blade on the wooden block was the buck's head. The other end of the sword was grasped in the thick veined hands of the priest, a well-rounded dark man, with eyes as bloodshot as the floor. A vermilion *tilak* on his forehead looked like blood. From where he stood Tom reckoned that the sacrificial sword was a foot taller than his six-year-old height. As his eyes moved back to the freshly severed body, blood oozing from the cleanly sliced neck, it suddenly truly dawned on Tom that the red substance he stood on was not paint, it was blood.

At the time, that extreme exposer so shocked Tom that he was bedridden for a week with high fever, aggravated by nightmares of spurting blood from severed necks, and the looming bloodshot eyes of the priest.

That sight struck his heart again that very moment he stepped into the Japanese bunker. Momentarily swept back to the past and caught off guard, an involuntary convulsion rose in Tom's guts. In front of him, different shapes, some animate, some abstract, emerged from the crude walls of the cave-like bunker. Blood randomly painted the mud walls, and a thick layer carpeted the floor. In a seeming lake floated nine headless corpses. Only their uniforms told Tom that they were his former enemy. Only his sense of army discipline helped him to control his convulsion and his previous evening's dinner stayed within.

He had known that sooner or later he would have to see and face death. But nothing could have prepared him to see such wholesale death, so brutal a massacre, so soon. Human bodies, so brutally butchered reduced him to a little boy, witnessing another large-scale massacre. In the temple it was animals, in the cave in front of him it was human beings.

Now, decades later, Tom was no longer that little boy. Playing hockey for the Doon School team in Dehradun, then for the Christ Church College team in Oxford, his frame had elongated and strengthened. His skin was no longer pale white but golden brown, toasted by the tropical sun in the foothills of the Himalayas. After spending his academic life in the best of institutions, amongst some of the finest minds, Tom ended up working as the manager of Tamulguri Tea Estate, in a far-flung corner of India.

"Tom, are we expecting a good production this year?" asked the visiting general manager from Calcutta.

"Yes, Henry, rains have been good since March, so I think we're up for a bumper second flush."

"Are the labourers supplying enough cow dung?"

"Yes, Henry. Your idea to give them low-interest loans to buy livestock was a stroke of brilliance. Now we're getting enough manure for the plants locally."

Hearing one of his ideas was working, the General Manager beamed. "So the quality of the dung is good?"

"Yes," Tom replied, wincing inside. He wondered if his boss

had come all the way from Calcutta, travelling for six days by train, boat and horse to take stock of the dung for the plants. After a few years as the manager, Tom was finding his work and life in the tea estate somewhat mundane.

When war broke out in Europe he felt he should join the army out of patriotism. Yet another part of him had wanted to join to add more excitement to life. The routine of tea garden existence had become a little grinding – the morning garden visit, the late morning factory visit, noon lunch and siesta break, and then in the afternoon repeat the visits to the plantation and factory. The only break from this routine was a weekly stopover at the Tea Club on Friday evenings, where all the neighbourhood managers and their wives came together. Even there, however, the conversations revolved around tea, albeit over untold glasses of wine and spirits.

His wife, Sandra, didn't particularly enjoy going to those gatherings. Yet being the manager's wife, she had to make her appearance. And she did play her part pretty well. No one ever guessed how much she actually hated it. At the club they were the perfect couple. At home Tom and Sandra's relationship had, however, become quite mechanical. Both lived in their corners of the house, meeting only at the dining table and in bed at night. Sandra had a broad perspective that yearned to explore life beyond the estate. She subscribed to books and magazines from around the world. Tom too subscribed to different journals and books, but all were related to tea and factory equipment. Their dinner table and bedtime conversations never veered far beyond their tea-growing life. In bed, Tom always fell asleep moments after a goodnight kiss. Initially, during their courtship years, Sandra had respected Tom because of his passionate dedication to his job. But within a few years, his work had actually caused a rift. So much so that the bedtime kisses were their only physical contact. By the time Sandra stirred awake in the morning, Tom was up and about, inspecting the work of his labourers.

He would have liked her to be more involved with his work. Show more enthusiasm for the lifestyle they led. Instead Sandra grew aloof, lost in her own world once she realized there was no hope of pulling her husband into an alternate world besides his tea plants and brews. To her husband's annoyance, Sandra was also very much involved with the labourers, spending her days with the cooks, the gardeners and other assistants around the house. Sandra took interest in the tea-estate labourers, photographing them, and learning about their lives. When she was with Tom and managers from the neighbouring gardens came visiting, Sandra acted the part of the perfect wife. Sandra thought she had married the wild man from the East, but Tom lived in the wilderness without a wild heart. If they paid him well he would have been as happy pushing files sitting in the Williamson Magor head office at 4 Mangoe Lane, Calcutta.

Living the lavish life of a tea planter in Assam, it took Tom a while before he finally had to show his patriotism towards his birth country, England. Four years after the British prime minister, Neville Chamberlain, declared war on Germany, Tom volunteered to join the war effort. He was chosen to train in jungle warfare in Central India and his blond, wavy hair turned a few shades darker; his face already toughened by years, responsibility and experience working at Tamulguri, took a step from serious to stern.

Tom's father had good connections in the British Indian army. Even outside Assam he was well known and held in good esteem for his hunting expeditions and the after-parties for which wine, food and waiters travelled a thousand miles from Calcutta.

"Mr Hastings, excellent food! I don't miss Calcutta Clubs dining at all when I come here. In fact I miss your parties out there. Good food, good hunting... What else does a man need? Ha...ha...ha!"

"Good company, General Williamson, good company is what else a man needs! It's a pleasure to host you every year."

General Williamson nodded and, smiling, he said, "Wish I could return the favour sometimes. Food and wine, not a problem. But where the hell do we arrange the excellent game you have here to hunt?"

"Ha! If only the generals before you had thought about that and left a few animals for you to hunt out there!"

Those parties that Tom's father hosted for the high and powerful, came in handy for Tom. When the time came for Mr Heisting's son to travel one thousand miles in the guests' direction to train as an army officer, those who mattered – the top brass, instructed those who mattered immediately over Tom, to go easy on him. On a day when a tough training session was to take place, he invariably had a cold or a sprain in an ankle and was allowed to rest while his fellow trainees trained, crawling in mud, running ten miles carrying their fully loaded gear of fifty pounds on their backs on the hottest days of summer. Those rest days he spent by having quality cups of tea from his garden along with his superiors, while his fellow trainees sweated it out in the muck of the tropical heat. Throughout his training, he took it as just role play – he was the officer and his job was to command.

And once he was commissioned and posted in the frontier town of Kohima, it was a life similar to the one he had in the tea estate. From his red-roofed bungalow, he commanded his men, soldiers in place of tea garden labourers. Albeit there were a few less orderlies in the Kohima bungalow than he had in the tea garden to order around. In his tea garden bungalow he had a helper for every job around the house – a cook, gardener and cleaner were a given. He had a man to polish his shoes and keep his clothes in proper order. He had a man to dress him up and tie his shoelaces. Someone else was there to bring him his newspaper and tea. Another help followed him around in the humid tropical heat to fan him. There was a servant to even help him get on his horse and look after it. And when he bought a car, he had a driver to open the door of the car for him and drive him around. And for every manservant the man had, his wife, *Memsahib* Sandra, had an equal number of maids to help her move though her day. Tom's posting in Kohima was as Captain of a battalion of the Assam Rifles. As an officer he had men to do his dirty work, at home and at work. It came naturally to him to delegate, to let others do the job for him.

But Tom was no soldier. He had joined the army partly to bring some excitement into his life and partly because he felt he had to answer the call for duty when war came to his motherland Britain.

"*Saahab*, this *jaangli* savage did the job for us! I think he is the thing we saw; good I didn't shoot him." Chetri burst out, looking very pleased with the outcome.

Wide-eyed, Tom followed Chetri's rifle pointing towards a dark corner in the cave. At the deepest part of the bunker, four bayonets cornered a man as bare as the raw earth he leaned on. Tattoos covered his body and face. Curious, unafraid, his small slit eyes darted from one soldier to the other. Beneath the dark blue ink of tribal tattoos, Tom made out a well-proportioned face – raised cheekbones and a well-defined jawline, as sharp as his gaze. The savage's head was shaved except for a tuft of straight hair on top of his smooth skull, tied neatly into a bun. A porcupine thorn held the knot together. More tattoos curved up and down the contours of his lean, muscular body. Around his waist slung an ornate belt made of cowrie shells and gemstones, holding a wooden scabbard. Below the belt, pubic hair partially covered his placidity. In his lowered right hand, he held a blade that glistened silver and red in the weak light. Tom noticed that it was a *dao,* the traditional Naga machete. The fingers of his left hand clutched the shaved severed head of a Japanese officer whose body lay beside him. Next to the body the headless officer's Samurai sword was snapped in half – its fine steel alloys no match for the crude brutality of a cast iron Naga *dao.*

"What to do with him, *Saahab*?" Chhetri asked, his rifle and stare never veering.

Managing to maintain his poise, Tom suggested they find out from where the savage had come.

"*Kot pora ahise tumi?*" asked Chetri, echoing Tom's question in Nagamese.

The savage did not reply. Just then the six new recruits walked in. The novice, who had mistakenly fired his gun earlier on, stepped on the coagulated blood that covered the floor and slipped and flew onto one of the headless Japanese soldiers. The collision gave him such a fright that he involuntarily screamed, "Aammaaa!" Seeing the non-soldier like act, the savage burst into giggles. More guns came up at him.

Tom intervened, "Hold it, soldiers. It's not a crime to laugh." The fallen soldier was the only one who didn't seem amused by Tom's comment.

Chetri was no stranger to savages like the one in front of him. He knew they were fierce. He read more into the savage's laugh than anyone else. He read that if he could laugh even while surrounded by men who could take his life any moment, he would have to be extraordinary.

With the bayonet on his 303 rifle, Chetri tapped the *dao* and the savage let it drop from his hand without resistance. The savage disarmed, the five Gorkhas flung their guns across their shoulder and each laid a hand on the man.

Chetri took Tom aside. "Think we should let him go, *Saahab*. Though he seems to have something against our enemy, I don't think he's a threat to us. Or if he wanted, he could have easily chopped a few of our new soldiers." Chetri smirked.

"You are right, Chetri." Tom answered thoughtfully. "We should observe him first to make sure he is not a threat to us. Have the men tie him up! We will take him with us for now and see what we do with him."

One of the fresh recruits brought forth an ample length of rope and, with another novice, ran in circles around the savage, engulfing him in a twirl of the rope.

"Oye, what are you doing?" Chetri cried. "Is he an elephant that you are wrapping so much rope around him? Let go. Bahadur, Shankar, you take over."

Two of Chetri's Gorkha soldiers took the rope and tied the man's wrists. The savage didn't resist; only a slight frown crinkled his forehead as he was forced to let go of the severed Japanese head. The savage's possession dropped on the ground and splashed in the mud blood. Stooping, Chetri picked up the head, took it to the officer's body and placed it on his chest and offered a firm salute. In the gloom, Tom gave Chetri an approving nod. The savage's eyes had followed Chetri's actions. At Chetri's salute, his eyes brightened for he perhaps understood that action as a gesture of respect to the dead victim.

"Do you think we should cover him with something before we take him to the garrison?" Tom asked Chetri, gesturing towards the savage's nakedness.

"Okay, *Saahab*, but what do we have?"

"How about your towel, if you don't mind?"

"Oh, yes, my towel. No problem." Chetri wasn't too happy to be using the towel with which he wiped sweat from his face to wrap around some savage's genitalia. He unwrapped the handloom woven red-and-white chequered fabric from his neck. Bending over the savage, he wrapped it around him. For the first time, the savage's expression grew stern. His black eyes grew fierce, and he began to shake his trunk frantically.

"*Saahab*, *Saahab*, I don't think he wants the towel around him!"

"Yes, that looks very clear. Okay, okay, take it off. We'll take him as is."

Once the towel was removed, the savage calmed. Chetri was pleased to have his towel back unworn. Encircling the savage, the party set off downhill. The savage strolled, while his captors slip-slid down the steep path. Once they were far enough from the Japanese bunker, the savage took one last look up the hill marked by the bow-shaped branch of a rhododendron tree as the signboard declaring the way to the man-made cave. To the eyes of any other man it would be difficult to find any outstanding object to use as a landmark amidst the identical mass of green.

A savage being escorted amidst a circle of the civilized, the journey through the forested path passed without incident. As they reached the garrison, all eyes turned to the returning patrol. Soldiers and townsfolk alike stared at the party as if they were escorting a prehistoric creature from the jungle. Soldiers and labourers digging trenches and commanding officers froze and stared at the passing contingent.

Naga workers looked at the savage with apprehension; they knew something about him of which the rest in the garrison didn't have any idea. One of the workers came forward and asked the whole group and no one in particular, *"Kot pora dhori anise, taike?"*

"He is asking where we captured him." Chetri explained to Tom.

"Tai bhal manu nohoi. Bhogoban chara ase." The Naga worker explained to Chetri that the savage wasn't a nice man, a godless man. Chetri translated for Tom, omitting the comment that the savage was not a nice man. For Chetri was a man who believed his instinct, which told him otherwise. Chetri knew a number of Nagas around Kohima whose families had been Christians for two generations. Being zealous early converts, they despised the savage people, seeing them as devoid of Jesus and Christian ways. Some of Chetri's Naga friends who practised Christianity also kept links with their old ways of Nature worship. From them he knew that the rituals of head hunting had more to it than mere acts of savagery.

"Ask this chap if he can communicate with the savage?" Tom interjected.

"Oh, he won't be able to, *Saahab.* This man is Angami and the savage is from the Konyak tribe."

"How do you know?"

"I too have lived in the Naga hills, *Saahab.*" Chetri smiled.

A British officer from the Assam Regiment approached. "Good morning, Captain Tom. What the hell have you brought back from patrol?"

"Hello! Captain Smith. Yes, he is quite a specimen!" Tom exclaimed, immediately realizing his un-officer-like excitement. Composing himself, he gave his moustachio a quick twist between the index finger and thumb. "We caught him in the act of slaughtering the Japanese intruders."

"Oh, then he hasn't done too bad a job, has he?"

"Of course. That's why we…I mean, I thought of bringing him along."

Captain Smith's junior, Lieutenant Peter, arrived on the scene. "Is that thing human?"

News of the savage travelled through the garrison like wildfire. Closely trailed by the now confirmed news that the Japanese had indeed reached the periphery of Kohima. Even before Tom could reach his command post, the garrison commander, Colonel Hugh Upton Richards, had him summoned. Deciding to arrive alone, he looked at Chetri, "Take him with you and don't let him out of your sight."

Only too pleased to have full possession, Chetri saluted and took Tom's leave, proceeding through the maze of soldiers and civilian workers. The hills within the garrison periphery were a beehive of frantic activity. New paths were being cut, trenches were being dug across the hills and spurs of Kohima by labourers and non-combatants; first to their own specifications then some were re-dug to army specifications. Previously dug trenches were being reinforced with timber and tin sheets. Chetri looked at the commotion of working men teeming through the hills as he passed by along with his eleven men and one exhibit of a man. The *Subedar* felt they were in a good position to defend the garrison, if at all the Japanese came raiding.

Tom stepped into the Commander's bunker and gave him a firm salute, re-adjusting his palm slightly, thinking it had shot a little too high. He enjoyed perfecting his salute. Commander Richards has been Tom's boss for only a couple of weeks. Before Richards's arrival, Tom had been his own boss. There had been no higher ranking officer to whom he had had to salute. In truth, Tom felt like an unpractised saluter. When his juniors saluted, he merely nodded, most un-armylike. A year of army training for a tea plantation manager didn't transform into army mannerisms.

In early March of that year, before the arrival of Commander Richards to Kohima, Tom was given orders by the Assam Rifles headquarters in Guwahati, to take his company on patrol to the borders of Burma to check on the Japanese advance into India. Instead, he had sent his Lieutenant, John Smith, along with most of his company. None returned.

"Morning, Tom. I hear you had a successful raid."

"Yes, sir. We accomplished what we set out to do."

"I hear you had help completing your mission."

Hearing that comment, Tom's chest deflated. "Yes…yes, sir. Before we could attack, a savage had finished off all the intruders."

"I believe he beheaded ten fully armed men. Quite a skill."

"I think so too, Colonel. That's why I decided to capture him and bring him along."

"So, what's your plan?"

"Plan, sir? Well, I think I will observe him and see if he can be trusted."

"Okay, good plan. Any man we can find who can fight for us, we should use. He should definitely be superior to the bunch we have had to recruit so far."

"Very true, Colonel..." Tom thought of telling him about the accidental firing while on their way to the raid, then decided against it.

"Has he been aggressive?"

"Nothing we can't handle, sir. I thought when we were coming through the forest he might try to escape; he didn't even attempt it."

"So where is he now?"

"I think I'll get my *Subedar* to keep him in his bunker, till I figure him."

"But won't that delay things? No, no, no, since he has shown no signs of aggression, why not keep him right next to you? You can speed up your assessment of him."

At the end of the conversation, Tom gave a half-hearted salute and, cursing the commander under his breath, walked out.

He wasn't used to being ordered around, let alone the Garrison Commander telling him to sleep beside a savage. How could he get out of it? He had agreed with Sandra, who volunteered at the hospital nearby, to stay separately so they didn't cramp on each other's space in the confined space of bunkers. Who was the Commander to order him around? What did the Colonel know of headhunters? Probably nothing, having just moved in from Delhi? With those thoughts in his head, Tom stalked his way down from Garrison Hill.

Garrison Hill, as the name suggests, housed the headquarters of the garrison. It was the centre of the garrison's activities and also its highest point. Colonel Richards's command post was located there. To the northwest of Garrison Hill lay the hospital in which Tom's wife worked and that hill was aptly named Hospital Hill. To the south, opposite Hospital Hill, Tom and his reduced battalion, which was down to the size of a company, had their bunkers in Field Supply Depot Hill or FSD in short. To get there Tom had to negotiate through the hill called Kuki Picket, named after the Kuki tribe of the Nagas. Field Supply Depot Hill housed the field supply depot. The hill next to FSD, housed the daily issues depot of the garrison and was thus named – Daily Issues Supply Hill or DIS, which sat on a ridge below which ran the road going to Imphal and beyond. And across the road, further south still, was Jail Hill. All six hills had army units deployed and formed the core of the garrison. The outer margins of the garrison encompassed Hospital Hill to the northwest; to the northeast the Deputy Commissioner's bungalow, and beyond it, across the Dimapur–Meriama road was a Naga village where a platoon of soldiers from various army divisions had been gathered. And to the south, Jail Hill formed the southernmost outpost of the garrison's core. To the west of these hills a deep gorge offered natural protecton to the garrison's defence. The garrison occupied a fourth of the total area of Kohima town.

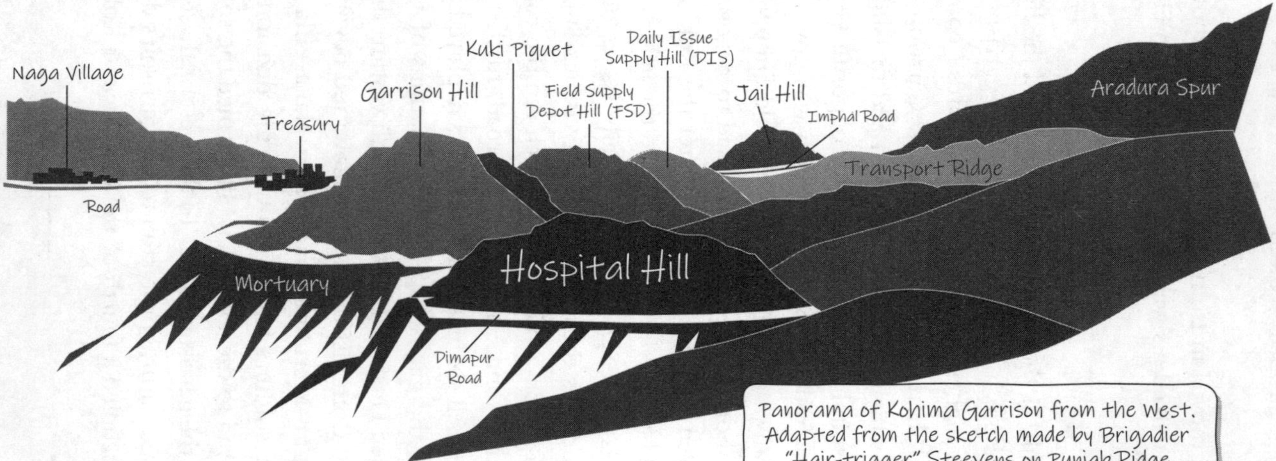

Panorama of Kohima Garrison from the West.
Adapted from the sketch made by Brigadier
"Hair-trigger" Steevens on Punjab Ridge

From where they entered the garrison it was only three hundred yards to Chetri and his soldiers' bunkers in Field Supply Depot, but it took them almost an hour to reach there. All the residents of the Garrison, curious about the captured savage, coming around with their questions, delayed their arrival. When they arrived at his bunker, to arouse no more excitement, Chetri had his men tie up the savage inside his bunker. With the Japanese on their doorstep, there already was enough going on.

With all the commotion, Chetri could sense that the Konyak warrior was becoming slightly agitated. When his men left, Chetri tried to remember the few Konyak words he knew. He tried them, but got no response. The warrior stood erect, his strong bare feet spread out and firmly placed on the damp mud floor. When offered a stool to sit, the figure merely raised his chin and cast his eyes downwards. There was none of the amused Konyak warrior that Chetri had seen after the slaughter.

Considering whether he should untie the savage's hands, Chetri reckoned it would definitely be a friendly gesture. Before coming to a conclusion, one of his men called out to inform that Tom was on his way. He would have liked some more time with the warrior alone. Tom entered and, somewhat exhausted, assumed a squatting position on the stool that the savage had rejected moments ago.

"Did you manage to learn anything from him? Where he is from and why he killed all those Japs?" Tom fired away, while Chetri sat down on his bedding roll, and the savage kept his stance.

"No, *Saahab*, he hasn't uttered a single word. If you leave him with me for a day or two, I should be able to make him talk."

"Can you speak his dialect?"

"Not much. I just know a few words."

"Well, then, you better teach me those words so you can get on to other more important things I have lined up for you. Bring him over to my bunker, let me see what I can get out of him." With those words, Tom stepped out of Chetri's bunker, striding away like it had all been his idea.

On Field Supply Depot Hill, Tom's men occupied four bunkers. Tom's was the biggest and top-most bunker. Below it was Chetri's, and ten metres below were two more bunkers, side by side. These four bunkers were a fraction of a few hundred such bunkers that dotted the Garrison defence perimeter like pockmarks on the face of the hills. Yet, from a distance they were made invisible by the pine, cherry and rhododendron trees spreading a green carpet above them. Some of the bunkers had a roof of corrugated iron sheets, some had wooden planks, and the forward trenches were mostly left open to offer a clear line of sight to enemy movement. Under the lights at night, the activity in the trenches felt like a gloomy fair going on underground. While, until that time very little was going on over ground in the hills, the storm was building momentum silently. Tom and his men found first-hand proof of it at Aradura Spur; where the savage had turned a grim picture grimmer.

In accordance with his rank, Tom had ensured that his bunker was dug slightly longer than most. Tom had moved into the bunker a week ago with his orderly, Raan Singh, who was from United Provinces, the largest province of British India. Raan, being Tom's attendant and cook, had to spend most of his time inside the bunker attending to Tom *Sahib's* domestic matters, now that Sandra *Memsahib* was away at the hospital. He could comfortably stretch his arms across the bunker's breadth, but nothing much more than that. Each time he thought of the three-bedroom bungalow that Tom had lived in after they first arrived in Kohima, Raan frowned – although his servant's quarters hadn't been much bigger, beside the detached kitchen built behind the bungalow. However, the long covered corridor, which ran from the kitchen into the main bungalow, had made him feel connected. He missed the dull yellow glow of the light bulb in his room. He missed his bare creature comforts. He even missed the electric bell that alerted him to duty every morning, a gift that Sandra, on her last visit to London just before the war, had bought for him. That bell acted as his alarm clock to get bed tea ready for his *Sahib* and *Memsahib,* every morning at a quarter past six.

When the *Sahib* went on tour with the Deputy Commissioner to Naga villages, the *Memsahib* didn't like staying in the house alone. Then Raan got to sleep in the bungalow's third spare bedroom in amongst the *Sahib's* hunting guns, polo sticks and *Memsahib's* tennis rackets, knitting needles, and the crockery specially ordered from England; those items made his bed feel like an island amidst a raging sea of sports and household items. In spite of its storeroom-like feel, he enjoyed those nights in the bedroom and looked forward to them. He felt privileged to be sleeping under the same roof.

Now, in the bunker, Raan had mixed feelings. Still privileged to be sharing the same space, it somehow felt more disadvantageous than anything else. In the stifling space inside the bunker, Raan was always conscious of his *Sahib* and forced to be prim and proper. He missed the moments in his room by the bungalow when he could be by himself and do what he felt like. He missed, for example, humming songs from Hindi movies, which he considered a hobby. Now he could only indulge in them when Tom was out of the bunker. And he did indulge with gusto whenever he could, mostly to shut the voices in his head from scaring him about the future.

But all considered, Raan revered Tom. Especially the way he looked. Raan reckoned that if he hadn't worked in the family fields so long, every day, early in life, he could have been almost as fair. Almost as tall as his *Sahib*, and once as slim, now Raan's own cooking, and his habit not to waste food, served up too many leftovers that had him a little soft and round around the edges. Before the garrison barber had clipped his hair, he too had long flowing hair, like the *Sahib*. Tom's was blond; Raan's jet black to match his shining eyes. On his upper lip Raan also grew a replica moustachio. Being a naturally hairy man, he had a thick crop, but as a sign of respect he trimmed the ends shorter than his *Sahib's*. When twirled up, the ends always fell a few millimetres shorter.

Another activity Raan enjoyed in the loneliness of his room was practising Tom's ways and mannerisms. He twisted his limited English vocabulary to flow in similar accent as his *Sahib's*. In front of his small dull mirror he would bring an empty cup up to his mouth with a flourish, emulating his teatotalling superior. After the lunch and dinner chores were over, Raan also liked to collect the best pieces of charcoal from the hearth and sketch vegetables on a pad Sandra had brought for him in Shillong. He particularly loved sketching bitter gourds and pumpkins, his two favourite vegetables. In the bunker he couldn't practise his art, as he had to cook over a stove fuelled by kerosene instead of wood.

Wondering where Tom could be, he looked out of the trench and was pleased to see him coming out of Chetri's bunker. Following Tom were Chetri and his men encircling someone between them. Raan quickly moved to the steps to receive them.

"Good afternoon, *Sahib*! Tea?"

"No, Raan. But move your stove from the corner to the middle. We will have to make more room."

As the circle parted, Raan saw him! Trying his best to hold back surprise mildly marinated in fear, quickly he reminded himself that they were at war. As an army operant, he must be prepared to see men – dead or dying, civilized or savage, uniformed or naked.

"Oh! Who is this? Where did you find him, *Sahib*? What will you do with him?" Out of nervousness, questions rang out.

Tired from his expedition, mental fatigue and physical exertion, and after answering so many questions, Tom simply replied, "Well, let's see what he can do for us."

"What can a naked *jaangli* do for the *Sahib*? He could be dangerous."

"I hope to use his fierceness against our enemy."

"Will you keep him for long, *Sahib*?"

"We will see."

Observing Tom's nose starting to twitch, his thin moustachio throbbing like the head of a praying mantis about to strike, Raan realized that question time was over. His *Sahib* had had enough. Raan busied himself placing the stove as a border between himself and the savage, further cramping his portion of the bunker. This arrangement did not encroach upon Tom's space.

THREE

THE SAVAGE SAT ON TOP OF A BOX FILLED WITH RIFLE AMMUNITION, below it was a crate of grenades. Chetri's Gorkhas had brought in the boxes and tied the savage to the handle of the grenade box. The tattooed warrior looked at the knot attaching him to the handle of the box. Secretly he smiled, knowing he could untie that knot any moment he pleased. The soldier who had tied him had used a simple overhand knot that he probably used back home to secure his cow from straying. Perhaps the soldier had equated the savage's intelligence to that of his cow.

The warrior's eyes roved around the bunker. He didn't think much of his captors' house. It was hardly a house. Didn't these white and brown people know how to build? They seemed to cover their bodies well; their second skin seemed finely woven. Yet they lived in burrows like rats. He observed how Tom's pale skin contrasted to his khaki uniform. Tom reminded him of another white man. A man who was the reason he had landed up there amidst the circus of brown and white men. A faint smirk appeared on his otherwise stern face. That other white man had taught him the white men's tongue. Pretending not to understand, he wanted to play his ignorant act for a while longer to see if he could trust his captors and partner with them.

The savage was no meek man. He was called Mongseng, the fiercest warrior of Poilung. Not many people dared to visit his village. Only one man from outside his community visited often. He could because *Wangba* – the *Ang* or king of Poilung – gave him his protection. The *Wangba* liked three things in life: One, being the *Ang* of Poilung; two, leading his warriors into battle to bring back prosperity for the village; and three, to drink rice beer made by the fine hands of the Poilung women. The *Ang's* last two interests led to his early end.

Once, returning with his warriors after a successful expedition that earned them ten heads for Poilung, his troop crossed paths with a white warrior and two rows of brown warriors from the plains. The king restrained his men from attacking. He had come across such white and brown warriors before. He knew their short spears had magic; they spat fiery iron that made even the toughest elephant-hide shields defenceless.

Like the white man he saw in front of him now, Mongseng remembered how the white warrior had once come forward in their village. He didn't have a weapon and wore a peculiar second skin that went from neck down to cover till his feet. To the *Ang* the white man's dress seemed like an upturned bamboo basket; the kind that the women of Poilung used to carry their produce from the fields. The white man's dress was also white. Instead of challenging *Ang* and his men, the white warrior bowed before them and introduced himself as 'The *Padre*'. He offered the *Ang* a gift, some liquid the colour of dark earth, retained within a container as transparent as water but solid like a dry bottle gourd. The white man figured that the *Wangba* didn't know what to do with the gift. As a serving suggestion, the white man tilted back his head and gestured with an imaginary cup to his lips. Understanding this universal gesture for a drink he took the bottle respectfully with both hands, removed the cork off as instructed, and brought it to his lips.

The transparent container was cold, the liquid inside bittersweet. While he didn't quite like it, he couldn't stop himself from sipping a little bit more. It neither looked nor tasted like his familiar rice beer brew, yet after a few sips he felt a head rush as strong as a few mugs of rice beer. He was high and happy. And in that intoxicated state the white warrior became his best friend. The *Ang* invited his new companion to Poilung and hosted him in his own house, while his men stayed in different village houses. The next day he threw a huge feast and sent them off with abundant gifts of rice beer and game birds slung on bamboo poles. The white man went away happy, promising to return soon with more wonder liquid.

Sure enough, carried from a far-off land in a bag slung across a bamboo pole on the shoulders of two porters, led by his new white friend, a steady supply of bottles started pouring in every month. Soon the golden brown liquid in the transparent container became the king's constant companion. Its taste grew so enticing that he became addicted, giving up on the rice beer brew of his village.

As time passed, the white man started mixing with the villagers. He carried gifts for all – tobacco for the men, salt for the women, and for the children treats hard like stones and sweet like honey. He began telling stories to those who would listen. His stories were about an Almighty. That Almighty was something like the powers the Savage, his *Ang* and the rest of the villagers believed in. The Energies they prayed to, which existed in their streams, in the forest, in the fires, in the rocks – the spirits that lived in nature, which guided them through their day-to-day lives. The new white friend said that they were only slightly mistaken about the source of that Power. The Almighty was not invisible. It didn't live in objects. It had a form. It was not an 'It', neither a 'She', but a 'He'. He didn't exist in the forest, streams, fires or rocks, but in their hearts. That Almighty had a son too. He had a form, not very different from theirs, but perhaps a little paler, with no tattoos, and more facial hair than any men in the village could grow.

Raan pushed a cup of tea towards the savage with the caution of a caretaker putting food into the cage of a tiger. Mongseng's mind floated back to the present. In Tom's corner he noticed a photograph of the bearded Almighty that the Padre touted to his villagers. He concluded that Tom must be from the same faith as the Padre. The Padre had promised a better life for the villagers if they followed his new bearded Almighty. The warrior wondered if the better life, the prosperity the Padre promised would lead his village into rat holes like his captors. Seeing the cup, the savage hopped lithely down from his perch, sending Raan flying back five paces. Tom chuckled under his breath. Then mindful not to put down Raan in front of the savage, he pretended to busy himself with a withered map of

Kohima and surrounds, leaving Raan to adjust to the savage on his own.

Greedily downing the sweet tea in a few gulps, it was lighter and sweeter than Mongseng was used to, but he didn't care. He hadn't had a drink or eaten a morsel since he finished his ration of smoked meat, roasted sweet potatoes, taro pods and sticky rice a couple of days before. On the journey from Poilung that began ten nights ago, he had supplemented his meagre ration with small game, but hadn't gone out of his way looking for them, as he had been keen to reach Kohima at the earliest. That was one reason for travelling light. Whatever small game crossed his path – a bird, squirrel, rat, snake – he shot with his bow or chopped with his *dao*. Depending on his hunger he had either roasted them where he hunted them, or kept the kill to eat later. But as he approached Kohima, wild game had become scarce, driven to hiding by strange noises or killed and eaten by the ten hungry Japanese soldiers the savage had slaughtered inside the cave. For a couple of days they had been on the same path as him, as he approached Kohima. They were a day ahead of him, a day extra to live. They ate any game they came across, leaving only trees, bushes and shrubs for Mongseng to look at and satiate his hunger.

Initially on their way towards Kohima, across the Chindwin River, the Japanese army encountered friendly Nagas. Their similar skin, similar eyes, similar hair and similar height had endeared the hungry Japanese army to the Nagas. Villagers offered them their food, even some of their meat. But small villages with small food stocks could not satiate the growing giant. As the Japanese army grew bigger and food became scarce, the Naga offerings stopped. The marching army started taking food forcibly, letting their guns do the negotiation. The

Naga villagers, accustomed to packing up and leaving their villages empty when attacked by more powerful neighbouring villages, didn't take long to adopt that same technique with the Japanese. When the wind brought in news from their log drums that the Japanese were approaching, all they left in their villages for the arriving army was thin air.

Instead of satiating Mongseng's thirst, the cup of tea turned his mind and growling stomach on to food. Just then, an unfamiliar smell began to engulf his nostrils. A small cauldron wearing a thick outer skin of black ash sat on some kind of hearth made of metal. He looked at Raan and then at Tom, wondering whether he would be offered some food too. So far his captors had seemed hospitable, hence he didn't untie the cow knot binding him to the metal trunk and escape.

The sun beating down on the hot metal roof of the bunker began peeping in from the west. Busy near the stove, Raan asked Tom, "*Sahib*, should I serve lunch? It is past one o'clock."

Tom looked up from the map he was engrossed in, "Oh! Didn't realize it was past thirteen hundred, yes, yes..." Pausing, he indicated with a nod of his head towards the savage, taking a moment to observe him, "Serve him some too."

Mongseng returned Tom's gaze with an apprehensive appraisal of his own. Tom quickly turned back to his map.

Out of habit, Raan had prepared a little extra food. When he cooked in the bungalow there were invariably unexpected guests or helping hands around the house that meant more mouths to feed. While cooking in the bunker, with Tom's men always coming by, the likelihood of unexpected guests was expected. But that day Raan's appetite had been ravenous. Having suffered a mild spell of dysentery the previous day, he was hoping to make up for the lost food. Grudgingly, however, he prepared an extra plate and with an almost steady hand offered it to the savage. Like the tongue of a lizard catching a fly, Mongseng shot out an arm and grabbed the plate. Both limbs, giving and taking, retracted like a recoiling spring.

After lunch Tom tried out the three Konyak words Chetri had taught him. Unknown to Tom, the words layered in a Nepali accent, then his own English accent, created a totally fresh new language that had no resemblance to Konyak. Trying harder, Tom repeated and re-repeated the words, managing only to amuse Mongseng, and behind his back, Raan. As Tom realized he was going nowhere, he dropped the idea of communication and went back to being a commander, ordering Raan to make more tea. Mongseng was enjoying Tom's efforts at communication. Before opening his mouth and making life a little easier for his captors, he wanted to wait and watch, before deciding whether to stay or leave.

In the middle of the night, through the thick blanket of darkness, which only Mongseng's eyesight could penetrate, he found his captors sleeping blissfully like babies. When he was sure his captors were sound asleep, Mongseng untied his hands so that he could sleep comfortably on the metal trunk. He spotted Raan's kitchen knife next to the stove. The two comatosed necks on either side of the bunker seemed easy prey. He could cut off their heads with the knife and disappear. But then, their heads wouldn't do. He hadn't come all this way to collect that kind of head. And besides, they had fed him. It wasn't in his culture to kill the hands that feed. Beyond tying him they had not ill-treated him. Should he focus on the one count of enmity or believe their friendly gestures? With those conflicting thoughts he drifted back to sleep.

Just before dawn Mongseng woke up and quickly retied his own wrists so that his captors wouldn't become alarmed at seeing him free. In his hurry he slipped the knot a little too tight. Now, with the sun chasing away the moon he needed to go and relieve himself badly. Both solids and liquids were threatening to disobey. With aching hands he couldn't loosen his own knot. It hadn't occurred to Raan at night to take the hostage out to relieve himself. After dinner Tom had been away at the Garrison Command Post to discuss strategies, and once he was back had been too preoccupied with war tactics to think about such basic considerations. Even so, for the naked warrior, no possible future event, however immense, overshadowed his present need, however mundane it might have been.

Mongseng at the brink of his threshold frantically pulled at the ammunition box, which finally dropped, awakening Tom. Half asleep, seeing the scene, Tom rolled out of his bedding, sprang up and hit his head on the roof of the bunker. From Tom's yelp, Raan woke up groggily. His body, aching from the semi-crouched position he had had to sleep in, became suddenly alert the moment he noticed the nearby naked man in a state of heightened agitation. Noticing his captors awake, Mongseng pointed to the rope, motioning that it needs to come off so he can attend to the call of nature. Frantically he uttered the universal sound, "Pisss, pissss, shisss, pissss…" and pointed towards his morning erectness.

"Did you take him out last night?"

"Oh! Didn't think of that..."

"What?! Do I need to tell you everything, Raan? Can't you use your head every now and then?"

With accusing eyes Raan looked at the savage who simply stared him down.

"It's your fault, not his! Tom retorted, "Take him out immediately."

With that instruction, rubbing the bump on his head, Tom walked out. In the tiny, damp space the fumbling Raan couldn't untie the rope, so had to use his kitchen knife. He knew Chetri would be none too pleased and made a mental note to cook him a special something in lieu of the split rope.

A good night's sleep and recovery from dysentery had emboldened Raan who led the savage out as if he were a pet dog. Along a muddy path Raan led the savage, zigzagging between the bunkers. At the attention they received from the inmates of the bunkers they passed by, Raan's chest puffed up. He waved and shouted at the soldiers he knew, drawing the attention of others to his object of display. He could have taken the tattooed warrior straight down the hill to the pit latrines below their hill. Instead he had decided to visit the farthest facilities above Dimapur Road, near the Deputy Commissioner's bungalow.

Suddenly feeling cocky, every few metres Raan stopped to chat with a soldier or orderly he knew and told them how his *Sahib* had captured the savage. Adding that it was now his responsibility to train this warrior in the ways of the modern world. Mongseng tolerated it all well. He looked at the hand clasping the rope that bound him; those hands didn't look like they could hold down a domesticated cat, let alone the big wild feline that he was. Along those arms there was more fat bulking them up, than muscles. If he had wanted to, Mongseng could easily yank the rope and go his way. But he had a plan and he wanted to stick to it. Though every hard tug at the rope and Raan's condescending commands made Mongseng's resolve to stick to the plan weak.

Amid Raan's oratory spills and the long winding path through terraced bunkers, plots not so long ago used for cultivating rice, Mongseng finally could hold no more. This time when Raan yanked at the rope, the wild man returned the yank with one of his own. The powerful tug sent Raan flying backwards on to the muddy ground, landing on his back with a splutter. As he regained his senses and turned around, he found the savage relieving himself in full view of the bunker residents surrounding their path. Raan turned deep red, embarrassed for his fall from grace into mud and the collective embarrassment he felt for the savage's act in full public view.

Once Raan was sure that the savage was done, he gently pulled at the rope and the relieved savage followed behind. The red-faced Raan made no further conversation or eye contact from then on. They crossed Kukie Piquet and climbed up a small hillock to reach the tennis court above the District Commissioner's bungalow. Spotting a tap Raan took the savage to a mature cherry tree. It was one of the first cherry trees that the British planted in the Himalayan foothills along with their rule, half a century ago. Raan had to use almost the whole length of the rope to tie it around the cherry trunk, leaving hardly enough length for Mongseng to move freely.

Mongseng was not quite sure what Raan was up to tying him to a tree.

In Mongseng's village they usually tied animals to a tree to graze or to sacrifice it to a God. He was certain Raan didn't expect him to graze. Looking at the lines marked out on the ground he suddenly regretted not escaping when he had his opportunity. Sizing up the lines of the tennis court Mongseng reasoned that this was some sort of a sacrificial site. The lines dividing the earth into different sized boxes looked menacing to him. He wondered if he was to be sacrificed and his body dismembered into different parts and each part place into the different boxes on the tennis court. The net across the court he concluded must be to capture any sacrificial offerings that try to escape. Mongseng reasoned his captor must have changed his mind and really meant him harm. With rising alarm Mongseng looked Raan up and down, searching his captor for a hidden sacrificial sword.

Raan wondered what was going on with the savage who pulled at the rope, only managing to tighten the knot. With open palms facing down, Raan waved and gestured, hoping that the savage would again calm down. That gesture only managed to confuse the savage. Raan tried another gesture; he took out an imaginary penis out of his pants and making a hissing noise pointed to the savage, requesting him to relieve himself once again. Mongseng looked carefully around Raan for a *dao.* If he was to be dismembered, it seemed that they start by chopping the penises first. Like the Konyaks valued heads, his captors must value penises. Ah, that is it, that is why they kept their dingily dangles hidden.

With only a soft whistle as warning, suddenly, seemingly out of nowhere, a mortar shell dropped on the cherry tree, bursting with a deafening boom. The broad trunk of the tree took the whole force of the blast splitting through the middle, blowing the half furthest away from Mongseng into shreds. The rope that bound him was ripped apart, throwing him a furlong away. Luckily for both of them, the standing portion of the tree had protected them against the shrapnel. Raan lay face down on the ground, too stunned to move, his face contorted like ripples in sand. Mongseng thought his captors had very powerful Gods. They directly struck from the sky and killed their sacrificial offerings. A smirk escaped his grim expression, the foreign Gods were powerful but their aim wasn't that good. Seeing Raan lying on the ground face down, Mongseng decided he must take that opportunity to escape while his captor's attention was diverted. Stopping to take one last look at Raan lying flat on the ground, he made off towards the opposite end of the hill, diving into the bushes to be swallowed up by the undergrowth.

No matter how much you prepare for an eventuality, when it does materialize, it catches everyone by surprise. The sudden Japanese mortar attack on the garrison caught the new recruits off guard and most left their position and ran in the hope to find better cover. The seasoned soldiers tried to hold their position and their nerves, but seeing the general commotion even some of them lost their composure. Caught unaware, the whole garrison scattered for cover like a colony of ants running from the randomly darting tongue of a pangolin. The shelling went on in spurts. The Japanese mortar company fired in random directions and watched where the majority scattered and then fired again.

While the British Commander General Slim and other generals immediately over and under him had debated on possible entry points for the Japanese and where to hold them off, a whole Japanese division had slipped right under their eyes into the thick tropical jungles and mountains of the far Northeast. Unknown to General Slim and his cronies, the Japanese were now closing in on Kohima, and making their presence felt. As the days ticked by, they had converged on villages around Kohima in batches. The myth about an attack had become real when Tom's patrol had discovered the Japanese soldiers entrenched in the bunker atop Aradura Spur. While they were regrouping, a company of early enthusiastic arrivals, having settled comfortably into their trenches, had decided to fire off a few trial shots. Of which one mortar landed on the cherry tree where Raan Singh had tied Mongseng.

The Kohima Garrison was equipped for peace not war. Rather than fighting soldiers, there was more administrative staff. The defence of a town barely visible on a map of the British Raj would be left in the hands of a mixed bag of soldiers, paramilitary forces and civilians, who had hardly held a gun in their life. Besides the 1st Assam Regiment and a handful of Assam Rifles companies, only broken companies from shrunken battalions had arrived in Kohima just as the Japanese were closing in. The rest of the garrison comprised of non-combatants. Instead of guns they held thick wads of red-taped files, steering wheels, whips and ladles. They were clerks, drivers, mule herders and cooks, issued with guns to fight against the Japanese imperial forces.

By itself Kohima was of no importance. However, the easternmost borders of the Raj, Imphal – where the IV corps of the British Indian army was headquartered were connected with Dimapur – a major supply depot of the Allied forces in the North Eastern frontier, by the arterial road that went through Kohima. That made the protection of Kohima paramount.

Now whether the arterial link would be saved or severed from the British Raj depended largely on a ragtag band of defenders.

While the game of mortar shells went on, Mongseng climbed to the top of Aradura Spur and observed the chaos from there. He realized the gods hadn't tried to claim him. It was his captor's enemies, whose ten heads he had collected, trying to kill him with fire from the sky. He didn't feel bad for taking those heads from whose bodies he had no personal animosity. But now that they tried killing him, he could go on slicing them.

Mongseng watched the ruckus for a while, then he made his way back into the hidden foxhole he had visited the previous day. In the dark stretch of the cave his conquests still lay, partially claimed by ants, the bodies strewn on the damp earth in the positions they had fallen. He picked up his *dao* and replaced it in its wooden scabbard inlaid with cowrie shells and semiprecious gemstones.

With a show of dexterity, the warrior deftly gathered the ten heads, stacking them up like a house of cards – four at the bottom, then three, two, and one on top. He carefully lifted the pyramid, balancing them in his folded arms, supported by his body, the top head cupped under his chin. A leopard returning to the cave, whose den the Japanese had converted into a bunker, spotted him stepping out and ran for its life from the eleven-headed monster that emerged from the cave.

Outside the bunker, Mongseng retrieved his spear from the undergrowth. It was a work of art. The teak wood handle was six feet long; the middle of the spear was covered with ornate furs in different colours from different animals. One end of the spear had a conical sharp metal point and the other end had a flat double-edged blade. Shifting the spear to his left hand, Mongseng confidently made his way to a small rocky cavern he had discovered on his way up. In this hole he hid the ten heads, carefully closing the mouth with a rock. With a glint in his eyes, he plucked some triangular leaves from a bulbous shrub and crushed them with a stone. They emitted a foul smell. He smeared the rock covering the mouth of the cavern with the paste. This would safeguard his possessions from scavenging animals should they come looking for his bounty once it started emitting rotting smells.

For a Konyak Warrior there was no bigger humiliation than to be captured alive. Those heads were the first of the bounty in search of which destiny brought him so far from his village. For those prized heads he had tolerated the humiliation of being held captive.

FOUR

REMOTE DIDN'T ADEQUATELY DESCRIBE THE VILLAGE OF POILUNG where Mongseng came from. Sitting on the flat tip of a mountain range, the village was surrounded by tall and short, wide and thick vegetation. Flanked by sharp cliffs on two sides, it was impossible to see the houses on top. The village was so high that men passing through the gorge by the snaking river below looked like rolling pebbles. The cliff faces were of solid rock, a smooth, natural protective wall. The narrow third face of the mountain was a steep ridge that offered the only approach to the village. Hidden amidst the natural vegetative barrier, was a tightly woven twenty-foot bamboo wall with sharp poles tilting at a forty-five degree angle amidst the trees that circled the village, forming another protective layer from invaders.

Mongseng was the prince of Poilung. He was the eldest son of Poilung's *Wangba,* the king. He was the son from the *Ang*'s third and youngest wife, Naro. The tenth child; the first boy after nine girls. But the *Ang* didn't stop with him, going on to produce another ten girls and three boys. And yet, among his twenty-two siblings, Mongseng became the *Ang*'s favourite child. Being the first boy to be born after nine girls, the *Ang* didn't want Mongseng to imbibe any feminine traits from his sisters. Early on his father initiated Mongseng into his affairs of administering the village. He would let Mongseng count the pumpkins, chickens, pigs, goats and occasionally a cow or a *mithun* – an Indian bison, which villagers paid to the *Ang* for settling a dispute, over land or love, quarrel or theft. The fee paid to the *Ang* was commensurate with the case he judged. Settling a minor dispute usually earned him a fee in produce from the fields of his client. This kept Mongseng busy counting pumpkins, corn, and such smaller value items that came in large quantities. Mongseng looked forward to the days when his father passed bigger judgements in matters of land or love, because then the settlement fee was big, and his counting job, small. The *Ang* was a just ruler. He never stipulated or demanded a fee; he received payment that was given. Quantity of payment varied from subject to subject depending on the wealth they possessed in terms of agricultural land and livestock.

Besides Mongseng's time with the *Ang,* the rest of it he spent growing up much like any other village child. He played with all of the children, his face covered in dirt, his feet bare on the ground – he looked no different. It was only when they played games that needed someone to lead that he became a leader. Not by force, not by influence, but by nature. He had the natural demeanour of a Konyak prince. By the age of six his formal tuition began. First with wood-edged spears, throwing them at banana stem targets. By age eight, when spear-throwing had made his arms strong, he was initiated into the art of targeting those same banana stems to slice them with a *dao* or pierce them with a bow and arrows. Soon a skilled marksman, by the age of ten, he accompanied men twice his age on hunting expeditions.

At the age of twelve, when many children of his age were still looked after by their parents, he on the other hand, had become his mother's bodyguard. Mongseng started escorting his mother to the terraced paddy fields of the village. While she worked alongside other village women in their fields a kilometre from Poilung, he stood guard with other male warriors. On one such occasion, in the middle of a hot day while the other guardsmen had gone to the stream to quench their thirst, Mongseng heard a rustling in the woods. Quickly he alerted his mother and the other women toiling in the sweet potato patch. Moments later, a Himalayan bear sprung from the undergrowth and charged the gathering with a fierce roar. Mongseng, the young boy of twelve, stood firm and tall with a spear in hand between the group of women and beast. Erect on its hind legs, the bear came straight towards them. The white 'V' marking on the chest amidst the bear's otherwise black fur grew bigger and bigger. Then, just when it looked like the six foot, three hundred kilogram giant would crush the four foot, thirty kilogram boy, Mongseng turned his spear, let out a blood-curdling shout and gave a hard jab with the blunt end of his weapon right in the middle of the 'V'. The sudden jab and shout stopped the bear in its tracks. Breathless and squealing, it turned around and cantered off into the jungle in the direction it had come from.

Despite the king's best efforts, Mongseng did imbibe the trait of compassion from his mother and sisters! He never killed for fun, only when necessary.

Unlike other boys his age, he didn't feel the need to show off his skills with a spear or a bow and arrows by unnecessarily shooting and killing live targets; his confidence didn't need the bolstering or approval of his peers. Despite his strength, he never bullied the weak, instead taking them under his wing, trying to relieve their fears and replace it with courage. A friend of his, Sangkok, never dared to venture outside the village on his own. Even into his late teens Sangkok feared to go hunting. He became a laughing stock. On wet rainy days when the boys couldn't go out into the open to play games and were instead confined to the limits of the *morung* – the communal gathering shed for boys, they always found entertainment at the expense of Sangkok. Mongseng decided to correct the matter.

One day Mongseng convinced Sangkok to come along on a hunting trip promising him that he would not let him out of his sight. Knowing Mongseng would be true to his word Sangkok agreed and accompanied Mongseng and four other friends into the forest. It was March, yet heavy showers throughout the winter meant the forest had a thick blanket of green. Evergreen trees were greener, deciduous trees had sprouted their leaves early, ferns and shrubs whose roots and pods usually lay dormant, had erupted into dense bushes. The jungle was so fecund they could hardly see a few paces beyond them.

At one point, as the forest engulfed the group of six, Mongseng and Sangkok were momentarily separated from the rest. Just then, they heard a shriek and ran towards the source. It was the village jester Pemba, the one who poked the most ridicule at Sangkok. From a distance they saw he was lying in a pool of blood, his stomach ripped open by a boar sporting six-inch tusks, which now stood near its quarry. As the boys watched, the wild hog charged again, intending to finish off the jester. Thinking on his feet, Sangkok shot a trembling arrow. Just behind him Mongseng also let off a shot on the same trajectory, just a fraction of a second later. Sangkok's arrow sailed an inch over the boar's shoulder and disappeared amidst a cluster of rattan vines. Mongseng's arrow pierced the heart of the boar, which was dead before it dropped to the ground.

The young hunting expedition returned to the village triumphant and sad. Two members of the hunting expedition carried on their shoulders the boar hanging from a bamboo pole. The jester, barely alive, was slung across Mongseng's back with a vine wrapped around his abdomen to keep his intestines in place. Sangkok rode on the shoulder of the last expedition member. In the thrill of the kill, Mongseng had given all credit to Sangkok. Sangkok, unsure where his arrow hit, had accepted his friend's verdict with awkwardness.

The village medicine man sewed up Pemba's stomach with a thread made out of the fresh intestines of the swine that was responsible for the rip. Over the stitches he applied a paste made out of a concoction of herbs. To keep the pain at bay while the wound healed, the medicine man prescribed Pemba a good dose of rice beer to be taken five times daily. As the jester's wounds started healing and the scars faded away, so did his jokes about Sangkok. Though Mongseng and Sangkok never discussed the hunt, secretly Sangkok suspected the truth. But he knew why his friend gave him the credit and was ever grateful to him. With respect from his peers, Sangkok's heart became bolder, maybe not as bold as Mongseng's, but much, much more than what it used to be.

Before Mongseng turned fifteen he became the commander of a *khel* of boy scouts in his village. He made Sangkok his assistant. When the elder warriors went out to hunt or fight with neighbouring villages, the defence of Poilung was left to the responsibility of these young warriors.

In time, when the *Ang* was away, Mongsen became the junior *Ang.* Matters that couldn't wait to be settled till his father's return were provisionally ruled by the junior *Ang.* Once his father came home, he rarely revoked Mongseng's judgements, which were mostly a mirror image of what the *Ang* would have conferred. If not, then the *Ang* often found them better, more just. The people of Poilung never had to wait for justice, and knew they would have an uninterrupted rule of law even when the present *Ang* was no more.

The village closest to Poilung was Wokcing. It lay about ten kilometres south, but for all of their differences they may as well have been a thousand kilometres apart. At one time both villages were close. Quite a few families inter-married their children; in fact, Mongseng's mother, Naro, was a maiden from Wokcing. At one time, both villages were equally prosperous, until the main stream supplying water to the fields of Wokcing mysteriously dried up. That was the same year that Mongseng was born. The people of Poilung silently believed that the villagers of Wokcing must have done something wrong to incur the river god's wrath.

Before long, the *Ang* of Wokcing decided to try and correct any wrongdoings by borrowing some of Poilung's prosperity. He sent warriors to snatch some agricultural land. The Poilung *Ang,* Mongseng's father, wanted to settle the matter amicably. Those fields the Wokcing warriors occupied were anyway plots that were far for Poilung farmers to go and attend to daily. He decided to rent that land to Wokcing on the condition that the Wokcing people would pay rent in the form of labour by helping in the other fields of Poilung. To discuss those terms, the Poilung *Ang* sent two of his wisest village men. The Wokcing *Ang* received them warmly. Between the talks, rice beer flowed freely. But by the end of the day the outcome wasn't very good. The wise men from Poilung, well and truly intoxicated, didn't remain wise. Throwing diplomacy out the window, they told their host how they really felt on the issue of grabbing land.

The two wise men were returned to Poilung, silent and headless. The *Ang*, with no inkling of how his wise men had behaved was infuriated. That same evening the *Ang* sent twenty of his best warriors to talk a little more, this time with spears and *daos*. At dawn the party returned, the five leading warriors each carrying a head in their left hand, and their glistening blood-smeared *dao* in the right. Since that time, *daos*, spears and arrows were the only forms of communication that went back and forth between the two neighbouring villages.

When the first heads started coming from her village, Naro realized that the path to her parent's home had been cut off forever. She bore no grudge towards her husband, for she knew he was looking after his people, which was her home now too. Instead of mourning, Naro became busy with her own growing family, first giving birth to Mongseng, who was welcomed into Poilung with celebrations that lasted two full nights and days. Compared to this, the birth of her next five children, three boys and two girls, was a low-key affair.

Time passed and Mongseng grew to the height of his mother's ears. Time turned, and Naro reached up to her son's shoulders. Then news came from Wokcing, first through the log drums, then through messengers, that Naro's dying mother wished to have one last glimpse of her daughter. After consultations with her husband and a few village elders, a decision was made. Naro should go, but it was best for her to go alone. Among the Konyak people it was an accepted custom that warriors from a village did not hunt heads of people whose roots were the same as their own.

Naro felt guilt and excitement simultaneously. Guilt, because she felt she was betraying her husband's village by visiting their enemy; excitement at once again seeing her parents and childhood home. She dressed in her queen's attire – a knee-length white cotton wraparound decorated with cowrie shells and the hair of human, goat and bear. Multiple strands of necklaces in symmetrical lengths of red, blue and green beads formed a layer from neck to chest, covering up her breasts. Above her elbows, four-inch thick ivory tusk armlets adorned both arms. More beaded red and blue beads wound around her calves completed her visiting attire. The queen, anticipating a feast to welcome her, set off for the short journey with a pauper's ration of a few roasted taro and sweet potato pods.

As she set off, Naro hummed a lullaby her mother used to sing to her when she was a little girl. Down the jungle path she trod, across terraced fields, on to the ravine, and across the stream. It was a path she knew, but in the still of the morning, unknown to her, long shadows concealed Mongseng, first becoming a tree, then a cluster of rice reeds in the fields, then a rock in the river. His instincts had told him to go with his mother; he trusted his intuition more than tradition. As Naro walked, the log drum of Poilung reverberated throughout the hills with the message of her impending visit. The Wokcing drum responded in welcome. Still keeping his distance, Mongseng allowed himself to relax once his mother reached the wooden arched gate of Wokcing.

At the gate, there was a beeline of people to welcome Naro

into her parents' home. The pathway from the village's log gate to her parent's house was lined with women dressed in their traditional garb. They performed a merry dance and sang in rhythm to their footsteps. A noble *mithun*, the local cattle, and two pigs were slaughtered for the feast. The village came to life as if spring had arrived in the middle of winter. The mood was so infectious even Naro's mother found temporary relief and arose from her bed for the celebration. With stealth and curiosity, Mongseng observed the proceedings from the shadows of a tree across the village fence.

After hours of merriment and reunions with family and friends, it was time for Naro to depart. The sun had moved unnoticed from the eastern sky to the west, and she wanted to reach Poilung before dark. On reluctant feet, after a tearful farewell, she retraced her morning steps. After the rekindled warmth of family and friends, once the excitement of the day had faded, she felt a little uneasy walking alone. As a woman, and especially as a queen, she was used to an entourage of women and warriors guarding her whenever she stepped out. Being the giver of birth, women were the most important, fertile possession of a village. If a warrior brought back from a hunt a woman's head, it was considered the most prized trophy. Hence, women were highly valued by rivals and preciously protected by allies. The thought that she could cross paths with a warrior from another village, other than Wokcing, crossed her mind. For the first time in her marriage, she felt anger towards her husband for having overlooked that possibility.

Mongseng, sensing her unease, closed the gap between them and decided to let his company be known. When Suddenly, up ahead, Naro came face to face with a warrior. By the way he tied his tuft of hair he unmistakably belonged to her parents' village. Momentarily, Naro felt relieved, reckoning that her parents had sent the warrior to escort her back to Poilung. But then, why was he approaching from the opposite direction? And why was he approaching with a raised *dao*? The tweeting songs of the birds disappeared. Only the glint on the *dao* blade shone against the blue barren sky. As the blade came down, Naro observed the shimmer of the setting sun slid over its narrow end.

The next sound Naro heard was the metallic 'cling' of the *dao* – not against bone, but against stones on the path. The world came back to her. And with it the familiar comforting figure of her son, standing in full stead behind the crumbling figure of the warrior. With the return of birdsong came a final muffled gurgle as Mongseng's spear pierced the warrior's life out. As relieved and happy to see her son as when she had given him birth, she hugged Mongseng who turned her face away from the dead killer. Over his mother's shoulder Mongseng observed the dead warrior. He had tattoos on his face, hands and feet, but none on his chest. When a Konyak warrior took a head, his chest was denoted with a special tattoo. The absence of any tattoo on the dead warrior's chest could mean only one thing – that his mother would have been the warrior's first head. Mongseng was surprised; the dead warrior was his father's age.

When Naro eventually turned around she realized she recognized the dead warrior. It was Chingmak. A long time ago, before the *Ang's* proposal, he had professed his heart to her and offered himself as a suitor. Unfortunately, Chingmak didn't have the heart to fetch her a human head to prove that he was man enough to protect her for life. It now seemed he never could acquire a head or a wife, as the tattoos that adorned a man's arm that proclaimed him a married man were missing too. Naro felt a pang of sadness for him, but no sooner had sorrow arrived it was replaced by anger. How could he think of taking her life after proposing to spend the rest of his life with her even though it never came to fruition? Naro's grim face relaxed as Mongseng let out a high-pitched war cry as he took Chingmak's head with one clean swing of his *dao*. Mother and son performed a traditional war dance matching step for step, completing three circles around the body.

Through the ravine, Mongseng's war cry travelled miles to reach the ears of the log drummer of the men's communal *morung* in Poilung. The drummer then relayed the arrival of a fresh head to the world. Poilung bloomed with activity. Men busied themselves with preparations to receive the head. Women busied themselves to feed the festivity. The *Ang* supervised the reception committee of warriors that gathered at the entrance to Poilung. As Mongseng arrived at the gates with Naro, the shrill war cries of the tattooed warriors armed with their *daos,* spears and shields could be heard for miles. For a moment even the birds stopped singing in the woods and listened. Children jumped with joy, following Mongseng holding the head by its tuft of hair. A boy poked at the head with his fingers making it swing like a pendulum. His mother quickly pulled him away and threw an embracing smile towards Naro, wishing one day it would be her son in the middle of a similar procession returning after winning a similar gift for the village.

As Mongseng placed the head on the log drum inside the *morung,* a village elder struck the drum with his club headed sticks, shiny from years of use, extracting the gruff melody. It was an intricately carved, fifteen feet long cylindrical wooden drum made from the single trunk of a mature *sesam* tree. Multiple woodenheads jutted out from the sides. A tree which had lived its full life before dying, drying and falling to the ground on its own accord. The hollow inside of the drum was high enough for a five-year-old child to easily stand erect. Its amplified boom easily reached Wokcing, where the sounds created a different atmosphere, the ripples of which would move back and forth between the two villages for a long time to come.

Proudly, *Wangba* handed his son a rooster. It had crowed its 'cooook-raak-cooo' that morning, waking the *Ang* too early, for the last time. In one motion Mongseng twisted and plucked off its head and offered the dripping blood from its neck to the human head. Elders sitting around the log drum hummed a prayer to bless the village with fertility in the days to come. Then one by one they broke an egg over the head and wished prosperity for the village, their individual families, and for themselves.

As the ceremony and celebrations continued, the eldest queen, Saningla, smiled at Naro and tapped her ink needle on Mongseng's chest. As the eldest queen it was her responsibility to decorate the chest of all village warriors who claimed a head. Saningla had become an expert, decorating many chests with tattoos symbolic of fertile fields, sheds full with livestock, and rivers and streams brimming with water to feed the crops. With years of practice, Saningla didn't need to trace the designs on Mongseng's chest. Beginning the proclamation of his status as a successful warrior she straightaway inked the designs on to his amber chest. Elsewhere, the blacksmith of the village busied himself with a small glob of brass, shaping it into the form of a head. Each head a warrior claimed was rewarded with a small brass replica, worn as a pendent on a red beaded necklace. In another corner of the village, other craftsmen were shaping a headdress. To a round, finely woven cane hat they attached a pair of *mithun* horns, one on each side, with a pair of boar tusks forming an arch in the front. To finish it off, hornbill feathers woven into a circle were attached to the back of the wicker crown.

Saningla's son Sangting, five years younger to Mongseng, came and looked curiously at the design his mother was creating. He had his first facial tattoo and his front teeth had been chiselled to represent a tiger's fangs, proclaiming him an adult at the age of ten. Saningla looked at her own son and wondered when she would have the privilege of decorating Sangting's chest. Enjoying the display, Sangting moved to the other side and admired the blood-stained *dao* lying next to his elder brother. Smiling, he picked it up, barely managing to hold it upright. Saningla smiled, her dream would have to wait.

Once the tattoos were complete, the *Ang* led Mongseng and the village elders to the head-tree where a few skulls in various states of decomposition already hung. It had been months since the last head had arrived. Deftly, two elders removed the oldest skull, free from all fragments of skin or hair, to be taken back to the *Ang's* hut and hung from the bamboo wall at the entrance. Then, with ceremony, Mongseng placed the fresh head into a netted bamboo busket and hung it to a branch of the tree. Throughout the night, rice beer flowed by the bamboo mugful from bottomless earthen cauldrons. The *Ang's* white friend, the Padre, didn't participate in the proceedings and looked on from his guest hut, scarcely hiding his disapproval. Endless songs praising Mongseng and the warriors of Poilung continued from indefatigable throats, until the light from the glowing wood fire embers was replaced by the amber of dawn in the eastern sky.

By the time Mongseng became of marriageable age, another eight brass heads had been added to the red-bead necklace. Almost every eligible girl from every *khel* – division – in Poilung vied for his attention. *Wangba,* his father had married three wives; his grandfather had married twenty-five. Mongseng was free to marry as many wives as he could afford to look after. But by then he had already given his heart to Meailing. Mongseng reasoned, since he had only one heart, he could give it to only one woman. Dividing it into pieces could lead to pain; he saw his father go through hurt every few days when his mother or one of his step-mothers went through their monthly mood cycles. When that happened the *Ang* sought refuge in the intoxicating liquid gifted by his friend the Padre. Mongseng revered and respected his father, but on these occasions he didn't like what he saw. He himself, even in celebration, always remained a teetotaller.

Being the eldest son of the *Ang* and having expressly stated his will to marry only one wife, the king arranged a lavish wedding, sparing no expense. On the day, five *mithuns,* three stags, ten pigs and untold chickens and wild birds were slaughtered for the feast. Neighbouring villagers arrived from afar and, for the day, even Wokcing forgot its hostility. But amongst the guests from Wokcing were the family of Chingmak – Mongseng's first kill. Seeing much love between the newlyweds, old, repressed resentments began to rise. Like dry wood burning from inside, not a spark was visible, yet the red-hot embers simmered within.

A week before the wedding, with help from his friends and

other skilled villagers, Mongseng had cut a step on the hill, just below his father's house. He would build a love nest for Meailing. A frame was built with the split branches of trees, whose trunks were used as stilts. Double bamboo mats became walls. *Takou,* palm leaves woven in the shape of a longish arc, with a narrow front, like the pointed head of an arrow, became the roof. When the newlyweds moved in, not a single joint creaked under their playful feet. Even when they made love the stilts stood firm, as strong as their bond of love.

Once the honeymoon was over, the young couple settled down to their life together. Being the king's son and bravest warrior did not exempt Mongseng from mundane day-to-day work. During the day he used his head-chopping skills for chopping firewood, one skill polishing and perfecting the other. When Meailing went to the fields, Mongseng went with her to watch out for rival warriors. While Meailing cultivated, he shot at birds and squirrels with his slingshot to add to the evening's pot. Mongseng still went hunting for bigger game, but now his responsibilities continued after returning with the hunted animal to the village. If it was a communal hunt he carried his share of the animal home, performing the cleaning and chopping before Meailing cooked the meal. Left over meat was cured with salt before beading the chunks into necklaces of green bamboo vines. Then Meailing hung the meat over the kitchen fireplace to dry and preserve for later.

Meanwhile Chinmak's family after attending the wedding and returning to Wokcing had kept the embers of hate burning. They slowly kindled the hate amongst their villagers and the ambers spread, festered and turned into hot lava, spreading around the village, burning any newly found peace. In Poilung however, there was no heat of hatred, and life resumed as usual. Perhaps pacified by the well-attended wedding feast, the warriors of Poilung became a little casual, thinking they had quenched their neighbour's hunger for blood. Sometimes hunting parties went only with their spears and bows, leaving behind their unwieldy shields. At times, women toiled in the fields, plough and prodding with scant protection, while the men preferring to drink rice beer in the shade of the *morung*. As the day's passed, the *Ang* too got into the habit of taking an extra helping of the leftover rum stocks, brought by the Padre, especially for Mongseng's wedding.

Routine was however hard to maintain for long. There were always heads to be accounted for. Life felt gentle, until one afternoon, like lightning in a tranquil blue-sky, tragedy came unannounced. Out in the fields, shrill war cries filled the air. The women and children of Poilung ran towards the narrow village path as Chingmak's brothers, friends and cousins launched their attack. That day, Sangkok had been the only warrior to escort the group to the fields. Hearing the piercing war cries froze him in his tracks. But before he had even seen them, a Wokcing warrior's *dao* pitched him to the ground, headless. Along the heavily forested track, running in single file, those at the end of the queue never made it back to the village safely.

Sitting in the *morung,* the *Ang* and a few old warriors who had been sharing the Padre's gift since morning unmistakably heard the cries. While the elderly only wielded a *dao* for chopping wood or peeling cane, intoxication and anger made them feel young and brave. The men helped themselves to what they could. Slotted into the bamboo weaving of the entrance wall of the *morung* were the *daos* of slain enemies. Years of disuse and slime from the fat of roasted meat had made the *daos* blunt, but the men were in no mind to know. Retrieving the weapons, the retired warriors moved with purpose towards the cries. Along the path, panicked, disjointed voices offered all that they needed to hear. "Wokcing warriors…" "Yes, they killed many…" They charged down the hill, *daos* at the ready.

Anger sees no reason. And laced with intoxicants, it goes blind.

By the time Mongseng had gathered his warriors and reached the outskirts of Wokcing, a scene of carnage lay before them. On the path they found four headless women. Another lay headless in the fields and besides her body lay Sangkok's. Bent over a rock, propped up by a broken spear from behind, the iron head of the spear protruding out between his collarbone and neck, Mongseng found his father's body. But his head remained intact. Not far lay the other seven of the party, their blood mingling with the wet, fertile earth. None of the eight bodies had been beheaded. The Wokcing warriors had maintained the custom of not hunting the heads of the old and frail. The *Ang* and his men had come as warriors to challenge them. Their challenge had been respected and they were given a warrior's death. Mongseng understood what had happened, keeping his own head and stifling his weeping heart he ordered his men to carry the bodies of his father and fallen tribesmen back to the village. Chingmak's family had taken revenge for their fallen brother. It was an eye for an eye, a kill for a kill; and he had made the first kill with Chingmak. If he did not stop his men then and there, this blood feud would have no end.

In the mourning village, Mongseng was greeted with hostility. The villagers wanted him to bring vengeance and heads, but all he returned with was reason. Even Meailing felt betrayed. She wondered if her love had made Mongseng weak. Wouldn't a man avenge his dear father's death? Not to mention Sangkok, who also happened to be his wife's brother? Not knowing what else to do, Mongseng maintained his stance. In the privacy of his home, he patiently helped his wife understand his point of view. If they started taking heads for revenge, the killing would never end. How could heads taken in hate really remain auspicious and bring the village fertility?

In time, Mongseng's reason and love calmed Meailing. Even his mother, Naro, understood Mongseng's reason. She had lost her husband, but at least he had had a warrior's death. The powers that be, in the sky, in the streams, in the trees, would accept her husband and embrace him, for he had been an honourable man. In the rest of the village however, among Mongseng's stepmothers and villagers alike, there were no feelings of love or patience. They remained restless.

FIVE

MYSTIFIED, MONGSENG LOOKED ON FROM ATOP ARADURA SPUR. Below him mortar shells blew up soil, and occasionally fragments of men. For some odd reason, the gore reminded him of a calming sight; the welcoming showers of spring, when the first nascent, pregnant raindrops hit the thirsty, barren earth and sent the dust flying up. He wondered why the gory sight unfolding in front of him reminded him of such a tranquil memory. He could tell there would be no spring after that show of fiery blast from the sky.

Was he going insane staying amidst the madness that was unfolding between the two warring sides? He could take his ten heads and disappear. No. He told himself. He couldn't turn away from such destruction. He was a warrior, he wouldn't run from a battlefield however alien it might sound and look. He had come here to settle a purpose back home; he had to achieve that purpose, or else he would definitely not be a worthy son of the deceased *Wangba* of Poilung. He would not let go to waste the purpose with which his father, the *Ang* had raised him. Mongseng made up his mind to stay on and keep himself focused on the reason he had travelled so far to this foreign people and their culture. The warrior retraced his steps downhill after taking one absorbing glance to note the different bushes, contours in the soil and shape of stones around the cavern where he hid the heads.

Using his Zeiss field glasses (gifted by an Australian Captain who had lost his eyesight in the Second Battle of El Alamein), Tom focused on pinpointing the Japanese position on the hill across the road. His fine pair of field glasses transported him almost into a Japanese bunker. The enemy seemed to be swarming into the Kohima hills like a colony of ants converging around a cube of sugar. The ragtag bunch of Tom's garrison would be a sweet target for any organized army to devour. Immediately in front of his lenses there seemed to be at least a company which was entrenching themselves just across their side of the Garrison. The rumours of a full-scale Japanese army approaching Kohima was materializing in front of his eyes.

Out of the din came a nearby voice, "Goot ebening!"

Tom jumped backwards, fumbling to retrieve his Sten gun, almost hitting the roof of the bunker. Doubling back, he tripped over Raan who cushioned Tom's fall. The accent of the words had sounded to Tom like a Japanese soldier trying to speak English. That, coupled with the powerful focus of the binoculars, made Tom think he had been discovered by the enemy. Recovering from their impromptu wrestle, Tom recomposed himself and looked at the entrance. Silently and casually, the naked warrior stepped into the bunker and leaned calmly against the mud wall, looking amused at the tangled pair. "Goot ebening," he repeated.

"*Sahib*, he spoke! He spoke English!" exclaimed Raan, mouth wide open, turning from the savage to his boss.

Looking at the savage, both men echoed, "You speak English?"

"Lil'thil, lil'thil." Mongseng replied, stepping further into the bunker, now with caution, making sure that his captors wouldn't try to tie him down again.

"Why didn't you say anything when we found you?" Tom asked, straightening and stiffening somewhat, trying to regain the posture of the officer that he was supposed to be. Following his boss's lead, Raan stood to attention next to his *Sahib*.

"You *amake* chance *nidi*, *sidha* tie me. What speak?" Mongseng replied in a dismissive tone, complaining that he was immediately tied up without a chance to explain himself. He looked away from them to see where their fire-spitting spears were kept.

"But you had the whole day after that?" Tom reasoned sceptically.

"I see, think, speak *na* run." Mongseng answered as a matter of fact.

Adding to Tom's interrogation Raan rattled, "You... you should have told me at least where you were going this morning. You left me there to die! You made me look bad in front of my *Sahib*." He looked at Tom for approval. Tom nodded and he continued, "I thought I let my *Sahib* down by taking you out and getting you killed." While he rattled off his objection, head swaying from side to side, Raan rubbed his ears with the palm of his hands, trying to relieve the ringing noise still going on from the blast.

"I think you pray, so I go. If you tied, you get free, you not go?" The unfair accusations helped Mongseng remember more of the white man's language than he would have mastered, had they been having a normal conversation. Mongseng's solid logic in broken English shut Raan up.

"Then why have you come back?" Tom intervened.

"I help. Kill enemy."

That was what Tom wanted of him and when he heard that, he found Mongseng's reason to stay hard to believe. When a situation unfolds in a way that it seems too good to be true, it is hard to believe it to be true. A doubtful fear arose in Tom's mind. Maybe this savage was being planted in their midst by the Japanese. Were those he killed even Japanese? Tom was too repelled by the sight to take a closer look at the severed heads. Now he regretted his momentary lapse of judgement back at the enemy trench. He should have examined the massacre closely. Were those men killed by the savage actually Nagas dressed up by Japanese soldiers to look like themselves and asked the savage to kill them and make him their bait to throw into the British Garrison? How else could a savage with his primitive weapons kill ten soldiers armed with machine guns and the latest rifles? The gory sight of the massacre in the cave played back in Tom's mind and an involuntary convulsion rose in him. He steadied himself by immediately trying to take his mind elsewhere.

"Where did you learn your English?"

"O, we have one man like you visit village. Same, same, very white like you." The savage emphasized on 'very'.

And Tom took offense on the word. He liked the privileges that came with his colour in a colonized country, but he never liked to be considered pale. "What is that white man doing in your village?" Tom asked coldly.

"He try give us something call god. He say we pray wrong power. He say nature power no good."

"Oh. A missionary, a padre?"

'Yes, yes. He like we call padre him. First English word he teach us is padre." Mongseng humoured himself, recollecting that instance from far back in his memory.

"Padre is not an English word. It is..." Raan tried to show off his knowledge but found himself unsure. Cutting short Raan's intrusion, Tom threw him an angry stare, raising his left eyebrow, which made the right end of his moustachio tilt down. Tom continued, "Did the Padre tell you to come here and help us kill the Japanese?"

"Ah! No, he say no kill. No enemy. All that god man's people. Kill is sign, sine...something like that he say. No bad do, go somewhere he call hav...an, some good place after die." Mongseng scratched his head trying to recollect the name of the place the Padre mentioned where good people could go after death.

Tom left Raan to get to know the savage better. Now that one issue was solved, he returned to the larger issue at hand. He had to strategize and organize the rest of his men and prepare them for what was inevitably approaching.

Raan and Mongseng spoke – Raan expressed his curiosity, Mongseng tried to answer Raan's curiosity with his limited ability in English. He could comprehend much better than what he could speak. He was a good listener and the white friend of the *Ang,* the Padre had always liked to lecture, not teach. The Padre had used a fair bit of Assamese with his English while preaching. Mongseng learnt his English by picking up the Assamese words the Padre threw in between his sermons and joined them together to get a gist of what the Padre spoke in English. He grasped everything Raan asked. And when he wanted to answer, his English vocabulary clashed with his Konyak and Assamese words with the same meaning. Living in Assam for a while, Raan could understand Mongseng in scattered bits.

A commonality in language can make a stranger seem acquainted. A savage, civilized.

Speaking the English language helped Mongseng in another way that night. It made the rope restraining him disappear. Though he could lie down freely to take a nap, another issue stopped him. It wasn't pain that was troubling him; it was comfort. After his captors realized that he was not a 'savage', they began treating him more humanely. Instead of making him sleep on a bare metal trunk, Tom sent Raan to DIS Hill to bring in extra bedding. It was the softest bed Mongseng had ever slept on. It was so cosy it made him uncomfortable.

In contrast, there was no chance of peace or comfort that night for the Imperial Japanese forces brimming around the garrison. After their long march from Burma across the Chindwin River, they were keen to get down to business, shelling the garrison intermittently. What saved the garrison from a relentless bombardment was the terrain the Japanese had traversed to reach Kohima. On arduous jungle slopes they had lost half their ammunition and equipment and had to ration their supply.

As well as his mattress, Mongseng's keen sense of hearing wasn't proving a gift under the circumstances. The commotion also kept his two not so gifted bunker companions wide-awake. That night, Tom could have sent Mongseng to stay with Chetri, but he thought the native might prove useful. Tom looked at Raan, whose eyes replaced the full moon hidden by the smog of the explosions.

"Raan, how about you make some tea for us?"

"Yes, *Sahib*." As he squatted on the floor and pulled out the stove, Raan snapped out of the dread that engulfed him.

Meanwhile, Tom pulled out a map of the surrounding area from his duffle bag. He intended to use the map to pinpoint enemy positions and also if need be, to find an escape route from the Garrison. It was a project he had kept to himself and intended to keep that way till the hour of need proved otherwise. But perhaps Mongseng could help to point out the accuracies and inaccuracies of the map. On a makeshift table of piled high ammunition boxes Tom spread the map and drew Mongseng's attention.

"Hey, Mongseng, do you know what this is?"

As the glow from a blast added its light, Mongseng took a look and replied in a monosyllable, "Haw?"

Tom understood it was going to be a long night.

"You know what a painting is?"

"Ha?"

"*Sobe*." Raan called out the Assamese word for picture, to try and help out the cause.

To their surprise, Mongseng did understand, "Ah! *Hoi, jane*."

"He understood, *Sahib*!" Raan's face glowed, not just from the light of the stove. Tom let a smile escape from his otherwise serious face.

Outside around the periphery of the Garrison, the battle raged on as a series of skirmishes between the Garrison frontline defenders and Japanese forces. Each testing the other's mettle. While inside the Garrison, in a bunker, an Oxford-educated British officer was waging another battle. A battle with words. Tom was trying to explain what a map was in as simple language as possible. As the incursions on the periphery ceased, so did Tom end his expedition on the map.

Letting Mongseng keep an eye on the developments outside and asking Raan to keep an eye on Mongseng, Tom, exhausted from the battle with words, decided to take a nap. It was 4.30 am. He set an alarm for 6 am. While his *Sahib* slept, Raan busied himself with cleaning. Slowly the sun's golden rays crept up the hill and into the bunker, oblivious to the horrors that defaced that patch of earth. Yet, Mongseng observed one thing was missing. There was no chorus of birds welcoming the day.

Bathed in sunlight, the protruding stones and roots on the wall of the bunker cast shadows of ephemeral forms, reminding Mongseng of his own hut where, upon waking, he enjoyed gazing at shadows on the ceiling created by sunlight leaking through the gaps of the woven bamboo walls.

In his early morning reverie inside the trench, Mongseng thought of Meailing, his wife. How she woke up every morning long before the sun and finished the chores around the house. He always woke up to a cup of freshly brewed tea, made with tealeaf plucked and sun-dried from the bushes around their hut. Amid his reverie, Mongseng noticed a mortar resting on the wall of the bunker. That deadly human creation reminded him of the hollow cylindrical bamboo container they stored their tealeaves in – a gift from Meailing's parents on their wedding day. That bamboo container was an heirloom, having been handed down in Meailing's family from one member to the next for generations. Every new owner, every new pair of hands, and the smoke from the hearth over which it hung, turned the outer body smoother, darker, a rich golden brown.

By the time Mongseng sipped the bitter cup of tea, sweetened with a smile from his wife, she would be sitting in the corner on the handloom. In summer weaving a woollen shawl in preparation for winter, and in winter weaving a cotton wraparound for summer.

While Mongseng's thoughts floated to his love, another man, a man who had no love for him, was thinking of Mongseng. It was the Padre in Poilung. Since he had arrived in the village, a decade earlier, with a crate of rum, he had been observing and calculating his move. But the Padre was a patient man. He was waiting for an opportunity, rather than hurry. He knew the older generation would not be easy to convert. However similar he tried to make his bearded God to their nature Gods, they couldn't be convinced that a human could be the supreme power. They reasoned, how could a human be the power that holds the balance, when he is not even in control of himself. He needs the skin of animals in winter to fend from the cold, the shade of a tree in summer to shield from the heat. Whereas, even the tiniest living creature, the ant needs no such protection to survive? The Padre had no answer.

The *Wangba* and the other elders could be fooled when they were drunk, but in the morning once they regained their senses, they reverted back to their old beliefs. The Padre thought the younger generation would be easier to convince. In fact he would have long ago ploughed the younger generation with the seeds of his new god. However, even that did not prove so simple. His plough got stuck in a stubborn rock that was Mongseng's mind.

Mongseng did not ignore the Padre outright. He tried to imbibe the new with the old. But for the Padre's purpose, this was a dangerous combination. Neither did Mongseng reject the material objects or new thoughts the Padre brought from the new world. Mongseng weighed the new, and tried to see how it could enhance the old. How trend could fortify tradition. When the Padre started building a new *morung* it aroused Mongseng's curiosity. He was interested to know how mud cast into blocks and baked in fire could become strong like stone. How a type of rock broken down to dust could again become rock-like and hold the mudstones together. The *morung* built with those mudstones and rock dust became stronger than any bamboo or wood-built house.

However, once the *morung* was completed, Mongseng was not keen on the stories being told under the shadow of a log cross, tied up with cane. It was risky business to lift two huge pieces of log on to the slippery metal roof of the new *morung* and no one in the village was too keen to take on the job. The Padre had to pay ten men a pig each before they agreed to take on the job. The importance was beyond Mongseng's comprehension. When he asked the Padre why, he said it was the symbol of his God. It was symbolic of the supreme sacrifice 'He' made for mankind. It was a symbol to remind humans how benevolent a giver 'He' was. If they believed in Him, the Padre said their village would become very prosperous. Mongseng wondered why a God needed to be given a symbol. For Mongseng the natural bounties of Mother Earth and Mother Nature were actualities. There was no need for symbolism.

One thing Mongseng did comprehend clearly was the Padre was trying to tweak their old stories. Stories that have been passed on verbally for countless generations. Within these yarns the Padre tried to slot in his bearded God. Every time he managed to weave Him in smoothly with their ancient Gods, Mongseng would un-weave the new threads.

He argued with the Padre that, if his bearded God was so similar, why did his ways and preaching sound so foreign? Mongseng argued that what the Padre wanted them to do to become good followers and improve their lifestyle would destroy their traditions. When the Padre tried to reply to Mongseng's arguments, his reasoning sounded even more distant than the faith he was preaching. However, not all of Mongseng's friends and family were as stubborn or questioning as him. Seeing the good things the Padre brought for them from distant lands convinced many that his teachings and preaching must be good too. With those fresh young converts Mongseng fought on with words. Some saw their loss and returned to their old ways. A few stayed on in the new faith.

The most vocal, in favour of the new faith, amongst the fresh converts was Sangting, Mongseng's own brother. In spite of being the eldest queen's oldest son, he was younger than Mongseng and hence next in line after Mongseng, to become the king. Since the time Sangting was old enough to have a mind of his own, he had resented Mongseng. Sangting believed that it was Mongseng's fault he didn't get as much attention from his father. He was not only second in line to the throne; he believed he was also second in line to receive the *Ang's* love and adoration. In Sangting the Padre found an eager, younger, potentially powerful pair of ears, away from the *Ang* and the elders. The Padre filled Sangting's head with thoughts. Ideas of politics from a distant continent where being the eldest son was not enough, to become king you had to be the eldest son of the eldest queen. The Padre slowly instilled those thoughts, letting them find a permanent home in Sangting.

In time, the Padre managed to build a wall between the brothers, and then the *Ang* was suddenly no more. With the *Ang* gone and half the villagers enraged with Mongseng for not avenging his own father's death and the death of their relatives and friends, Padre finally had the playing field to unleash his game plan. It seemed Padre's aspirations of converting the whole village to his faith could suddenly be realized. He added fuel to the adolescent sparks in Sangting's mind.

With the *Ang* no more and with him his generation of elders wiped out, Padre became the only elder left in the village. Some of the youngsters and parents started looking up to him. But he was an italian and a foreigner could not be elected as the king of their village. But they wanted his active involvement in deciding their next *Ang,* since now it was a matter of dispute. A moment so opportune even Padre was confused whom to thank, God or luck. Padre reasoned that if he could make Sangting the next *Ang,* his dream to convert these wild people would become a reality soon. If the *Ang* followed what the Padre preached, it would not be long before his subjects followed in his footsteps.

Padre proposed that Sangting be made the next *Wangba* of Poilung. Saningla, the eldest queen, sided with the proposal. But Poilung did not fully buy in. Mongseng was older, and a much-loved and gifted warrior. The village remained divided. Though, they agreed unanimously that the bravest son of Poilung should become the next *Wangba*. Till the incident of the death of his father and his resolve not to avenge his death, Mongseng had been without doubt the rightful heir, with ten heads to his tally. Even Mongseng's father hadn't held that score when he replaced his grandfather. But the past events put the villagers' minds in doubt that bravery might have left

Mongseng's heart. In contrast, Sangting only had one brass head on his necklace. A warrior with a single head wasn't an exception, but this was a prerequisite to even be considered a warrior. The villagers could not accept Sangting as equally brave as his brother.

His proposal defeated, Padre took a leaf out of the book of older Konyak tradition. In the freshly constructed mudstone *morung* he called a village meeting to propose that over the next year the position of *Wangba* should remain vacant. During that period if Sangting managed to collect more heads than Mongseng, he should be made the *Ang*. A loud murmur buzzed around the *morung*. In groups the villagers discussed the pros and cons of the proposal. The next two warriors who had six heads each were good friends of Mongseng and they still looked up to him and would not think of sidestepping him to become the *Ang*. Though the villagers of Poilung were sceptical about Sangting matching up to his brother's heads tally within a year, they reasoned that at best the proposal meant more heads for their village's prosperity. With that prospect in mind, they unanimously agreed to Padre's proposal. While Padre didn't approve of headhunting, to make his candidate the ruler of Poilung he was willing to set aside that minor hurdle for now.

Mongseng didn't want to participate in the Padre's contest. He was confident his brother didn't possess a heart as brave as his and would struggle to bring home heads. Even the single head Sangting had managed to win was by accident. He didn't hunt for the head; he was out on a boar hunt with Mongseng. When after hours of searching they couldn't find a single quarry, he decided to take a break. Mongseng kept on with the search while Sangting found a cool spot to rest. Under the shadow of the cliff on which Poilung stood, Sangting took a nap. As he slept, a wandering warrior from a distant village, unfamiliar with the terrain bordering Poilung, had practically stumbled and fell onto Sangting's spear resting against a bush. A head was a head and nobody asked Sangting how he acquired it.

Mongseng did not hate Sangting like his brother hated him. Coming from a big family of twenty-three brothers and sisters with three mothers between them, they were like casual friends. Acquainted with each other, yet to some extent strangers. Mongseng, a naturally gifted child, was not in the house often. His father kept him busy. On the other hand, Sangting grew up at home, pampered by his mother, Saningla. At best, Mongsen had the usual love and annoyance that any elder brother has for his sibling.

The only other person, who knew the truth behind Sangting's headhunt, was Padre. In the zeal of following his new faith to the dot, during a session, Sangting confessed to Padre the incident behind his first and only headhunt. Padre had sworn him into secrecy and asked him never to tell anyone that his kill was by accident. During his years of visiting Poilung, Padre had found a few followers also because he doubled as a healer. When the village tiger man or healer could not cure an ailment, the ill went to Padre as a last hope. With verses from his red sacred book and some small magic white and yellow seeds he managed to cure many of them. The seeds tasted bitter, but many a times yielded sweet results. The cured became a believer in the powers of the padre and his God.

Unknown to Mongseng, after the meeting with the village, Padre summoned Sangting to his hut. He told Sangting that if luck provided him with one head, it would provide him with more. Sangting was happy to follow any path that could help him achieve his ambition. They planned another accident or a series of them to guarantee Sangting's appointment as the *Wangba*. Padre's bag of medicines could cure and a few could kill. In the dead of the night while the rest of the village slept, Sangting collected some water-soluble poison from Padre and headed towards a stream with four of his trusted friends. Their destination was half a day's walk from Poilung.

The stream flowed across a path frequented by people from two villages. They reached the stream at dawn and hid themselves atop a dense covering of grass, with a good view of the path. For hours they lay hidden without a soul passing by, except the occasional wild hog or wolf. In the afternoon their luck changed and they spotted a lone villager walking towards the stream. Sangting opened the bottle gourd container and measured half a bamboo cup of the poison, as instructed by Padre, and poured it into the stream. The five watched anxiously. They knew the poison would work because when it travelled downstream they saw small fish and crabs bobbing up from under rocks and crevices. The villager took a drink of water with his cupped hands and stood up. Nothing happened. He went over to a shady tree, unwrapped a woollen shawl he had over his shoulder and using it as a pillow stretched out to take a nap. The five waited patiently. They must have been waiting for hours since they saw the round shadow of the tree around the sleeping man become long and sliding away from him leaving him exposed to the sun. One of them threw a pebble on the sleeping villager. He didn't stir. Sangting slipped out from his hiding and approached the tree like a cat. With trembling hands he raised his *dao* over the blissful man who would sleep forever.

Within a couple of months, Sangting had crossed Mongseng's total headcount by two.

Mongseng could sense something was not quite right. How could his brother's shaky hands suddenly become so firm with the *dao*? Nevertheless, Mongseng didn't discredit him. But Mongseng had one firm belief – one head or twelve; Sangting would not make a better *Wangba* than him. Poilung needed an *Ang* who could keep up important traditions. Even though most were against him at that moment, he knew he was the right man for the job. He had to be the next *Wangba* of Poilung. Whatever was the source of Sangting's bounty, he had to find out.

By now he had got to know his brother well enough to guess that it wasn't an act of bravery that fetched him those heads. He had noticed the pattern of his brother's expedition to go hunting for heads. Always going with the same set of four, his closest friends. And none had the reputation of being a good warrior. Mongseng followed them to the stream and took up a position above them, observing them, hiding from the hidden. Nothing happened on the first two spying missions because no unsuspecting thirsty victim stopped by the stream. But he didn't have to wait too long. On his third lookout Mongseng found his answer.

Mongseng believed in a fair fight. Since Sangting had resorted to making the competition uneven, Mongseng sought remedies. He didn't want to go hunting in the neighbourhood and start another bloody competition. Otherwise the whole purpose in not avenging his father's death would go wasted.

From afar, trickling down through the villagers, he heard gossip that there was going to be a war. A war like no other, in the big village of Kohima. Mongseng knew Kohima was many moon's walk. Strangely enough, no one in the war actually came from Kohima. It was rumoured that neither warring side had even seen the other. No one knew why they were fighting.

Around the time Sangting returned to Poilung with his thirteenth head, news came buzzing around that a group of warriors from another village had come across one warring party heading in the direction of Kohima. Those warriors had looked almost exactly like people from around them. Those who had seen them had mistaken them for Nagas. Their build was similar – strong, sturdy and lean. They had the golden-brown complexion of a Naga. Their features were soft and their hair straight and black. Only from their second skins and the magic spears they carried, the villagers could distinguish the passing warriors as not being from their villages.

That piece of news struck an idea in Mongseng. An idea that could make him the undisputed *Ang* of Poilung. An idea that would help him achieve the feat to become the *Wangba* by not taking a single local head. Thus avoiding a blood feud. With his father's death he hoped to end all fighting and bring peace to the area. He wanted to return the practice of taking heads for the essence of what it was for his ancestors – a ritualistic practice to bring prosperity for the village, not an act to settle scores.

That idea led Mongseng to walk for nine starry nights to Kohima.

SIX

AN UNRELENTING NOISE DREW MONGSENG'S MIND BACK FROM HIS village. His radiant eyes moved to a makeshift shelf cut into the earth wall where he spotted a big silvery bug. Rattling and all the time slowly sliding towards Tom's head. In a single movement the warrior grabbed his *dao,* leaped past Raan, and sliced the bug in two. Just waking up, Tom swung to the side, sandwiched between his bedding and the wall. Raan dove from his kitchen corner and grabbed Mongseng by the waist, pulling him away from his *Sahib*. An otherwise timid human being, Raan was, of course, precious about protecting his own life, but any danger he saw to his *Sahib* made him fierce as a female tigress protecting her cub. He didn't think twice to put his own life on the line for Tom.

"What?" Mongseng stared down at Raan who was now gingerly clutching at his waist, "I kill insect." Mongseng pointed to the pieces of crumpled metal. Raan let go of Mongseng and moved away, processing the shattered clock. Finally exchanging a smile of relief with Tom, who actually looked a little annoyed.

"*Aare*, what did you do?" demanded Raan, switching his tone.

"What? I kill this. Or it is biting Tom head," answered Mongseng, his chin up.

"Good job." Tom exhaled, not wanting to waste the morning explaining just what he had killed. Now awake, he had other matters on his mind and far greater dangers than from a vibrating bug.

As a Captain in the sleepy town of Kohima when he was posted there a year ago, Tom wielded a lot of power but actually had to do very little. Now he saw there was a lot to do, he suddenly felt he lacked power. The scattered batches of troops and their officers trickling in were shrinking his position. The arriving troops consisted of parts of companies, battalions and platoons whose majority had either been killed in skirmishes or taken prisoner by the Japanese while advancing towards Kohima. The small initial garrison of a couple of hundred soldiers was swelling in size. There were a few Captains now and many men going about their different tasks. Tom felt increasingly frustrated, needing to know his role in the chaos.

"*Sahib*, tea?" Raan broke the awkward silence.

"No, thank you, Raan. I have to go see the Commander. Will have morning tea with him. And while I am gone, try explaining to this guy what he chopped." Tom flicked his head towards Mongseng who was fascinated, observing the inner parts of the chopped clock. Tom stepped out of the bunker leaving Raan with the arduous task of explaining the notion of time to a man who knew day and night, with no concept of hours, minutes or seconds.

"Hello, Tom, I hear you've made good progress with our Naga commando?" With a slightly sarcastic chuckle the

Colonel added, "Who literally lives commando, I hear." He greeted Tom in a manner that betrayed any hint of the current situation bubbling to a boil around Kohima.

While walking up to the garrison command post, Tom had observed the chaos of an unorganized crowd of men looking to defend the garrison, rather than a disciplined army. Seeing the chaos had further aggravated and frustrated him, yet the poised Colonel helped him get a handle on his own agitated mind. Besides, it was a pleasant cool morning in the hills, which also helped to put a calming balm on his aggravated nerves.

"Don't know how much progress I've been able to make, sir. But he does speak a little English and I am teaching him a little more, which is becoming quite helpful."

"Oh, bloody good show, Tom. That should make him easier to command."

"Oh, yes, Colonel, well maybe, but command is a concept very foreign to him. Even though he is from a primitive culture, that fact seems to escape him. He behaves as if he is an equal."

"Well, Tom, why are you the Captain? You will have to bring him to his senses and give him a position. He has to be useful, or else there is no point of taking on more work than what we already have."

Taking the Colonel's advice as a rebuke, Tom replied, "Yes, sir, I know it is my responsibility to handle him and train him, but with so much going on I have had hardly any time to focus singularly on him."

"No problem, Captain. Can you trust him? We need every pair of hands we can get."

Richards's open expression relaxed Tom into a smile, "I think so, sir. Just this morning he saved me from a violently attacking alarm clock – chopped it clean in two."

"Ha...ha! So we can trust his machete is still sharp after taking all those heads."

"Yes, sir. Though his English is a little blunt."

"Ah, as long as his machete keeps speaking fluently, we shouldn't worry."

"That's true. Sir..." Tom paused.

"Anything else to report, Captain?" The Colonel asked sensing Tom's unease.

"Sir, actually I also came to ask you about my position. Half my men are poorly trained, inexperienced, or have never fought before. Coming under fire, many have become totally paranoid, appearing to behave worse than civilians! I had a few with me on the patrol the other day, but they were practically useless and did what they pleased. If Mongseng hadn't killed the Japs...oh, that's the name of our savage." Tom replied when his Commander looked confused by the mention of the name, and continued, "I don't know if they could have put up a fight with the Japs or would have simply run. My Gurkhas are the only men I can rely on."

Colonel Richards was aware of the situation. He himself was experiencing a similar circumstance, albeit at another level. Tom at least had the advantage of being a little familiar with the territory, and the local ways. Richards had been in Kohima less than a month, having flown in straight from Delhi. Looking at Tom with a sigh, he knew there were no easy solutions.

"Yes, and the remaining non-combatants are not helping..." Richards began, "They won't volunteer to fight, yet they seem to think they have better information on the Japs. Their whispers about the enemy are making the new recruits jittery. They are making the Japs seem larger than life. As if they are some invincible demi-gods. Though the yellow bastards themselves seem to believe their Emperor to be some sort of demi-god and willing to die like dogs at his command. Our king must envy him." Richards contemplated with a smile on his face. His gaze travelled away from Tom, into a distant solemn place.

"Well the Japs didn't have a clue about a savage's machete back there in the bunker, that's for sure." Tom added.

"Yes, that Mongseng of yours, thanks to his exploits, now the civilians seem to think we have taken the help of the devil to fight the Japanese."

"Can we send the civilians away, sir?"

"That's the plan, if we can do it before the Japs manage to close Dimapur road." Richards paused to clear his throat and continued, "They have already blocked off the road to Imphal. But before all routes become impassable we are still hoping the West Kent troops will come through. If the West Kent battalion doesn't make it through, we will have to forcibly put a gun in every available hand and hope they don't shoot themselves, or us, before the Japs do. Let's just wait and see if the West Kenters arrive, before sending away the civilians."

From the situation on hand, Tom's attention went to the situation they could face in the immediate future, "A battalion, sir? That's all the reinforcement we will have?"

"If we are lucky."

Tom tried to hide his alarm and be soldier-like, "Okay, well, what are my orders then, sir?"

"Manage your own men, try not to lose any, and just ignore the non-combatants for now. Leave them to me."

This was not quite the response Tom had been hoping to hear. He didn't like what he heard. But more than that, he was pleasantly surprised; he was a little unsettled by the Commander's clear understanding of the situation. His Commander, who had been in Kohima only for a fraction of the time compared to Tom, who had plenty on his hands and bigger strategic issues to worry about, could analyse the brewing situation at ground level better than Tom.

"Right, sir!" mouthed Tom, offering a crisp salute, making his way out of the command post, feeling subordinate in position and intellect.

It was now clear to Tom that the enemy held much larger numbers than what had previously seemed possible. Somehow they had crossed the Chindwin River and made it through the mountainous terrain and dense jungles bordering India and Burma. Tom wasn't mentally prepared to face such a full-scale onslaught. He, like many in the small garrison town hadn't actually imagined that he would ever be involved in a serious battle. Who would have thought that the Japanese would launch a full-scale invasion on Kohima, when it sat between two more lucrative targets. Imphal, the IV Corps headquarters, and Dimapur, with its railhead and airfield, were both more obvious choices. He had mentally prepared only for minor skirmishes with a couple of companies of passing Japanese troops on their way to Dimapur. For that matter, even the whole exercise of preparing the defence of the garrison in Kohima had been more of a drill rather than an actual preparation for battle.

Tom walked out of the command post, happy that his superior stayed on Field Supply Depot Hill. The rising Kuki Picket that bordered with Garrison Hill protected Tom's north flank. Not being right next to the command post had its advantages too. He could pick and choose when he wanted to see the commander.

Before the Colonel had mentioned it, Tom had not known exactly what he had wanted from Mongseng. He wasn't sure how the garrison would react if he kept a savage with him. Richards's confident assumption that he could become one of his men landed an easy decision in Tom's lap. If the commander approved, who would be able to object? Reflecting back on the incident of the chopping of the clock, it certainly proved to Tom that Mongseng meant him no harm; if anything, he was being protective. A smile lightened his grim thoughts. Yet a savage was a savage, he would stay on his guard.

In the early morning quiet, Tom decided that he would kill three birds with one stone. His visit to his commander had borne some fruit, now he would attend to a couple of other things. It had almost been a week since he had seen his wife, Sandra. He would go and visit her at Hospital Hill just around the corner from Garrison Headquarters. And while he was there he would also get his knee checked by Doctor Robin. At the Aradura Spur when his novice soldier had mistakenly fired his rifle, as Tom dived awkwardly for cover he had sprained his right knee. The adrenalin rush of the day had kept the pain at bay, but recently, and with the damp weather, the pain had returned. Not to show any weakness in front of his men, he had suffered it in silence. It could be any day now that things take a turn for the worse and the Japanese close in on Kohima like a swarm of locusts looking for easy prey. He would need a fully functional knee should he have the occasion to run.

Initially, Tom had wanted Sandra to head to Delhi or Calcutta where they had family and friends. He wanted his wife to be safe. But Sandra, having grown up in the Assamese tea garden estates of the Williamson Magor Tea Company, of which her father was a manager, found Indian cities very wild. Besides, since they had moved to Kohima, Sandra had developed close bonds with many villagers. She had adopted the hobby of documenting their lifestyle in photographic memories. Instead of leaving, Sandra volunteered as a nurse, but Tom didn't take it too well. She had made her decision from the heart, but Tom took her refusal upon his ego. It seemed that she disrespected his competence at judging the situation as a Captain in the Assam Rifles. Since she had made the decision, until the time they moved from their bungalow to their respective garrison postings, Tom had been cold towards her. But a week apart had made his ego weak.

Sandra's mother had misjudged her date of conception, leaving it too late to travel to a better hospital in Calcutta or at least to the Mission hospital in Shillong. So Sandra was born in the dispensary of the Samsa Tea Estate in Upper Assam. She had wanted her first born (and only child) to be delivered by the hands of a competent doctor. But these were not easily available in the jungle. Despite her parent's apprehensions, coupled with the mysterious disappearance of the dispensary doctor just as she came into labour, a local midwife helped to deliver a perfect little girl.

Although born pure, as Sandra grew up, in the eyes of her parents, she did take on one defect. Sandra's parents, who had grown up during the height of imperial power in colonized India lived every day with the concept of white skin superiority. As a child, Sandra fought to stay immune to racial prejudices aimed towards the natives of her birth country. She spent her early years running at every chance among the tea bushes alongside the garden labourers children. In the tea community, with strict segregation between the management, staff and labourers, her parents, managerial friends and neighbours didn't look upon this kindly. They might have gone slightly easy on her if she had mixed with clerical staff's children, who were considered higher in breed, but this was not to be. As the years ticked by and repeated parental warnings landed on deaf ears, at the tender age of nine, Sandra landed up at a Darjeeling boarding school.

Despite all attempts at segregation, Sandra's love for the natives – as her parents put it – never disappeared. When she returned to the tea estate on vacations, old friendships came out of hibernation. As she matured into a bright young outdoorsy woman, her beauty also bloomed, somehow earthy, yet regal. She wasn't the typical teenage girl who spent hours in front of a mirror. Many visiting Londoners vied for her hand, but it was Tom, with his similar Assam tea garden upbringing, who stood out in her mind as allowing her to continue the life she loved uninterrupted. Her parents were only too pleased to accept Tom as their son-in-law; at least his was the right skin colour. Yet, the Indians with whom she shared her life were close to her heart. Thus, when it came to choose between safety and assisting the Kohima villagers, she chose with her heart.

Stumbling down Garrison Hill, Tom's lanky legs felt the strain. Somewhat relieved to reach the gutter between Garrison Hill and Hospital Hill, climbing up to the hospital was easier on his sprained knee.

The hospital's main entrance resembled a beehive. Flurries of people busily moved in and out. They were either coming in bloodied, or leaving bandaged, an equal mix of soldiers and civilians. The hospital grounds exposed Tom to the full-scale repercussion of the unfolding situation. From the casualties coming in on stretchers, leaning on the shoulders of others, limping in on tree-fork crutches, Tom realized this could lead to a full-scale war earlier than he anticipated. Naga porters helping carry some of the wounded, looked on with a mixed air of anxiety and excitement, as if they had come to a dark fair. It was indeed the beginning of a fair; a fair exuding the antonym of joy – where human flesh would be offered for free and only maggots would come to feast.

Amongst the multitude of dark and light brown faces there were only a few white ones, which made spotting his wife easier. Plus Sandra's long red, wavy hair stood out amidst a sea of black. For him she was a woman who stood out amongst any crowd. Her sea blue eyes were as alluring as any ocean. Her personality lit up any dull gathering. Her openhearted laughter was distinct enough to cancel out one hundred other laughs.

"Heyyy Tommy!" Sandra emerged from the other side of the room, gliding towards her husband as fast as her legs would take her. From her red hair Tom's eyes drifted down to her white nurse's gown, now red in parts, stained with different shades of blood. Used to seeing his beautiful wife spotless, creaseless, powdered, his excitement quickly turned into unease.

Without paying her appearance any heed, Sandra hugged Tom tight and kissed him flush on his lips and felt the stiffness in them. He reciprocated her move mechanically, not from his heart. Sandra could immediately feel the stiffness in Tom's embrace. He wanted to be released from the hug; revulsion for her blood-stained dress, the lack of familiar aroma he was used to, overpowered his love for her.

Sandra released Tom from her embrace, "What's the matter? Are you all right?" She asked, leaning away from him, resting her back on his unsure arm.

"It's my knee. Been troubling me for a couple of days now." Quickly shifting the blame from his nose, lower down.

"You should see Doctor Robin then, ask him to take a look." Sandra's face quickly exchanged love for concern.

"Yes, let me go see him first. Then I can be more at ease." He quickly moved himself away from the proximity of his discomforting closeness.

Sandra turned around and pointed to the corner. Spotting Doctor Robin attending to an Indian soldier, Tom disengaged quickly from Sandra, hoping she didn't catch the real reason for his discomfort. She couldn't pinpoint his stiffness but she could sense that the cause was not his knee. He must still be holding on to his ego over their disagreement, she concluded. Tom made a special effort to amplify his limping while walking towards the doctor. In the presence of his wife, he was no longer a captain but a boy trying to hide his misdeed. Sandra smiled at his back knowingly.

Tom and Doctor Robin had been good friends for a while now. They enjoyed going on several hunts together, when time had once allowed them to shoot animals exclusively. Doctor Robin spied his hunting buddy approaching and he left the Indian soldier he was attending, who sat patiently waiting for his return. He was used to being treated as second priority to a *Gora Sahab,* a white man. In the one hundred and eighteen years of subjugation under the British Raj, enough generations of Indians had lived under colonial rule to accept the situation had always been there. The wounded Indian soldier didn't know any other way, although just four generations before him, during his great great-grand-father's time, skin colour didn't determine priority. However, caste always did.

"Hello, Tom, you look like you have been stomped on by an elephant!"

Hearing the doctor's comment, Tom knew he was overdoing his limp, but now to suddenly revert back to his normal posture would expose his ploy. He could feel Sandra's eyes piercing his back.

"Think I twisted my knee while ducking for cover under fire, Robin." Just then an amputee on crutches moved past. He seemed to be walking better with one leg than Tom was managing with two.

"Hmm...let's have a look." The doctor squatted down, lifted Tom's trousers and turned and twisted the leg. After tapping it a few times with his rubber hammer but perceiving no major problem, he gave Tom a couple of syrettes of morphine.

"Only to be used if you are under extreme pain. Otherwise, try to rest it for a few days, old chap."

"Rest? Under the circumstance we are in that might be a little difficult, Robbie."

The doctor dispelled his anxiety with a smile. "Do you think there might be a lot of them coming our way?"

"Not sure of the exact numbers yet, but may possibly outnumber us." Tom told half a lie. He didn't want to worry his friend more than he already was.

"Isn't some more reinforcement coming in from Dimapur?"

"There are, but the Japs might block us off before then. We might come under siege before further reinforcement breaks through. I just hope we'll be able to hold them off till then..." Tom leaned closer to his friend; he felt he shouldn't keep him in the dark, "This is strictly for your ears, Robbie. We don't want the situation to become more panicked than it already is..."

"Of course, of course, Tom. You needn't tell me *that*," he grimly nodded at Tom.

The noise of patients howling in agony, doctors shouting instructions to nurses, nurses instructing stretcher bearers, relatives of wounded civilians greeting each other, exchanging notes – were all suddenly outpaced by a bigger, louder thunderclap. A moment later, another whistling, booming crack sent the stillness into panic. Everyone – patients, doctors, nurses, ran for cover. Only the infirm and a few firm doctors and nurses tried to stand their ground. One of them was Sandra. Seeing her standing amongst the chaos, Tom grabbed her by her waist and swung her to shelter under a heavy teak wood table.

The bombardment went on across the garrison with clockwork precision – an explosion every few minutes. Patients, doctors and attendants tried to synchronize their living moments with it. Doctor Robin, an American, tried to stay calm by imagining they were firecrackers from the fourth of July – even though it was the fifth of April. A few Indians tried to console their nerves by imagining it was *Diwali*. Slowly, the military-trained doctors and nurses who had taken shelter came out of their hiding to help those who stood their ground. Reluctantly, Tom loosened his grip around Sandra and let her join the brave duty-bound medics. Seeing them, others, Tom included, who were well enough physically, started helping the totally helpless. In the grip of danger, colour, caste and creed all became one. Some ran out of the hospital, some ran in, not sure where it would be safe.

Minutes seemed like years and forty-five years later, Tom spotted two shadows creeping in through a window. Could it be enemy infiltrators? Removing his revolver from the holster, but aware he couldn't make a clear shot, Tom eased his finger on the trigger. Suddenly there was Raan, followed closely behind by Mongseng. Spotting Tom, Raan's stern face split into a broad smile, "*Aare, Saahib!* We were worried. We looked for you all over!" Raan shouted through the clamour.

"You shouldn't have come looking for me. Could have killed yourselves." Tom shouted back.

"*Aare, Saahib,* this *jaangli* is an expert. He brought us through the shelling as if it was just rain."

"What do you mean?"

"You will see when we go from here." Raan smiled, happy to have a little grip on the situation in the battlefield over his army Captain *Sahab*.

For a moment the hubbub in the hall died down to stare at the stark naked warrior. By now, Mongseng was beginning to take people's gawks in his stride. Yet a hundred pairs of eyes, piercing at every part of his skin was a little too much to take. Tom caught Sandra staring at Mongseng. "Oh, this is Mongseng, dear. He is working for me."

Mongseng had learned, besides the white man's language, some white etiquette from his father's friend. He bowed his head and extended his right hand towards Sandra, relieved to focus on something else besides all those staring eyes. Raan and Tom looked on, totally impressed. Sandra placed her palm into his, and he held it as if he was holding a feather. "Hallooo, Mongseng." Her voice betrayed her smile. She had native friends and was comfortable around them, but he was a breed apart. He looked from an unfinished mould – coarse, yet his gesture was so gentle that her formal, courteous smile turned into one of pleasant surprise.

"Nice meet you." Mongseng replied with an innocent smile. He was pleased to see a genuine expression on a person at last. Since leaving his village he was used to being received with trepidation. Sandra was the first white woman he had come across and she immediately created a positive impression. The femininity in Sandra was a little different to the women of his village. She was different from Meailing, his wife. Meailing's femininity and beauty was close to his own handsomeness. Meailing's femininity was there; however it was carved out from chiselling and smoothing a masculine mould. Sandra's femininity was different; it was cast from a totally different mould. She didn't have any trace of masculinity in her.

Flexing his injured knee and deciding against injecting himself with a syrette of morphine, Tom spoke to Sandra and convinced her to take a break from her duties and come and rest with him in his bunker. During a break in the assault, led by Mongseng in a single file, the four of them headed out. Sandra was sandwiched between Tom and Raan, with Raan covering the rear flank. All three pairs of eyes were on Mongseng, while he used all of his senses to see. During the first bombing he witnessed from atop the Aradura Spur, he had observed that the sky fires never landed in the same place twice. In a zigzagging formation, he took the line from one fresh crater to another, in the direction of Tom's bunker. Moving only for the first thirty seconds after a shell landed. Then for thirty seconds he listened. Whenever he could hear an incoming shell, he fell flat inside a crater or took cover behind a tree. The others followed his lead.

Heavy shelling made the air dense, metallic. Gunpowder fumes mixed with dust dimmed the sun's golden rays to a dull rusty yellow. The heavy foreign air brought Mongseng to the point of dizziness, but his instinct to survive was stronger. He had never before inhaled such foul air. As they moved up the hill, something landed in front of Sandra. Taking a closer look she saw it was a foot, severed at the ankle, still inside its boot, the shoelace neatly tied. Despite her courageous attitude and nurse's training, the fright proved too great. She passed out right by the bodiless appendage. Seeing his *Memsahib* faint, Raan almost passed out too. Tom cradled Sandra's head in his hands, hands that were shaking uncontrollably. Sensing he was the best man for the job, Mongseng hauled her onto his back. He had enough experience returning from successful hunts carrying animals twice her weight. However, he did treat her more gently. Tom was impressed with Mongseng's expert handling of Sandra and also grateful, reasoning that he couldn't assist with his troubling knee.

Ears ringing and spent after the initial rush of adrenaline, finally the group reached the comparative safety of the bunker. Not once did Mongseng misjudge the direction of a shell, and all fell at a safe distance away. Swiftly, Raan unrolled Tom's bedding on which Mongseng laid Sandra down. Then he retrieved a jerrycan of water so Tom could revive his wife. Since Mongseng had shaken Sandra's hand at the hospital, till now when he gently laid her on the bed, Tom's opinion of Mongseng had been changing. Raan, too, after being guided by Mongseng to and from the hospital through the bombardment, was becoming a Mongseng admirer.

Coming back to consciousness with a start, in the confined bleak surroundings, Sandra found everything unfamiliar, except Tom's anxious face. Relieved, she hugged him, clinging on like a child seeking comfort. Tom a captain, and not one to show much emotion, especially in front of his men, held her awkwardly. Realizing his stiffness, Sandra tried to compose herself, moving out of the embrace. Her dazed eyes looked around while her hands tried in vain to tidy her dress.

To give them a moment alone, Raan asked, "*Sahib*, shall I go and check on Chetri and his men?"

"Ah, good idea, Raan. Yes, do that and report back. Take Mongseng along too, he should get to know all my men better."

Nodding, Raan took Mongseng by the hand and led him towards the exit. Mongseng didn't understand why Raan was leading him out again. Just moments ago, he had risked his and their lives to bring them in there.

"Where we go now?"

"We let *Sahib* and *Memsahib* have some time on their own. They have met after long, no?" Raan whispered.

To a man to whom a display of affection was as normal as a smile, it made no sense, yet he followed Raan. There were a lot of things that didn't make sense to him since he arrived amidst the foreign culture.

The intensity of the shelling was down from one every few minutes to a few every hour. Still Raan, not willing to take chances, crawled on his belly. When he saw Mongseng's crouched walking, reducing himself to the size of a foot and a half dwarf, Raan adopted that posture, a more agile way to move. The odd retaliatory fire of mortar sounded from Kuki Picket and around the Tennis Court. Raan led the way down to a trench thirty metres from theirs. Crouching that way seemed to Raan as if they had come at least a kilometre. Mongseng recognized the occupants, but their first meeting had not been so pleasant.

Showing no surprise, Chetri greeted Raan, "*Aou, aou;* come, come, Raan!" and smiled at Mongseng, who apprehensively returned the smile. The other five occupants also greeted them warmly. They hugged Raan and folded their hands and bowed to Mongseng.

"*Aur, Saahab,* good?" Chetri enquired, "I went looking for him some hours ago, just as the shelling started, but none of you were in the post."

"*Aare, Sahib* had gone to meet Commander *Sahib* before the shelling started. We went looking for him and found him with the *Memsahib* in the Hospital." Raan exchanged a knowing smile with Chetri. "Only the *Memsahib* fainted on our way back. But now she is fine too, by the grace of *Ram…Hari Om…*" Raan shut his eyes, raising his head upwards, shuttling his right hand index and middle fingers several times between forehead and heart.

"Hmm… Well, there was not much need of *Saahab,* thankfully. All we did was sit out the shelling and shot at the Japanese *chutiyas* who tried to infiltrate our position…" Chetri added with a chuckle.

"They attacked?" Raan's eyeballs expanded.

"Yes, but not many got through. The forward positions took care of them before us. We only shot at three. Two went off limping, carrying the third. *Madarchodd,* motherfucker, must have died by now." Chetri concluded with an air of satisfaction.

"There was so much *dhul*, oh, it was dusty, we could hardly see what was going on."

"Did the *jaangli* get frightened hearing all that bombing?" Chetri asked with no hint of condescension in his voice.

"*Aare,* no, not at all. In fact he guided me through to the *Sahib.* He's like a sniffer dog." As the comment came out,

Raan remembered that Mongseng was right beside him and bit his tongue. He threw a sideways glance at Mongseng, unsure if the savage had understood. Raan smiled at Mongseng apologetically and added, "Oh, by the way he is no *jaangli*. He can speak *Engrazi,* and his name is Mongseng."

"*Aare wah!* Why didn't you speak to us that day?" Chetri asked. Mongseng merely caught his eyes and smiled. Understanding English was easy for him. But to speak was a little like fighting a battle inside his head. Konyak, his mother tongue fought with Nagamese and Assamese, and all three languages fought with English, before the right words in the right tongue came out. So far he had faced enough struggles for one day. He let his smile do the talking.

Chetri stooped his eyebrows at Mongseng's smile, then turned back towards Raan, "I will have to go and see Tom *Saahab* for another matter. Good news is some more troops have arrived. Bad news is, some of them were trying to take over our bunkers. But I told them nothing doing, I won't move my men an inch, let alone vacate our position without my officer's orders." With a serious look he continued, "They got my message clear and began digging their own trenches oooo'ver there near Garrison Headquarters." Through the trees Raan barely made out one long bunker dug with four smaller surrounding ones. The fifth bunker on the western flank was out of sight, but the proportion of the three protective bunkers around the main one made it easy for Raan to imagine there might be a fifth.

"*Aare, Sahib* met the Commander *Sahib* before going to meet his real commander, the *Memsahib*, at the hospital before the bombing." Raan concluded with a mischievous grin.

"Oh, yes, yes, then I am sure *Saahab* knows about their arrival. Then I..."

"You call Tam, '*Sahib*', he call Tam, '*Saahab*', what he actually is, *Sahib* or *Saahab*?" Mongseng interrupted.

Raan and Chetri looked at Mongseng coming into their conversation arbitrarily. Raan replied, "*Aare*, I am from the United Province and Chetri's from Nepal *na*, so we speak like that. '*Sahib*', '*Saahab*', same same. Like for you Tam, Tom, same same."

"Ah, like Ang, Wangba, same same." Mongseng smiled to himself. Chetri and Raan didn't understand what Mongseng meant, but they let him be.

While Mongseng was getting to know his former captors and present allies, another development was unfolding along the Dimapur road. At Colonel Richards's orders, almost a thousand civilians had been sent on their way. The garrison may have been their home, but they were now needless bodies to worry about – just extra worry to add to the panic amidst the chaos. From the garrison the chaotic crowd of non-combatants formed a beeline out of Kohima. While from the other direction, moving into the garrison, marched step-for-step a disciplined lot – the 4th battalion of the Royal West Kent and 4/7 Rajputs finally made it from Dimapur to Kohima.

To Lieutenant Colonel Laverty, Commander of the Royal West Kent battalion, the sight on the road of the unorganized non-combatants, and later in the garrison, didn't impress him greatly. As a defence position under immanent attack, no one seemed prepared. He saw essential provisions, like water reservoirs, food godowns, left exposed, making them vulnerable targets. Trenches had been dug seemingly wherever, by whoever wanted to dig. Except for a few, there were no definite formations. Upon the potholed earth, soldiers ran around like headless chicken, fear and excitement danced in their inexperienced faces. Local Naga vendors moved freely around the positions, selling their produce to the distracted defenders. Laverty considered that any of those vendors could be working as informers for the Japanese, giving away the garrison formations to the enemy. Thankfully, he mused, there's not much of a formation to report. A smile appeared with the thought.

To Laverty, a man who was leading an experienced and disciplined battalion of some four hundred and fifty men, Kohima looked more like a town getting ready for an ill-organized theatre, than an actual army of men preparing for their defence.

Even before Laverty met the garrison commander, he had judged Colonel Richards in a bad light. Though, on a man who had been given command of the Garrison only a month ago, it was an unfair assessment. To command an inexperienced bunch of men was no simple task. Even though Laverty was to report to Colonel Richards, West Kent being part of the 161st Indian Brigade, he decided to take charge of his own men. Without breaking his stride Laverty decided to set up his own independent command post and seek orders directly from his Brigade Commander stationed at Dimapur.

The battalion of West Kent and 4/7 Rajput was the last hope to trickle through the watertight grip of the Japanese

31st Division blockading Kohima. Kohima was now officially under siege.

When they had given enough time to Tom and Sandra, Raan returned to the bunker with Mongseng. As there was no door to knock, Raan thumped his feet hard on the damp earthen steps leading into the bunker.

"Come in, Raan." Tom called. Since they had moved to the bunker he was used to his orderly's improvized way of announcing his arrival.

"Good afta-noon, *Sahib...Memsahib.*" Raan's face brightened up, seeing his masters together.

Mongseng was silent when he walked in. Sandra thought he was homesick. Actually his stomach was growling. He hadn't had any proper food since breakfast, which was also light by comparison to what he was used to. Back home he ate three well-proportioned meals with meat, sticky rice and vegetables.

As if on cue, Raan asked Sandra, "*Memsahib*, are you hungry? Should I prepare some dinner?"

"Oh, that would be lovely, Raan! I'm starving. Haven't eaten a decently prepared meal since the last one you cooked for us in the bungalow."

"Yes, prepare a gourmet dinner to welcome Sandy." Echoed Tom, pulling Raan's leg, knowing there were very few options he could offer.

"I will try my best, *Sahib*!" The joke eluded Raan, his expression turned serious.

Raan cooked the best meal he could with dehydrated potatoes and bully beef (canned beef) and served it with trepidation.

"Sorry, *Memsahib*, cooked what I could. Even becoming difficult to find some basic spices I need."

"Oh, I understand, Raan. This is wonderful…yes, it is really good…thank you." She nodded her head and dug into her plate.

For Mongseng, it was a feast. With his right hand he scooped up two mouthfuls for each of Sandra's. Seeing their enthusiasm Raan was relieved. Even Tom gave him an approving nod.

Mongseng particularly loved the bully beef curry. The canned meat was so different in taste to fresh meat that he deduced the bully beef cans to be a meaty fruit of some tree; he made a mental note to look for the tree. He intended to take a few seeds with him to grow back home.

SEVEN

IN CHETRI'S BUNKER, EVERYONE TOOK TURNS TO COOK. COMING from a society where men and women shared responsibilities equally, each Gurkha, including Chetri, could cook well. In the garrison under siege, their meals turned out as tasty as their food rations would allow. Chetri's men being a mix of Indian and Nepalese, their food ration was different to that of the white officers. Instead of bully beef, they were supplied with rice and *dal*, and on the odd occasion a portion of horse or mule meat was supplied to supplement their simple vegetarian ration. Compared to what the Japanese had to sustain themselves with, Chetri and his men's ration was a banquet. However, it was nothing close to what they were used to back home in the Himalayan mountains.

Chetri's father, grandfather, great-grandfather, great-great-grandfather, nine generations before him, had all lived and died in Bahadurpur, a small Nepalese village near the town of Gorkha in the Kingdom of Nepal . Being the first born of his family's tenth generation, his father had named him Bahadur to honour their village. His full given name was Chatur Bahadur Chetri. He was a bright child, a source of pride and joy for his young parents. From the age he started speaking full sentences, he helped his parents in the small family farm, growing vegetables and grazing the family's livestock of cows, goats and a few mules. As Chetri grew, what he lacked in height, he made up for in physique. Like all Gorkhas, he was built well. He also loved to explore. On days when he finished his chores early he would explore the neighbouring villages. When he could manage it he loved to go for half-day hikes, though he longed to travel further.

Amongst the previous generations in his family, his father had been the only man to travel to the town of Gorkha, a full day and a half's journey on foot. When Chetri's father had turned eighteen, his father had sent him to Gorkha to buy tin sheets for the roof of their house. Hence their house had been the first in Bahadurpur to sport a silvery metal roof amidst the thatched roofs of grey-brown. It was a matter of great pride for his grandfather. After the new roof was installed he made it his morning routine to climb the nearest north-facing hill at dawn to watch the sunrise reflect off his roof. Chetri's father inherited the same habit. But by the time Chetri was eighteen, full of life and strong like a bull, the tin roof had become old, rusty, and stopped reflecting the sun, instead leaking in places.

On a whim one day, Chetri's father decided that since his son was the same age he had been when he set out to buy tin sheets from Gorkha, Chetri should set out for the same journey to replace them. The little money he had in silver and brass coins were anyway gathering dust inside the hollow chamber of a bamboo pillar in their bedroom. Bahadurpur's economy being sustained by barter, the villagers had little use for money. Whenever traders came from Gorkha to buy produce from the villagers, the traders paid the villagers in kind. They brought along essential supplies the villagers needed like salt or utensils for their kitchen or other household items made of metals, fabrics or shapes that the village blacksmith or weavers couldn't produce. Occasionally when a household didn't have any need of items a trader brought along to trade, they exchanged their produce in return for shiny silver and brass coins. They accepted money more for it's novelty than its practical use.

The evening before the journey, his father handpicked two of his strongest mules to carry back the tin sheets, and decided this was an occasion to celebrate for the family. He killed a goat and shared the meat with his neighbours. Chetri's mother prepared his favourite mutton curry with cinnamon and cardamom spicing. His father decided that any son old enough to go on his own to Gorkha, was also old enough to drink. Father and son downed jugs of *chung*, brewed from red rice grown in their terraced paddy fields. By dinnertime father and son were well and happily drunk.

During the night it rained heavily. In the morning when Chetri woke up it was still raining, so he was happy to sleep off his hangover a little longer. When the downpour finally stopped in the afternoon, Chetri felt fresh and ready to leave, but his father's mules baulked at the slippery path. Or maybe their refusal was a premonition of something bad to come. Chetri still thought about it till this day. As he wouldn't have enough light to go too far, his mother advised him to stay overnight at her brother's house in Taple.

When finally he was able to coax the mules to set off on the journey, suddenly the sun appeared in a clear blue sky as if it has been shining brightly since morning. His mother bid him a tearful farewell, reprimanded by his father, saying it was bad luck to send off a loved one with tears.

Working his way downhill on the path, when he could see

the waving hands of his family no more, Chetri tried to pick up his pace, realizing that the mountain's paths had turned more into sludgy streams. Slip-sliding on the sloppy ground, his mules were unsteady, the slippery ground threatened to roll them over the cliff's edge. To avoid any such calamity, Chetri decided to lead his mules off the path into the thicket on firmer ground. Once he was sure that he had cleared the floodwaters, Chetri looked to return to the path, but the thick mountain vegetation upset his sense of direction.

By the time he relocated the path, the sun had set. In the mountain forests, with their very small window between dusk and nightfall, it soon became totally dark. Fumbling through the blackness he decided to take shelter for the night just off the trail in the burrow of a *kadam* tree. Tying his mules to a low-hanging branch, he gave them enough rope so they could forage on the leaves and green tender reeds growing in abundance around them. Once Chetri was happy with the arrangement, the moon appeared. In its silvery light he removed the sling bag strung across his shoulder and took out a parcel wrapped in leaves. After untying the bamboo twine, he gingerly unfolded the leaves to reveal *phapar ko roti* that his mother had packed for the journey. Along with the pickle, *muli khorsani aachar,* the *rotis* tasted like *amrit* – nectar descending directly from the heavens. After quenching his thirst, and washing up in a nearby stream, he returned to the tree's hollow and, in no time, the warmth of the food inside lulled him into a deep slumber.

Some time in the middle of the night, Chetri felt a deep pain on his chest and woke up. He couldn't move his hands and opened his eyes to find three masked men standing over him. The moonlight trickling through the canopy revealed that they were wearing monkey caps that covered their faces up to their necks. Through the small slit around the top Chetri could see their greedy glistening eyes. His blissful snores had caught the attention of passing robbers.

Trying to put up a fight with his feet, Chetri landed a few kicks on the two robbers nearest to him. But together they easily pinned him down. His feeble attempt hadn't helped the situation he was in. Instead, angered by his resistance now they tied up his feet, as they relieved Chetri of his father's savings and his two mules. Not satisfied with that, they then stripped him of his clothes, and the one to whom Chetri had landed his hardest kick, unzipped his pants and relieved himself on the young Gurkha. The only thing they left him with was total humiliation.

Laying on the ground shivering, Chetri watched the stars through the canopy, until he could hear the robbers no more. Slithering back into the tree's bosom for warmth, he begged for the darkness to pass. Swinging between anger, humiliation, sleep, pain and fear, Chetri came to the sound of footsteps. From the noise, Chetri guessed that it must be a cow herder passing with his mule to gather fresh grass for his animals. In the sky, light was taking over from darkness. Chetri crawled out of the burrow and slithered towards the sound.

In the scanty light the cow herder was startled to see him. His initial thought was that it was a short fat python and he contemplated whether to fight it with his stick, or flee. But the moment he discerned the boy, his fear turned into compassion. The young cow herder untied Chetri, and taking pity on him offered a gunny bag to wrap around his nakedness. He fed Chetri some of the *dal-bhat* meant later for his lunch. After thanking the cow herder profusely, Chetri started walking.

He couldn't bear to return home, so continued on towards Gorkha, now feeling aimless and empty, lost materially and emotionally. With no respect for himself, he didn't know what to do. But amid the chaos inside his head, one thing was clear. He would never return home until he won back the money and mules from those robbers.

At Gorkha, another kind-hearted soul took pity on him and gave Chetri some of his son's old clothes, and offered him a job in his small shack of a restaurant. For that old man, Chetri worked in the restaurant in exchange for clothes, food and shelter, sleeping on a bench after the day's business was done. The restaurant was at the edge of town, at the end of the path from Bahadurpur.

For months Chetri lived scuttling between hope and hopelessness. He tried to feed the travellers passing by with the best food he could cook and served them with the best manners he possessed, in the hope that they would become friendly with him and burp out some news about the robbers. Often there was promise of a path leading to the robbers. Then, as always, the dense forest swallowed it up. He lost any hope of redeeming his honour and spent endless sleepless nights; his dreams spun different yearns out of the humiliation he suffered in the hands of the robbers. Then one day Bishnu Chetri came to Gorkha. He was a *Subedar* in the Assam Rifles. After eating his food, Bishnu told Chetri that a recruitment drive for new soldiers was being organized in a town called Tezpur in the state of Assam in India, where he was stationed.

For Chetri, this was the first piece of news that made him feel good. Even though the chance of getting back his mules and money from the robbers looked bleak, by joining the army he reasoned he could at least earn back his pride. From Nepal into India he followed Bishnu, who lodged him in Tezpur at his sister Parul's house. To dispel the loneliness that he felt inside and to brush up his Assamese fluency, Chetri enjoyed talking to his hosts and their two children, who took an instant liking for their new uncle. On the day of the recruitment drive, Chetri's desire to leave his humiliation behind saw him come first in all the obstacle courses the recruiting officers had set up for the unwitting hopefuls.

Chetri was posted with a battalion in Tezpur. Whenever he had a day off, he visited Parul's family. There he met Chandrika, Bishnu and Parul's youngest sister who was finishing her Bachelor in Arts from Cotton Collage, Guwahati. She was academically brilliant, and Chetri was brilliant at any job that required hands and feet. Chandrika was impressed how Chetri had risen from adversity as a simple village boy to become first a *Sipahi* in the Assam Rifles. Then within a short time rose to the rank of *Subedar*. Before long they were married and Chandrika bore a baby boy, just as Chetri's battalion was relocated to the Kohima Garrison.

As sunlight warmed the landscape, the heavy fog that had encased Kohima overnight rose like a blind covering the screen in a movie theatre, to reveal the scene that awaited the defenders. In war movies, most scenes show action. In real battles, the mundane day-to-day activities of 'normal' life intertwine with bombs and bullets.

The sound of trickling water caught Mongseng's attention. Curious, he peeped out of the bunker to locate the source as an Indian soldier attending to his early morning call. Once he was through the soldier looked up at the tree against which he had done his deed, broke off a pencil thin branch and started to chew one end. After his molars had reduced the end to a fine bristly pulp he proceeded to brush his teeth with it. Moving systematically, he made sure every tooth received individual attention. He finished up his dental hygiene with a deep guttural motion to summon all the mucus that had accumulated overnight, and spat it out with a coughing throw. As his head returned upright, Mongseng heard a cracking noise, and the soldier crashed onto the corrugated iron sheet of their bunker. Not a wise morning ritual to continue on a battlefield where hidden enemy lurked.

The crunch of the falling soldier woke the other three occupants. Blood trickled through a gap created on the corrugated tin roof by the dead weight of the lifeless soldier, and drop-by-drop blotted Sandra's already mottled white gown. She gathered her dress and pulled it up to her knees to prevent the fresh blood from colouring it any more. Mongseng was the first to hear footsteps, lots of footsteps. Again he peered out of the bunker, now standing on tiptoe, stretching his neck till his head touched the roof. Down below there was movement. To his untrained eyes it looked like rounded mossy river stones moving up the hill. Then, as his vision adjusted, faces appeared under deep-seated Japanese helmets. Mongseng grabbed his *dao* and spear. Tom, who had joined him, grabbed his Sten gun, Raan his 303 rifle, and Sandra, a long handled pan.

The crack of a second rifle ripped through the anticipation, the spark that started the defender's fire. A barrage of shots from both sides jolted awake the sleepy Kohima garrison. Out of sight the Japanese 58th Regiment built impromptu ladders and tried to climb the steep ridge on DIS. The forward positions of the C Company West Kenters used everything they had to stop the swarm of Japanese creeping up the slope. Grenades were hurled at men and ladders. Any who managed to climb up were swiftly dispatched with bayonets. Despite the large numbers attacking, not a single defender retreated. Some were killed in their trenches rather than evacuate.

The four in Tom's bunker, still a good way away from the action, watched as the green helmets dropped down one by one, and a few turned and retreated. After a pause, a fresh surge of shots rung out. Not a single Japanese managed to climb high enough to face the occupants watching from FSD Hill. In spite of their advantage in numbers, the Japanese failed to break through the stubborn defence.

What a start to the morning. All the preparation, all the anticipation, all the anxiety, all the dread, had materialised in front of their eyes. Their worst fears had become a reality. The four stood transfixed. The Japanese were there, in front of them. Just then Chetri appeared from behind the bunker. Sandra, the closest and first to react, almost struck a lethal blow with her pan, her reflexes restrained at the last moment by familiarity, "Oh, Chetri!" she cried out half out of embarrassment, half out of anxiety. Relieved at not having to become a fighter in the war.

"Ho, Madam! Are you fighting with us or against us...ha... ha...ha." Chetri was a typical Gorkha who never, under any circumstance lost his humour. But Sandra, Tom and Raan were not amused. Humour had been usurped by fear. Only Mongseng, built of similar material as Chetri, laughed. Sensing the sombre mood, Chetri stiffened to attention and addressed Tom, "Sir, my *jawans* are becoming impatient. Should I ask my men to move forward and launch an attack?"

"Just hold your position." Tom replied, irritated.

But Chetri could not hold his tongue. In a near pleading tone, he went on, "But, sir, my men are getting bored. They feel they are not in a war zone but in a cinema hall watching a war film!" Only Gorkhas could find so much excitement at the prospect of playing with death. Though another man in the bunker could understand Chetri. Only he didn't know to fight wars the way it was being fought. He was observing, learning.

"Tell your men we are lucky to be where we are. If they were in the forward positions, by now they might have wished they were indeed inside a movie hall, not on the battlefield. We will be here for another day or two without reinforcement. I'm sure they will soon have plenty of opportunity to engage with the enemy."

His Captain's flickering eyebrow and flared nostrils signalled to Chetri that there was no point pushing the matter any further. He saluted Tom, bowed to Sandra, smiled at Raan and Mongseng, and made his way back to his men.

EIGHT

TOM AVOIDED EYE CONTACT WITH SANDRA AND STARED AT THE ROOF where the dead soldier lay. He would have liked to pace around the bunker with his thoughts, but there was not much space. It was clear now that their garrison of less than two thousand fighting men was waging war against a disproportionately large Japanese army. Tom was in two minds – torn between self-preservation and duty. The previous day with the arrival of the battalion of five hundred West Kent men and the 4/7 Rajput company, his position as captain had been fractured yet again. For a fleeting moment he wondered if it would be a better idea to escape to Dimapur with Sandra. There were still some civilians trickling through. Should they too leave while they still had the chance? But he knew better than to suggest such a preposterous idea to Sandra.

By the time the attackers wound up for the morning, the sun had worked its way almost half way across the eastern sky. In the relative quiet, everyone's minds moved from the present to the future, to the coming hours and days ahead. Inside the bunker Mongseng felt a little lost. He listened to the noises outside of wounded soldiers; friends and enemies crying out in agony. He was happy with the opportunity the battle lent him to collect heads. But why were Tom and his men fighting this battle? Mongseng saw that the Japanese were attacking Tom's village, but he didn't see any point in trying to protect it. There were no crops, no children, and few women except Sandra. And the few iron-sheeted houses that did look worth protecting had already been laid to waste, broken down by Tom's people in order to see the enemy clearly as they approached. If not for food, heads or land, why were they fighting at all?

Mongseng looked across at the growing number of enemy dotting the surrounding hills. He reckoned Tom's villagers from Kohima might as well retreat into thicker forests and come back once the enemy conquered the little patch of forest and left after finding nothing to take from it.

Mongseng observed the killing of many warriors, but no heads were being taken. Although he would never claim a head from someone else's kill, the utter waste lying around tempted him to add a few more to his tally. He decided he would let Tom's villagers battle the way they chose, and he would fight in his style. The Konyak warrior knew it would be foolish to go hunting for heads in broad daylight. He decided he would become a nocturnal hunter.

With the break in crossfire, the thing foremost in Sandra's mind was to return to the hospital. She knew many more casualties would have come in. She peered outside and figured she wouldn't be able to find the path back to the hospital on her own. The paths snaking through the hills had totally been altered. First by the defenders of the garrison digging trenches all around and over the paths. Then by offence, as the mountains were dug up and shattered by enemy bombardment. With the enemy at their doorstep, she knew she couldn't ask Tom to leave his position and come to drop her. And to ask Raan to leave Tom's side would be wrong. Sandra and Tom exchanged an uncomfortable glance. She looked away and her eyes fell on Mongseng, who seemed to be elsewhere. He had no anxiety on his face as had the others. But she didn't fully trust Mongseng. Whether he was their friend, she couldn't quite tell. She wondered why he was still hanging around them when he could easily escape and return to the quiet of his own village.

She brushed the negative thoughts aside and smiled at Raan as she accepted her brunch – an egg sunny side up on a thick fluffy chapatti, along with a mug of tea. Finishing her first mouthful, she broke the silence. "Think I should get back to the hospital. Doctor Robin will surely need all hands on deck."

Finishing his mouthful, Tom spoke, "I think you will be more helpful at the forward dressing station. Why don't I speak to Doctor Young and have you moved there?"

Lieutenant John Young, commanding officer of the 75th Indian Field Ambulance had set up the forward dressing station between the Garrison Headquarter and the West Kent Head Quarter. Its location was considerably closer to Tom than Hospital Hill.

Being one of the only women in the garrison, Sandra felt she needed to assert her independence. "Hmmm, maybe. I can go and talk to him myself." She snapped. Sandra was no meek woman. Tom's suggestion felt patronising to her. She was not going to let him take away whatever little control she had over her life in this strange and hostile situation.

"Why do you have to take whatever I suggest in a negative light?" He snapped back.

"No. You are taking my comment negatively, Tom. I can speak for myself, is all I am saying…"

Mongseng and Raan, neither were much for husband-wife squabbles. While Tom and Sandra's argument continued, Raan busied himself cleaning the brunch utensils. Taking his lead, Mongseng set about sharpening his killing utensils with a stone. Raan used sand to scrub his pans and plates.

Fetching water was becoming precarious. The water tank lay exposed near garrison HQ. Raan took the opportunity of his employers' argument to do a water run. Cautious not to attract attention from the enemy, he held the metal buckets tight to avoid letting them rattle. Once Raan reached the tank he placed one bucket beside him, squatting down to fill the other. Within seconds a bullet clanged the empty metal bucket by his side. A Japanese sniper missed by a fraction. Raan froze for a second, unsure where the bullet came from. In that fraction of a moment of indecisiveness, his life flashed in front of him. Why did he need to leave his village to land up in this God forsaken place? He could have opted to stay back in the tea estate instead of following his *Sahib* like a shadow. Thankfully, a garrison soldier from a bunker nearby fired a retaliatory shot to distract the sniper and its noise snapped Raan back into the present. Taking his one intact bucket, half full, Raan made a lucky escape.

Raan returned to the bunker and sat down quietly in a corner. His 303 was resting against the wall. He looked at it. Though being in the middle of a garrison armed to the teeth, Raan had never shot this gun, and hadn't used any gun in a while. The last time he had fired a gun was a year ago, when the monsoon season had been the only frightful occurrence in his life. The Assam plains were flooded more than usual. Rampant landslides ravaged the hills, blocking the only road to Kohima. Raan hadn't been able to find any meat in the

Kohima market for a month. Since working for Tom, Raan had turned from a strict vegetarian into a strict non-vegetarian. He began considering cooking meals without meat as no cooking at all. With the road blocked, meat in the market had all but disappeared.

After cooking vegetables for a month for his masters, he could no longer bear to see the dismay in Tom and Sandra's faces any more. No matter how well he cooked, he couldn't please them with his dishes. An all-vegetarian recipe for lunch and dinner was making them both less appreciative of his cooking skills. He decided to address the matter head on and went into the nearby jungle with his rifle. After scaring almost the whole wildlife out of the jungle, he became lucky. Or rather a boar was unlucky enough to cross paths with him at point blank range. That night he prepared pork curry, pork fry and pork roast for his *Sahib* and *Memsahib*. He was happy to see his masters gorging on the pork, although he himself couldn't eat a morsel. Every time he raised a piece to his mouth he heard the dying squeal of the boar.

Tom found the air inside the bunker more risky and stepped out to meet Commander Richards. Sandra was not usually drawn into arguments. She was exhausted. How silly to quarrel over such a minor issue, while their lives hung in balance. Suddenly they were in the hands of an enormous enemy, surrounding them, waiting to crush them, coming close, maybe just two hundred meters away. Before she left, Sandra decided to try to get to know Mongseng, as Raan looked too shaken for a conversation. Besides, having brought her safely through the bombing, she felt she should at least be courteous.

"Mongseng, how far is your village?"

Startled by the unexpected query, before opening his

mouth, Mongseng managed to open an inch-long cut on his index finger with the spear's head he was sharpening. Not aware of the norms of the society he was living in since a week, he put his wounded finger between his legs and pissed on the cut. Sandra was shell-shocked. The crude disinfectant he applied to his wound pulled away an invisible layer of clothing that his mild manners had put on him. That bare act made him look more naked than he already was. Sandra looked away and didn't try continuing the conversation.

One good outcome of the incident was that it helped Raan come out of his death scare. Bringing a tube of Burnol, he applied a layer of the yellow paste on Mongseng's little finger and tied a piece of rag around it; lest Mongseng applied his own antiseptic on it once again in front of *Memsahib*.

Hearing the crack of a rifle, Raan ducked, Mongseng smiled. Mongseng's keen ears told him it was from nearby, it was friendly fire. A soldier at a forward position had let off his 303. He was just a boy, a soldier all of fourteen. To enlist in the army, he had lied about his age. He found himself a fresh recruit in the 4th Royal West Kent Regiment, to replace those who had been killed or maimed. A month after training, he was put aboard a ship setting sail for India. His father who had fought in the Great War of 1914 had been crippled. His mother, his father's childhood sweetheart had kept her word and married him upon his return. After eleven years of marriage, their only child was born. This boy blamed the enemy for the deprived moments with his father – to walk step-in-step in the fields with him, to go fishing, to play football. He wanted revenge.

He joined the war with a lie and now the battle was lying to him. It showed him the presence of enemies amongst shadows, in the movement of abandoned pets of the Nagas, in the sound of corrugated sheets rattled by the wind. Cooped up in a trench with two other soldiers, he suddenly asked himself what the hell he was doing. Asking how the hell this impersonal act could really solve anything. Everything seemed out of place. There in the frontlines, just a couple of hundred meters from where Sandra rested, no one could rest without someone watching out for them. Shutting eyes, except to blink, could kill. A nine-metre dirt road was all that they had between them and the enemy.

That morning, because of the intense Japanese attack, no fresh food was delivered in the frontlines. Usually they had a warm meal sent for lunch and dinner from the kitchen at Garrison Hill. By the time it reached them it only had the memory of warmth left in it. Yet it was better than eating canned food, which they had to that morning. The fourteen-year-old soldier found canned food repulsive. The war brought him away for the first time from his mother's cooking. He stood guard while his mates ate. The other two soldiers in the trench were twice his age. The three didn't have the luxury that a distance of just a couple of hundred meters offered Tom and his men. The little semblance of home comfort they received in their bunker; the satisfaction of cooking their own hot meals. Let alone cooking, soon the three frontline soldiers wouldn't even have the time to taste what they were eating from cans.

The boy soldier's firing made his mates in the bunker jump up to investigate. They were relieved to find a stray mongrel yelping way towards the enemy camp. The young soldier was glad he missed. The stray dog was gnawing away on a dead soldier. The dead lay on the dirt road like discarded gunny bags. The two experienced ones surveyed their surrounding and finding only dead faces staring back at them, sat back in the trench and resumed their meal while the boy stood guard. The young soldier heard another ruffling noise and this time he didn't bother to investigate. A lone shot echoed through the valley. The young boy slumped into the trench.

He fell to the floor like a sack of potatoes. The two older soldiers in the trench knew death when they saw it. They had lived through the middle of intense fighting in Burma in 1942, as part of the retreating British 17th army. Separated from the rest of their family for over four years, they took it upon themselves to protect this younger brother. Only a week ago he had joined them in Dimapur. They were just beginning to know him. Death took away that little familiarity. They stretched out his crumpled body and laid it lengthwise in the trench and resumed their meal. A long war had taught them to survive a battle, a siege; first they had to do the bare minimum to stay alive, finish eating before anything else.

When push came to shove, Doctor Robin was reluctant to let Sandra move from the hospital to the Advance Dressing Station, or ADS as it was known around the camp. Though he knew that being one of the best, she would be more useful in the frontline than with him. In fact convalescing soldiers in his hospital, who were almost fit, were joining up active duty in the Garrison's limited fighting force.

In her new role as a senior nurse at the Advance Dressing Station, no training could have prepared Sandra for what she saw. The hospital was one thing, and now, in the dressing station, injured patients were laid out lengthwise, a bloody train of beds. The not so badly wounded were given beds closer to the exit so that in case of a bombing they could evacuate the trench on their own, creating space for the stretcher-bearers to enter and carry out those who were immobile.

The first casualty Sandra saw had his leg severed below the knee. Suddenly she recalled the limb that had landed in front of her the previous day. She had imagined the worst for the owner of that limb. The patient in front of her looked worse than what she had imagined. The next soldier made the severed limb seem like a mere flesh wound. The dark-skinned man was practically been mummified in bandages. It looked like that was all that held him together. He had been ripped apart by shrapnel from an artillery shell. The pain he was in was beyond what Sandra wanted to imagine. His eyes looked beyond this world.

Nothing the Kohima garrison had prepared for would be enough to face what lay ahead. Sandra already knew that her paltry nurse's training was not enough, let alone to brace herself for the battle. Deep down Tom knew that his title wasn't much; his resolve wasn't strong enough. He should have stuck to the tea estate. Chetri was not a man who lacked courage. His spirit had been broken, but his experience dealing with adversity had taught him that he had it in him to come out alive. He wished he could have spent more time with his wife and new born child. He wished he had returned to his home village of Bahadurpur sooner. Now, as the war closed in, he vowed to dedicate his life to his family, if only he survives. Mongseng had wandered into someone else's war. He missed his family but held no fear. He vowed to keep his focus, while collecting heads and knowledge.

Inside the garrison, two thousand soldiers in their bunkers and trenches hunkered down. Surrounded by the unknown, they waited in trepidation for what was only beginning to unfold.

NINE

AS A GLOOMY SUN SET BEHIND A GUN-POWDERED HAZE, AN EERIE silence rolled over the garrison. Every movement, every heartbeat, every stare between soldiers, wondered, how big was the enemy? Would they have to face them all by themselves? Would any more reinforcement come from Dimapur? When would the next attack begin? There was no doubt in anyone's mind that it was coming.

From their position in Field Supply Depot Hill, Tom and his two companions observed frantic activity amid the enemy lines. On the facing hill, beyond their sight, they could only imagine the enemy numbers. Rather than let his imagination run wild, Mongseng began sharpening his arrowheads to an even finer point, rubbing them on the metal surface of a box of ammunition. The closed walls of the bunker amplified the noise, like fingernails screeching down a blackboard. Tom bore it. There was too little time to teach him how to shoot a gun. He should use what he knows, even though the maintenance would be less noisy. For Mongseng, in any other circumstance, killing with a bow and arrow would have felt like cheating; not giving the opponent a chance to prove their mettle. Against the fire-throwing spears of the enemy, he reckoned his bow was fair game.

Raan preferred pouring oil into a pan than into the barrel of his 303. But as there were no immediate meals to be cooked, and observing Mongseng busy with the tools of his trade, Raan was too fidgety to sit around idle, especially in the presence of his *Sahib*. Reluctantly he picked up his rifle, which had been issued to him for following his *Sahib* from the tea estate to the army. Raan looked at the pile of bully beef cans and lamented those days past; the days that were there just a while ago – ordinary, peaceful, sleepy days in the garrison town. Yet it seemed years had gone by since those happy carefree days. He shrugged his self-pity away and started dinner preparations as orders had come in to have a complete blackout within the defence perimeter after sundown.

The daily chores that didn't involve guns kept soldiers sane. The mundane kept their minds off the looming threat. It gave them some assurance to be in touch with the normal. A battle was fought half in the mind and half on the battlefield. Breaks from combat to perform daily routines gave the psyche of every soldier a small break.

After dinner Raan volunteered to stand guard while Tom and Mongseng took a nap, but Mongseng had other ideas.

"You cook good food. Now you sleep, I look after enemy." For Mongseng, in an environment where everything else was foreign, keeping watch for enemy attacks was one responsibility he had been familiar with since he was a boy.

Raan looked at Tom who nodded his approval. Only too happy to relinquish that responsibility, Raan laid out Tom's bedding roll and then his own. He was no soldier; he was happy to show off his skills over the cooking stove while others showed off their manliness in the battlefield.

But sleep that night amongst the besieged was the last thing anyone could have. Just as Tom drifted, the barrage began. From Jail Hill and Aradura Spur, mortars and 75mm guns opened fire. In the dark of the night it went on forever, an echoing symphony of terror. At the display of sparks created by the bombs as they hit their targets, Mongseng stared open-mouthed. To a man who knew little of the destruction of bombs and guns, it was an amazing display of lights and sounds.

"Better close your mouth, Mongseng. If some shrapnel goes in, it will not taste very good." Tom tried to expel the fear gripping his chest with a chuckle.

Closing his mouth Mongseng asked, "Shar…pel?"

"The pieces that bomb blasts throw around." Tom picked up his Zeiss binoculars and, with the aid of sparks of light emitting from enemy fire tried to locate the sites of the Japanese artillery guns and mortars.

"Bomb? Busts?" Mongseng turned fully towards Tom, curious to know what those words meant. He had frequently heard them in the last couple of days. He took the opportunity to ask their meaning.

Wherever he looked, Tom saw field guns and mortars blazing from the surrounding hills. Happy for the distraction, Tom asked, "Do you see those lights coming from the sky?"

"Yes, fire?"

"Right. Those are shots from a gun like this one..." He held up the Sten, "…but much bigger, and the bullets they are firing from those guns, are like this one…" he removed the magazine and dislodged a plump bullet from it, "…but much, much bigger." His blond moustachio twitching madly, looking into the savage's obsidian eyes, Tom handed over the bullet for consideration. Mongseng gingerly turned the bullet in his hand.

Just then, a mortar shell exploded only yards ahead. In unison all occupants ducked. Mongseng let go of the bullet and Tom threw out one lanky arm and made a good catch. Squatting down amongst the bully beef, Tom picked up three cans and held them out one on top of the other. Extending them towards Mongseng, he said, "That one that just exploded was a mortar bomb, about as big as these three cans."

"Cans? What cans? These no fruit?" Mongseng picked the top can from Tom's hand and examined it curiously, "Can, fruit, vegetable, all same same?"

"Well, fruit and vegetables grow on trees, but bully beef is made by men."

The intensity of enemy shelling and the defenders retaliatory bombing reduced substantially and Tom wanted to move on to other matters, "Shall we stick to the situation at hand? Raan will explain bully beef to you later?"

Tom stood up and, taking his queue, so did Mongseng followed by Raan. Tom handed Mongseng the binoculars. He didn't know what to do with them though he had been watching Tom use them often. Mongseng took the binoculars into his eyes while Tom adjusted the focus. As the enemy came into focus, Mongseng let go of the field glasses and leapfrogged backwards, grabbed his spear and took on an attacking stance. Looking around, he exclaimed, "Where enemy go?"

Seeing Mongseng's antics, Raan lightened up. Tom, who couldn't hold his Captain's composure, let out a laugh too. The perplexity of a simple man at experiencing a technology of modernity lent a moment of light relief. However, modern man's destructive ego had led them towards their own annihilation. Technology was one thing, but the technology of the new killing machines was a way to nullify everything humanity had achieved so far.

Tom returned to his corner, took out his map and started jotting down enemy locations. He would pass those locations on to HQ when he went for his morning briefing. HQ would tally that with information they receive about enemy positions from locals who were working as spies and guides. If the information from their spies and guides corresponded with his and other similar positional details marked by other garrison officers, they could be sure that the locals giving them information were not working as double agents for the Japanese.

After a second barrage of bombs the fighting subsided, replaced by the moans and cries of the wounded. The metallic smell of gunpowder pervaded the air.

"Tom *Sahib*, Tom *Sahib*..." came someone's urgent whisper. Raan peered out through the entrance. It was a messenger from the Garrison HQ.

"*Aare* Ratan Singh, *aao aao,* come come." Raan called him in, he knew the messenger well. They were from the same village of United Provinces in northern India.

Ratan Singh gave Tom a salute. "At ease, soldier." Tom responded and enquired, "Any message from Richard *Sahab?*"

"Commander *Sahib* has called you to Garrison Headquarters, sir! He also asked me to tell you that it is an important briefing and you must come immediately, *Sahib*!"

Tom tried to keep his eyes soft. Nodding, Tom tidied his uniform with Raan's assistance, as best as he could. As Raan tied Tom's shoelaces, he used a piece of rag and tried to remove some of the layers of mud from his boots. It was less than a month ago that Raan would fondly spend hours every Saturday polishing Tom's shoes. Tom tapped on his shoulder, and he reluctantly let go. Tom went away with the messenger. Raan saw them off and realized only when the peace of normalcy had left them, how much he actually valued the little things that add up to make life ordinary, normal, liveable.

With Tom gone, Mongseng and Raan occupied themselves by observing the stretcher-bearers running to and fro from the ADS. Like shadows popping in and out of darkness, picking up both death and life. Raan's mind went to his *Mem'Sahib.* He hoped that she was safe, and did not have to work too hard. He felt guilty to see her hospital dress in the state it was in. In the red-roofed bungalow if the washerwoman failed to show up some days, washing was his added responsibility.

Raan's eyes trailed a pair of stretcher-bearers carrying an injured soldier. They had to jump through fallen debris torn away by bombs – smoking chunks of tree trunks, mounds of soil dug out, craters the size of small ponds. To the cook ever present in Raan, it seemed as if the craters were huge cauldrons in which the devil was stirring a broth and the stretcher-bearers were lucky ingredients that were yet to be caught by the ladle and pushed into the hot brew.

While Raan was away on his vivid imagery of the battlefield, Mongseng spotted Tom beyond the stretcher-bearers. Tom emerged from the darkness looking worried and shot off an instruction, "Raan, get Chetri."

As Raan stood to leave, Mongseng stopped him, "Good cook stay. I go." Raan looked across at Tom who seemed irritated at having his instruction sidelined. Yet he nodded his approval. Mongseng grabbed his *dao* and spear on the way out. Raan busied himself with thin air, sorting out his already sorted items of cooking, till his *Sahib's* face returned to normal. The moon was yet to rise and the glow from the stars pierced down like millions of pair of feline eyes. Sleek as a cat, Mongseng moved through the darkness on all fours. His *dao* hanging firmly from the wooden scabbard woven into his cowrie shell belt. His spear became a part of him, clasped close to his body. Gliding over mounds of debris, melting through craters, smooth as a water strider gliding across a pond.

"Tam want you." Mongseng announced, as he entered Chetri's bunker.

Chetri and his five men swung towards the form that materialised from the darkness. Their anxious faces shaped into smiles, once startle was replaced by recognition. After the first unceremonious welcome they had extended to Mongseng at Aradura Spur, the Gorkhas had accepted Mongseng among them. From what they saw of him, they knew that he had been loyal to their Captain. If Mongseng wanted he could have left the battlefield. For Gorkhas, two traits that win immediate friendship and respect were loyalty and bravery. Both of which Mongseng possessed in ample measure.

Chetri welcomed Mongseng into the bunker as if he was paying a social visit to his house in the hills. "Mongseng! Haven't seen you for two days!" Chetri exclaimed, folding his hands and giving him a warm *namaste*. Mongseng returned Chetri's warmth with equal zeal.

Once the pleasantries were exchanged, Chetri enquired, "How come Tom *Sahab* wants to see me so late? Is it about our guests across the hill?" He indicated with his chin towards Jail Hill. From their position, under the moonlight the activity of the Japanese on the neighbouring hill looked like a colony of silvery ants busy around their anthill.

"He look worry worry, call you hurry hurry." Mongseng replied, scanning the horizon beyond Chetri's pointing chin.

"Oh, didn't know you are a poet." Chetri responded with a chuckle to Mongseng's lyrical reply.

"Poet?" Mongseng frowned.

"Song writer?" Chetri explained raising one eyebrow.

"I no write song. Nobody village write song. We only sing. Nobody write." Mongseng smiled.

"Oh, ho, ho. Don't worry, I also hardly write. Cup of *chai* before we leave?"

In the corner of the bunker a stove cut out of a biscuit tin held a kettle-brewing tea. The sides of the stove had been packed with mud to keep any light from the fire escaping towards enemy eyes. After the strict order came to not have any form of light in the bunkers at night, Chetri came up with the innovation. As long as there was no light escaping, Chetri and his men reckoned they were breaking no rules. *Jugaad* – inventiveness, kept them supplied with warm cups of tea in the middle of the freezing night.

"Ah, there you are, Chetri. How are the men? Is their morale high?" Tom asked.

"*Jee Hazur,* all are very motivated, thank you." Chetri responded. It was an automated response to an automated question that Tom asked him often when Chetri came to report.

"What took you so long?" Tom then questioned the returning pair.

"Oh, Mongseng had come to visit for the first time on his own, *Sahab*. I couldn't let him come away without a cup of tea."

"This is not the time for tea parties you know. We have a situation at hand. We have been cut off from the rest of the world. Orders are to fight to the last man. We have about fifteen hundred fighting men defending this garrison. The Japs have been estimated at fifteen thousand."

"Oh! All the more reason then, *Sahab*, that we enjoy our cups of tea. Soon we'll be too busy shooting and digging graves for the Japs. The more of them the merrier, no, *Sahab*?"

Tom ignored Chetri's attempt at humour. "We will stay as the second line of defence. Only West Kent has a full battalion, so our orders are to stay put and let them take on the first hand fighting. We stay in our defensive position and take on any Japs that might break through."

"But *Sahab,* the West Kent men arrived only yesterday! We know the area much better than them."

"What do you expect me to do with the handful of men that we have? I don't even have a full company. Just hold your position Chetri, that's an order."

Chetri knew he and his other Gorkhas were some of the best fighters in the garrison. They had been asked to sit on the benches while a new team played in their place. The addition of the new recruits had diluted his men's fighting capabilities a little, but still he thought his men would fair quiet well. With a salute and stamp of the right boot, Chetri nodded his displeasure and executed an about turn to pass on the disappointing news to his men.

As silvery rays disappeared behind the hills along with their oval projectionist, Kohima turned pitch-black and another, darker wave moved up towards the garrison perimeter from Jail Hill. The shelling beforehand had been a trailer. Suddenly, the damp thud of hundreds of boots, like the distant murmur of a thunder, reached Tom's bunker. One waiting game made way for another. As the second line of defence they must watch the enemy grow. Tom's bunker resonated with retaliatory fire and blood-curdling cries. Bren guns, machine guns, mortars and 303 rifles came alive. An orchestra of West Kent company engulfed the valley. The wounded lay where they fell, or retreated, but there were more replacements waiting. A new surge came bellowing their bloodthirsty cry. The guns of the defenders were patient; they allowed the enemy to grow in size, allowed them to come closer, become plump targets.

History kept on repeating itself – not within centuries, decades or years, but within the hours of a single night. There was an endless brood of Japanese soldiers waiting across the road on Jail Hill to come charging, to replace the fallen.

There was no respite. Runners brought news into Tom's camp that some Japs had managed to squeeze through the defence and had occupied a few houses around DIS hill. Those houses, evacuated of civilians, had remained empty. Edgy at the news, both Tom and Raan turned around together, to check behind their back.

The enemy attacking the perimeters of the garrison was so innumerable that they were visible even in the dark. A thought came over Tom that calmed him; to escape death now would be a miracle and he was no believer of miracles. They were living on borrowed time. With the threat of death looming overhead, Tom saw no point in upholding the hierarchy of *Sahab* and servant. He reasoned all three needn't keep watch over what was inevitable.

"Raan, you and Mongseng have a nap. We will each rotate and keep a two hour watch."

"*Aare Sahib*, how can I sleep when you stay awake? You sleep first. I will keep watch with Mongseng. Anyways, we better keep watch of our front and back."

"Oh, have you become the Captain of the bunker now?" Tom smiled.

In the low light, Raan missed Tom's smile and the noise of guns morphed the lightness in his tone. Raan heard only reproof.

"*Sahib*, even in my dreams I would never make that mistake. I will die if I have to, to fulfil your order. I was only thinking of you, *Sahib*."

"We are at war, Raan. Not in the tea estate now. Every one of us will have to be hundred per cent alert. All of us will have to do our bit to keep each other alive..."

Mongseng, who was being a bystander, brought the debate to end. "Both you eyes look red. Both sleep. I watch." There was no debating his point. Even in the dim light it was clear that Mongseng looked fresh. Raan and Tom suddenly felt ravaged by the war, even before they were headlong into it. Mongseng was happy to give up this night of hunting to allow his friends some sleep.

While his bunkmates tried to sleep, Mongseng focused his eyes on the repeating battle in front of him, while his ears deciphered every noise. He could tell from each noise what distance it came from. He could make out the difference between the sound of leaves when they fluttered in the breeze, whether insects crawled on them, a man brushed passed them, or if they were crushed under paws or feet. At that time, the feet of two West Kent runners made their way gingerly past, not knowing whether to greet or ignore him. From the battle cries, Mongseng figured that the Japanese position had not advanced.

All night, the Japanese soldiers kept coming relentlessly, group after group, like waves dashing on to a beach. To Mongseng, a warrior skilled at ambush, their frontal attack seemed senseless. It was like walking straight into the mouth of death. Mongseng also observed the defenders. Still, in their little holes they let death approach them. He neither saw any skill at sitting and waiting to stare death in the face. He wondered if death approaching in huge numbers made the living appreciate life a little less.

Mongseng's quota of the two-hour shift went by. He didn't know how a day was sliced up into smaller parts by that silvery insect he had chopped a few mornings ago. The sun and the moon guided his day.

TEN

AS THE SKY BRIGHTENED WITH THE PROSPECT OF SUNLIGHT, THE Japanese stopped their assault and retreated from their exposed positions, stumbling down below the ridge where they had some cover.

The rising sun revealed the cost of calm in the Kohima hills. It seemed as if a hurricane of immense magnitude had destroyed everything. Till that morning Mongseng didn't know that humans were capable of such destruction. The tree cover over the perimeter of the defence positions had received a haircut, a very close trim. Most of the canopy was gone. Worst affected were the trees around the battlegrounds; only stumps remained where the sky fires had blasted away their life. Scattered among the fatally wounded trees lay the bodies of many Japanese soldiers – the dead standing guard over death.

While the Japanese soldiers carried their killed and maimed comrades to the bottom of the hills, the defender's stretcher-bearers were busy on top, moving around the pits, picking up siege casualties. While the Japanese stacked their dead into a pile and cremated them in petrol, the stretcher-bearers carried their wounded to the dressing station, and the bodies of the dead to shallow, hastily dug graves.

Through all the turmoil, for the first time in days, two

souls let their bodies rest, not forever, but for a few hours. It was Tom and Raan. Only the impassive glitter of the sun that refused to dampen its glow for the foolery being enacted on earth, and the equally aloof wind carrying the stench of burning human flesh, brought them back to life. Raan lost his drowsiness immediately, and realized he had slept all night. Feeling a little guilty, he went straight to the stove to make some tea for Mongseng as compensation.

The borrowed calm of the morning was shattered by a sudden burst of gunfire and grenades, possibly within the defence perimeter. Tom's scout and one of Chetri's men, Bahadur came by and reported that although many Japanese were killed, it didn't seem to have put a dent in their numbers. Tom took his Zeiss field glasses and scanned the horizon. Wherever he focused across the defence perimeter on the hilly terrain below, it was indeed teeming with Japanese helmets. Rubbing his eyes to shake off the last bit of grogginess, Tom wondered if Colonel Richards would call for him to send out men. As if in answer to his thoughts, a courier arrived with news. It was Ratan Singh, the runner from Raan's village.

"*Sahib*, Commander *Sahib's* wireless set has gone kaput! There is no link with 2nd division headquarter in Dimapur. All gone! Cut off! Now all communication coming through Laverty *Sahib.*" He paused, then added, "West Kent Commander, *Sahib*." Finished, without even stopping to have a word with Raan, Ratan about-faced and broke off into a run, his feet throwing up mud as he headed towards the next post to pass on the information. Some landed on Tom who was left rubbing away the fresh layer that now clung like a tree frog to the leg of his soiled khaki trouser.

The news about the broken wireless brought forth contradictory ideas in Tom. He surmised that since sooner or later the garrison would be run over by the enemy, was there any point defending? Maybe he should concentrate on an exit plan before the Japanese break through? The last order he had received from Assam Rifles HQ was to take orders directly from the garrison commander, Colonel Richards. Any orders from Laverty, Tom felt he would technically have the option to ignore. Unprepared and untested, he was torn between self-preservation and bravery. They were outnumbered ten to one and Tom reasoned his soldier's 303's wouldn't be fast enough to take out that many without everyone getting killed. It seemed to him, that the best course of action would be to stay away from the action as much as he could.

The blast of a grenade at close quarters broke into his thoughts. When Tom turned around, one body was missing. "Where is Mongseng?"

From the stove Raan turned around, equally perplexed, "Aare, don't know *Sahib*! He was here just now."

One hundred yards from Tom and Raan, a Japanese soldier lay dead, his upper body torn to shreds. He was one of the attackers who had managed to break through the defence at night and hid himself around Field Supply Depot, before being discovered. He had sneaked out from his hiding and as he tried to lob a grenade into a bunker, the stealthy assassin accidentally stepped on an empty can of bully beef and the squeak gave him away. A 303 bullet and a burst from a Sten greeted him. He dropped dead where he stood, falling over the grenade minus the pin. The grenade only managed to dismember his lifeless body.

The blown Japanese soldier was one among a few infiltrators who had positioned themselves inside empty huts in the DIS hill. His discovery led to the rest of the infiltrators. Their presence in DIS hill threatened to cut the C Company of West Kent from the rest of the garrison, as DIS became the garrison's last frontier after the Japanese seized control of Jail Hill. The D Company of West Kent, a reserve unit was sent out along with a platoon of Sappers to flush out the intruders. The enemy holed up within the defenders own perimeter couldn't be blasted out with any heavy explosive. Hence progress was slow and the Japanese infiltrators were stubborn. They were proving particularly difficult to flush out of the bakery, which was built of bricks unlike the other huts built with wood and bamboo.

A type 99-mm light machine gun inside the bakery was making the job of the defenders very difficult. Behind the barrel the Japanese soldier wielding the trigger was having a good time. All he had to do was shoot at any movement he saw. He had enough ammunition to kill all the defenders inside the garrison twice over. After a night's hard work, the infiltrators were happy with the role reversal of defending their position.

Just beside the bakery, a light flutter of leaves stroked the garbled trunk of a rhododendron tree. A shadow moved on to the roof and made for the chimney. Moments later the machine gun fell silent. Taking that opportunity, a D Company detachment of the West Kent's ran forward with an old hospital door stuck with bales of gun cotton. After placing it against an oven's wall that was less solid than the rest of the bakery, they ran for cover uncoiling detonating fuse as they went. Once a safe distance, one soldier lit the fuse and watched the spark slowly travel to the door. As the flame reached the door handle where the fuse was tied, a deafening explosion opened a crater in the wall. As the armed division rushed in through the crater, rifles on the ready, they figured they could have walked in through the main door. Four terrified Japanese soldiers greeted them, their guns dropped on the floor, next to the headless bodies of the machine gunner and his assistants.

As suddenly as Mongseng had disappeared, he returned. Raan greeted him like a long lost friend. The threat of death looming over his head made him value the protection of Mongseng. He started making a fuss.

"Would you like some tea? Some water then?"

"No, no thirsty." And before Raan could ask him the next obvious question, Mongseng added, "No hungry."

Mongseng acknowledged Tom with a warm nod. Tom returned a dry nod. He was happy to see Mongseng return, yet how he felt remained under his skin.

Tom couldn't help questioning his authority, "Where have you been? Why did you leave the post without informing either of us?"

"No door here." Mongseng pointed towards the entrance of the bunker, "No have to open or close, why have to ask, go and come?" With that answer and a smile, Mongseng simply rolled out his bedding.

Tom's face grew red with every word he uttered, but he was talking to thin air. Mongseng covered his face with his quilt. He had nothing in mind except catching up on some sleep. Soon long, soft snores were his only reply. Raan's whole body trembled into a silent, soundless laughter. A skill he perfected into an art form working for his white master.

As Mongseng snoozed softly, wide-eyed, Raan brought Tom's attention to the shimmer of blood dripping from Mongseng's *dao* resting on the wall.

Hundreds of men shot or blasted into bits over the past few days in and around Kohima since the Japanese crossed over from Burma was a casualty from a battle they knew how to fight and how to kill. Familiarity of how those hundreds were killed made that kind of brutality seem more acceptable. Three headless bodies lying in the bakery made them shudder.

The four remaining Japanese intruders were rounded up and allowed to cremate their dead in a spot between the Tennis Court and Garrison Hill. A few British Indian soldiers were assigned to assist in the cremation. While preparing for the last rites the Hindu Indian soldiers and the Buddhist Japanese soldiers had a disagreement on the exact steps to follow. The captive Japanese soldiers decided that since they were prisoners they would follow the cremating rituals of their captors. The Indian soldiers, seeing that their Japanese captives had given in, became benevolent and willing to follow the captives' rituals. Finally, Hindu and Buddhist rites intermingled and became one in death.

Taking advantage of the commotion in the burial grounds, Japanese soldiers still hiding around DIS hill made good their escape, carrying with them a few dead comrades. The dead Japanese soldiers from FSD and DIS hills were taken behind Jail Hill and heaped together over the pile of dead bodies from the previous night. A ceremony, this time a purely Japanese one, was held to honour the dead. It was a ceremony limited by resources available in the battlefield. Once the rites were performed, prayers recited, the bodies were unceremoniously doused in petrol and cremated. Cutting wood to cremate the dead was not an option. Bombing from either side had already depleted the tree cover on both sides and to chop off what remained and expose the bunkers of those alive wouldn't be wise.

To die for the Emperor was the highest honour for a Japanese soldier. Generations of soldiers following the Samurai tradition, made death in battle seem aspirational. Death was part and parcel of living. You lived to die, honourably. Thanks to the big war needing big numbers of soldiers to be recruited, even farmers and daily wage earners were given the opportunity to live the life of a Samurai. The Emperor, their demi God, gave them an opportunity to serve him. He wanted them to fight for the greater good, to bring more of the world under one roof – his ego-driven roof. Surrender was not an option in the Samurai tradition. The soldiers who surrendered inside the bakery were initiated into the Samurai tradition from their farming fields not that long ago.

The 31 Division of the Japanese Army had travelled through inhospitable jungles and across steep mountains to reach Kohima, running on sheer willpower and not much else. A general sitting in Tokyo had had an idea that on paper looked brilliant. The plan was to march through dense forests rarely if ever traversed by human beings, let alone a whole army division. His idea was to use bullocks instead of packhorses to transport supplies and equipment. When they needed meat, the idea was to slaughter a bullock – a two-in-one idea, packhorse cum meat. The general sitting in Tokyo liked to ride horses but had never come close to a bullock to know much about them, nor did he know the terrain in the Northeast corner of India. There were no paddy fields there. It was hilly terrain, challenging even for a horse or mule to negotiate. In the end the General's two-in-one idea turned out to be a three-in-one disaster. The 31 Division lost their equipment, their transport and their meal ticket long before they reached Kohima.

Hence, the Japanese army that reached Kohima was a gathering of quantity not quality. No army, however big, however well equipped with guns and ammunition could fight with an empty stomach.

ELEVEN

EVENING ARRIVED AS THE THANKLESS BARRAGE OF MORTAR AND artillery shells rained down with rhythmic consistency. Earth was blustered and blown up. Fat tree trunks were split down the middle. New victims fell – earth, trees, animals and men. As if an old gramophone record was stuck, the music of odium played on. An orchestra of 75-mm shells composed the base, and mortar and gunfire the crescendo. It was as relentless as a hailstorm on a metal roof, only ten times louder. That night too, Mongseng kept watch for most of it while Tom and Raan took a nap for as long as they could under the circumstances. Tom's order to Chetri and his men remained. They had to hold ground in their defensive position, no moving forward to attack.

Chetri and his men were annoyed to watch and wait it out, but Mongseng didn't mind. For the moment, he was content with his score. Thirteen heads within a few days was unheard of in Poilung. It could be a warrior's lifetime achievement to have reached the total number he had reached by then. A total of twenty-three heads when you add the ones he already had before setting foot in Kohima. If the Padre hadn't been up to his mischief, his stepbrother Sangting would never have collected thirteen heads in such a short period.

As a shell blasted ten yards from their bunker, the silhouette of a burnt tree stump was illuminated. Mongseng wondered what harm that tree had done to fall victim to their war? Mongseng took heads to help his village prosper. He wondered why these men wanted to destroy every life form visible, for what gain? Naga battles were not so random and indiscriminate. Here it seemed everyone's motive was to annihilate.

Another mortar shell landed a couple of yards from the bunker throwing dirt and pebbles into the trench. A toffee-sized pebble clanked on a pan and dropped on Raan's forehead. He sat up in his bedding, his eyes darting from one corner to the other. Spotting Mongseng still on guard, he took a deep breath, easing into a sleepy look from his initial shocked expression. He left his bedding, trying to be as noiseless as he possibly could, not to wake Tom. It was a matter of habit rather than the need of the hour, given the noise outside which even a totally deaf person could start hearing.

Cautiously, Raan stepped towards Mongseng and stood on his toes to look through the viewing slit. As he peeped through the slit near the roof, a tracer lit up the sky revealing to Raan exactly what he didn't want to see. The fine hair on his neck, the narrow footbridge that joined the hair on his back with his head, stood up on end. Before the glow from the tracer aided visibility, Mongseng had already seen with his ears what Raan saw with his eyes. There were Japanese everywhere, advancing towards the perimeter. Throughout the previous days, Raan had been praying to Ram, Krishna, Shiva, Hanuman, and whichever other God caught his fancy, asking them to keep the enemy at as much distance from him as their powers possibly could. But now it seemed his Gods were becoming powerless against the relentless Japanese force.

At that moment, Raan cursed the day he had shown up at Tom *Sahib's* door to apply for the job of a cook. He wondered what bad karma he had accumulated in his past life. Why did he have to die so early in the prime of this life. He had never even had the privilege of knowing the comforts of being in close proximity of a woman – skin to skin. Who would relay the news of his death to his parents? How would his otherwise strong mother take the news? Would she be proud of him? She had never liked the fact that he worked for an *Angrez* beef-eater as a cook.

While thoughts of death and its aftermath skittered around Raan's head like rats captured in a trap, as many thoughts were mounting in Mongseng's mind too. He felt excited to sense so many enemy heads marching towards him. How many would he be able to collect? How many would he need to become the *Wangba* of Poilung? Surely Meailing would be as happy to see him with the heads as she was on their wedding day? Would his mother be proud? He checked the blade of his *dao* and stiffened and relaxed his muscles and swung his arms, readying them for the occasion that lay ahead.

Raan had no such trust in his own capabilities. Shell-shocked, he picked up a shovel and cut a ledge under the viewing slit, then opened a box of grenades and one-by-one placed them on the ledge he had dug out. In his hurry to be ahead of the enemy, he pushed on one too many. As it rolled off the ledge and dropped on to a metal ammunition box, Raan gritted his teeth. Holding his forehead, he thanked Lord Ganesha that the noise didn't wake Tom. But the grenade wasn't done yet. It rolled off the trunk and bounced off Tom's right shoulder and landed right in front of his eyes. As he came to, his eyes popped open and he sprang up like a jack-in-a-box. Then the light from an explosion outside illuminated the friendly shape of the British grenade, with safety pin still attached. Heaving a sigh of relief, Tom spotted Raan frozen midway with a grenade in one hand, and his forehead in the other.

"What the hell are you doing?" Tom yelled as his fear turned to anger.

"*Saahib*... I was... no actually... well, yes, I was... p-p-preparing..."

"What?! What?!"

Tom's outburst dried up all words in Raan's aural well. Mongseng had found the whole episode hysterical but knew better than to laugh.

Tom covered his embarrassment with further irritation, this time directed at Mongseng. "What? Why are you grinning? What is so funny? That could have gone off you know. The drop could have easily dislodged the pin!" Tom pointed at the grenade on the ground.

Mongseng managed to keep his grin from getting out of hand. He found it amusing that his war chief was a man who feared battle. He wondered what his father would have thought. In some ways he found Tom similar to the padre in his village. Both men seemed uncomfortable in the surroundings where they chose to establish their homes. And both men were prone to judging situations without fully comprehending the realities on the ground. Tom's fear for the fireball reminded him of how the padre had reacted to seeing his first head. Mongseng also recalled how the padre tried, like Tom, to hide his fear with disgust.

Keeping his thoughts to himself, Mongseng lifted his hand and pointed outwards, "Look, battle come close. Raan just prepare for battle."

Wide-eyed, Tom peeped out in the direction of Mongseng's pointing finger. Tom's relief and anger evaporated. What he saw was what he had been dreading all this while. The enemy were at his doorstep.

Initially when the garrison was being fortified and Tom moved into the bunker along with Raan, Chetri and his men, he had taken it all in his stride. It felt like rehearsing for a fire drill. He had not seriously thought that the garrison would ever really come under fire. Slowly he had realized that he might have to send some of his men to fight. But he never really imagined that he would need to fight himself, ever have to raise a gun and aim it at a man and squeeze the trigger and take the life from a stranger. The morning he had taken the patrol party out to Aradura Spur, even then he had not really expected to encounter any enemy. After his initial shock, he was relieved that Mongseng had done all of the work.

A West Kent Lieutenant came running towards them crouched and started shouting, "What do you think you are up to? We need more men to defend the perimeter! They are swarming like flies and you guys sit up here like rats!"

Raan went red but Tom didn't change colour. Feebly he answered, "My orders are to be the second line of defence."

"Whose orders? When you can clearly see the first line is crumbling, aren't you backing us up?"

"Careful officer, you are addressing your superior. My orders from the Garrison Commander are to hold my position." Tom answered with a cold look.

Raan looked at Tom, perplexed. After the phone lines had gone down, the only way Tom received communication from Richard's HQ was through runners, yet none had come by since the attacks began in earnest. Raan knew when Tom wore his poker face that he was most probably lying. He also knew better than to interfere, and left the matter alone. Anyway, he was with Tom on the decision. He didn't want any part in the madness unfolding. He was determined to live as many days as he could pull away from death's mouth.

Tom had his suspicion that there was a rift between the Garrison Commander, Colonel Richards, and the West Kent Commander, Lieutenant Colonel Laverty. Laverty knew he was in command of the best battalion of soldiers in Kohima and he didn't want his men to be mixed, diluted amongst the rest of the rag-tag bunch of defenders under the Garrison Commander's control. Laverty took advantage of his position and was not about to take orders from Colonel Richards. Deciding to take advantage of this unique position Tom made up his mind not to take orders from the West Kent Commander, and he would make sure the Garrison Commander couldn't find him.

Once the West Kent officer left, Tom sent Mongseng to fetch Chetri. He arrived with his characteristically broad smile. "So should we move forward and fight the Nippons?" Unknown to Tom, Chetri and his men had already been taking pot shots at the Japanese. It was Chetri who had directed the West Kent officer to Tom's bunker.

"We have to secure our position first, Chetri. Get your men, I have decided we are moving from here to Kuki Picket. We need to reinforce the garrison and Kent command posts." In Tom's mind this would secure his and his men's position. Kuki Picket being deeper inside the garrison, the Japanese would have to first take DIS and FSD hills before they came face to face with Tom and his men. Also with the two command posts behind them, they wouldn't need to keep watch over their backs.

"*Ji Hazur,* Yes, sir! I will bring my men right away."

Chetri had come with the hope of receiving orders to move forward, not to retreat. But he knew it was no point trying to argue with Tom. He also knew that sooner or later he and his eager band of Gorkhas would find more opportunities to engage. He maintained a tight camaraderie with other Gorkha soldiers serving in the different units around the garrison. From them he came to know that they were well and truly surrounded. He smiled to himself as he considered that after they move to Kuki Picket, if Tom ordered them to retreat further, their behinds would be at the enemy's front line. Raan, all too happy with Tom's decision, started packing up immediately. Indifferent, Mongseng put his *dao* back into its cowrie-shelled scabbard.

The moon had forsaken the battlegrounds some time back but the sun was reluctant to show. It was as though nature favoured the group of retreaters as they moved their post. Mongseng led the way, guiding them taking cover behind naked tree stumps, and in and out of trenches converted by bombs into craters. As the sky turned golden from grey, the group reached their destination. Streaks of cloud reflected golden hues, at the same time threatening to throw rain on the debauchery, perhaps to sooth their tempers. On the hill the trenches in the middle were a honeycomb of activity. Soldiers on alert with guns on the ready, and orders being passed back and forth. Empty trenches lay about the edges, most exposed to the enemy's line of fire.

Tom felt like an outsider gate crashing someone else's party, a gloomy one at that. As no rank insignias were allowed on the battlefield he had taken them off long ago. Now watching the activity, Tom took off his Assam Rifles badge. With its removal he became just another soldier in khaki uniform; only his skin suggested his identity as an officer. Tom wanted to blend into the crowd, preferring to lose himself in the khaki ocean. With the enemy attacking like zombies without any fear of death, Tom didn't see the point in showing any bravery. To fight the insane was not brave. He would not be ordered by his higher-ups to fight the insane. He would defend and save his life and the lives of his men.

Tom's men couldn't comprehend why their leader had removed all identifying tags, but Tom's expression told them he didn't want this action questioned or refused. Following suit, all the men removed their battalion badges and Assam Rifles insignia. Mongseng looked on and did nothing; he wore nothing, he took off nothing.

Then, the group led by the man who wore no clothes on his body and no fear on his mind, circled around the eastern edge of Kuki Piquet facing the ridge, to avoid any enemy fire from Jail Hill. By now Jail Hill had become an enemy fortress where many snipers lay. Mongseng crouched into a crater. The rest huddled in after him. As the last men followed in behind Chetri, a shot wrung out from across the ridge. It was impersonal like the hundreds of thousands that they had heard wringing back and forth, day and night. The last soldier stumbled into the pit clumsily and bumped on to Chetri's back. Chetri swung around; momentarily anxiousness made him lose his temper and he wanted to reproach the soldier. The soldier slid around Chetri's back and fell on the muddy ground like a piece of log coming loose from a pile.

So far Tom and his men had been in the war more like bystanders to the events that were unfolding in the besieged Garrison. Over the last few days they had heard and seen artillery and mortar shells being exploded in the thousands and the exchanged of bullets in hundreds of thousands. All those bullets were of a battle others were fighting, except one that nearly missed Raan. They had been lucky until now; a bullet amongst those hundreds of thousands came to change their luck. The fallen soldier had a clean hole running through and through his head. A tiny stream of blood was gushing out from the exit wound. Time froze in the pit.

The soldier killed was Bahadur – "It is a very common name. There are so many Bahadurs in Nepal that if you throw a stone at a group of Nepalis it will most likely land on a Bahadur." A joke Bahadur, the deceased soldier, loved to tell when a non-Nepali asked him his name. Now that stone from his joke came in the form of a bullet and picked him out amongst the group and no one was laughing.

He was a quiet type whom Tom only noticed at his death. They tried not to let their feet touch his lifeless body. Holed up in there, with a sniper looking out for any head that popped up, the Gorkhas couldn't cremate Bahadur according to Hindu rights. They wanted to offer him what little respect they could, within the cramped crater. Tom suggested they deepen the crater and bury him where he fell. Though Chetri, distraught, didn't want to agree, he knew that Tom was right. As deep as they could the men dug a grave with their bayonets and Mongseng joined in with the conical end of his spear. As Bahadur's body was being covered, Chetri took from his pocket a red-clothed booklet. It was the *Hanuman Chalisa*. He read a few verses as they laid him to rest in his foot and a half grave.

While the rest mourned the death, Tom mourned his decision. Would it have been better to stay put in FSD? Should he have changed their formation while moving, rather than walk in a queue, which left his man at the back vulnerable? Whatever was done, was done, he concluded they had to move on. With Bahadur's death, his resolve to distance himself and his men from the battle became even more resolute. Changing his mind he decided to take his men across Garrison Hill, to the tennis court, where they would have the Garrison HQ behind them. If Commander Richards sent out a runner to look for him, surely he will only look in his last known location. Early on in their march Chetri had informed Tom that Ratan Singh, the runner from Raan's village had fallen victim to a sniper's bullet during the night. For a new runner who didn't know Tom or any of his men, if he were sent to look for them it would be unlikely that he would be successful. With the Assam Rifles logo gone from their shirts, Tom and his men disappeared amidst a sea of khaki.

Everyone was shaken by the death, except for Mongseng, who since the day he was strong enough to wield a full-length *dao,* had known that death always moves hand in hand with life. While the others sat quietly in grief, Mongseng was busy trying to figure out a possible exit plan from the crater. Having already proved beyond any speck of doubt his warrior's capabilities, Tom was all ears when Mongseng laid out his plan, "I go this way. You half men go that way. Once men reach there, other half come to me. Fast, fast. Ok?"

"Okay." Tom nodded. By now Tom understood Mongseng's English fluently. Accordingly, Tom split up his men into two groups. Mongseng slipped out of the crater and slid across to take cover behind a mound of earth displaced by heavy explosives. The sniper's gun came alive. The shots tried to catch Mongseng, a trail of dust rose in clusters behind him. His agility helped him stay inches ahead. While Mongseng kept the sniper busy, the first group escaped into the safety of another empty trench to Mongseng's left. The sniper changed direction and got busy firing at the first group. Taking that as a cue, the second group escaped to safety behind the mound where Mongseng had taken cover. Outsmarting the sniper, Mongseng slunk to another cover. Every time Mongseng or one of the two groups moved, they didn't go more than five-ten metres at a time, just enough not to give the sniper time to readjust his position and the sights of his gun. The ballet of survival orchestrated by Mongseng frustrated the sniper out of his wits.

After a few twists and turns, he motioned for the groups to stop following. The created confusion had given Mongseng enough time to divert the sniper's attention and move right under his nose. With the stealth of a leopard he climbed up the slippery bark of the cherry tree towards the oblivious sniper. While the sniper fired at his enemy a hundred yards away, his real threat moved vertically, closing the few feet between them, an inch at a time. When Mongseng was half a spears length away, crouching down like a compressed spring he took aim, his feet firmly grasping the thick branch. Then, leapfrogging upwards he shoved the spear cleanly through the shooter.

Before the sniper knew it, he had missed his last target. The spear travelled up his anal tract, missing all bones on the way towards the heart. That it had been a heart torn between taking innocent lives and following the Emperor's command, did not matter. The flat blade of Mongseng's spear split the tormented heart in two. The rifle dropped from his hand and waved in mid air, dangling from the shoulder strap. With one flawless swing the *dao* separated the sniper's head, thus becoming his fourteenth kill from the hunting expedition. The head slid off the neck and brushed through branches and leaves smearing them red, finally coming to a rest with a dull thud on the damp ground below; the sound reminded Mongseng of a ripe jackfruit falling to the ground.

With the immanent threat eliminated, the relocating group covered the rest of the distance in single file. Tom temporarily relinquished his leadership to Mongseng. As they reached the bottom of Garrison Hill, Tom took back the lead and ordered them to move faster. He didn't want to be spotted by Colonel Richards or his men, who might wish to know their movements. Raan, who all the while had been carrying his pots and pans, using them as body shield between the sniper, wasn't too happy to quicken his pace. There at the beginning of the tennis court, on a slight drop below Garrison Hill…a gift from God, they found three empty bunkers.

They settled in for the day, exhausted. Exhausted not by the distance they had to cover, it was that burden of fear that rode in their heads. Death finally was living amongst them. It was no longer a stranger who lived in the neighbourhood. It was a familiar face that lived among them now.

Chetri and his men moved into the two bunkers in front. He ordered six of the new recruits to occupy one and he took the other with the remaining four Gurkhas. As Chetri slumped down on the floor of his bunker, grief also wore him down. He had been fond of Bahadur for his skills as a tracker and his no-nonsense attitude. He was all work and little talk. Chetri thought that if he had just walked a little faster into that fateful crater it might have given Bahadur an extra fraction of a second. Would that have saved him from the sniper's bullet? Did the dying soldier's last breath pick up a whiff of the scorn that Chetri had felt when Bahadur stumbled on to his back? A tear trickled down Chetri's cheek. He couldn't hide it from his men, two sitting on either side of him in the cramped space. They all shared his grief and let their *Subedar* have his moment. The teardrop rolled down his chest and was absorbed by his khaki shirt. And in minutes Chetri's emotions were dried up by duty that his khaki uniform donned on him.

In an adjacent bunker, Tom didn't think it would be appropriate to ask Raan to remind him of the name of the dead soldier. He knew all along that sooner or later he would lose one or more men. It was a game of hearts; it was only a matter of time before his team would be dealt a queen of spades. How long they had to play, and how many times they would be dealt that costly card, they had to wait and see. Raan hadn't known Bahadur that well, but his death had roused the fear that Raan had so far managed to keep encased within his heart. He wished he had heeded his brother's request and taken up farming instead. He was scared. Unlike the others around him, Raan had been trained in the art of sustaining people, not killing them. He was born into a strict vegetarian family, and seldom killed an animal. Only after joining Tom's service as a cook did he begin to eat meat. He was afraid of being killed. And the thought of taking another life also sent a shiver down his spine.

Across the bunker, Mongseng looked at his spear and made a mental note to find a slate stone to sharpen it that night. He liked to keep his equipment pristine. As pristine as his conscience, which put no stain on his soul for taking a life that could otherwise have taken his. He had left his fourteenth trophy hidden inside a burrow of the same tree from which it fell. From his thoughts, Mongseng's gaze fell on the battlefield where bodies lay strewn – some disfigured, others dismembered. He had never known people to fight for so long, over so many days. Back home, their battles were always fought in a day, collecting the heads of the defeated, and returning home. Warring parties never travelled for so many days and nights to fight in a foreign land, and evidently over nothing. He wondered how much longer the battle would last. His intention to come to Kohima was to defeat the purpose of the padre. Though, another thought was starting to bother him. His plan to counter the padre's trickery was going well but would taking so many Japanese heads back to his village really bring their Konyak village prosperity?

TWELVE

ONCE SETTLED INTO THE NEW BUNKER, MONGSENG, RAAN AND TOM engaged themselves with other activities. Mongseng began to stitch two big pouches for carrying water. He was amazed that these white and brown people had a cloth that could hold water, a discovery he made while walking past a bunker after a heavy downpour. Water had gathered on the roof that had a tarp covering over it. When he came across a long piece of canvas discarded by soldiers from another trench, it gave him an idea. As the canvas had multiple shrapnel wounds, it had become useless as a rain cover. He had dragged the canvas with him to the bunker and with his *dao* carved out two intact pieces, skilfully manoeuvring between the holes. He now stitched the damp fabric with a needle he had carved out of a thin sheet of metal, again with the help of his trusted *dao*. When Raan saw him stitching with the concentration of a seamstress he couldn't help a little jibe, "*Aare* Mongseng, what are you doing in the middle of the war? Instead of looking after your weapons, are you sewing a skirt for your wife?"

Ignoring Raan's taunt, Mongseng focused on his job. Partially because he didn't understand what a skirt was. Not receiving a reaction to what he thought was a perfectly contrived dig, Raan attended to his impoverished kitchen.

When Raan finally saw what Mongseng was creating he was pleased. As the West Kent Commander Laverty had predicted, the Japanese had blown up the garrison's exposed water reservoir at the first opportunity. Now, the airdropped water supply was not enough, and the only stream to fetch water was located in the middle of enemy territory. When stealth was required, clanking metal buckets weren't ideal.

While his two assistants worked with their hands, Tom was working with his head and heart. Both were pounding with thoughts and feelings for Sandra, of bravery, of treachery, of defence and attack, of running to hide. Through it all however, Tom tried to maintain his brave face. As he sat there in the bunker he didn't let the thoughts or situation brewing reflect on his face. Before his emotions got the better of him, and his vulnerability became exposed, Tom upped and left under the pretext of going to report to the Garrison Commander.

In the relative peace, and once it was sufficiently dark, with a canvas sack strung across each back, Raan set off with Mongseng to fetch water from the stream. Passing Kuki Piquet by the crater that was Bahadur's grave, Raan wanted to pay his respects to the quiet soldier. Raan could barely spot a blade of grass anywhere, let alone a flower to place on the grave. Everything around them was pulverized and raw. The fighting continued around DIS and FSD, with the enemy entrenched across Jail Hill. In the process of trying to retain ground or gain ground, the actual ground was demolished. As a replacement for flowers, Raan picked up a couple of perfectly smooth oval stones and placed them on Bahadur's grave.

Excellent stealth training for Raan, together they crawled across Daily Issue Supplies Hill, on to the road below. Then, lying flat on their bellies they shimmied across on to the other side, and into enemy territory. Mongseng was thankful that he had his deerskin on around his groin or else the rough stones on the dirt road would have ripped his manhood apart. Careful not to make any noise, they attempted to step with tiger's paws, and progress like a sloth. Invisible as a tiger, its stripes blending into a sun-chequered forest, Raan shadowed Mongseng's moves, stuck close to him like a bur on fur, and the two men disappeared into the darkness, dissolving in with the sounds of the night.

At a curve below Jail Hill lay the stream. Protected from shellfire, the area was still covered by thick foliage, rendering it undetectable from above. After risking his life to reach there, Raan felt disappointed to see their reward. The stream had hardly a trickle of water flowing in it. Local Naga guides working for the British had known the existence of the stream long before the war. It was a stream that flowed steady with the same amount of water, be it summer or winter. He was thankful that the water was at least crystal clear; finding clean water was a blessing. Keeping one eye towards the surrounding darkness and one on the sack that seemed to tease him, taking forever to fill, Raan held his patience.

Among the familiar sounds of the night, Mongseng could hear the unfamiliar murmur of Japanese voices. As Raan's sack filled up and Mongseng placed his in its place, a commotion flared up at close quarters. While it was Raan's instinct to run, Mongseng grabbed him by the shoulder and gestured him to stay put. Heart in his mouth, Raan watched as Mongseng slipped away to investigate. Not far from the stream Mongseng spotted a foraging Japanese soldier, plucking bulbous stems of a variety of weed that grew around marshlands. When he saw the plant the soldier was plucking it reminded him of his childhood when he and his friends used to go and pick those stems. Peeling back the bark revealed the tender, sour flesh within which they chewed and sucked on. Once the Japanese soldier had an armful, he headed up Jail Hill. Mongseng followed out of view, keeping a safe distance, his steps as nimble as feathers being blown along a path.

After a short time, a small fire came into view, looking as miserable as the four occupants squatting around it. A barrier of leafy green branches created a wall around the fire, to muffle the light and avoid attracting the attention of the wrong pairs of eyes. Sustained with a few twigs from dry shrubs, the fire accommodated a single deep pan. As Mongseng looked on, a streak of flame escaped its well-built barricade, illuminating the contents within. To the bubbling pot of rice the forager added his stems and leaves, shredding them with the sharp edge of his bayonet and covered the brew with a piece of wooden plank. While the subdued men waited for their meal to be ready, they whispered amongst themselves. From their expressions Mongseng could guess that they were not discussing events from the battlefield. Their wistful laughter took him along with them to distant lands, far away from there, close to loved ones.

Once the weedy rice broth was ready, one of the men produced a can of condensed milk from his overcoat pocket, pierced it with his bayonet, and added a little cheer to the otherwise miserable dinner. Eating the broth using their bayonets as forks, Mongseng felt a pang of compassion for his trophy givers. If they came to attack his territory across the road, he might take their heads tomorrow. But for now he would let them be.

As Mongseng made his way back to Raan, he scanned the

night-veiled mountain. All around he sensed misery, starvation, filth and disfigurement. Many shadows resembled mere skeletons. Looking at their numbers from afar, Mongseng had assumed the enemy was powerful; he hadn't expected them to be even worse off than those holed up in the garrison. Again Mongseng wondered what these soldiers would gain by defeating an enemy who had very little food and now sat on desolate land. Leaving the enemy in their plight, they retraced their steps, now wrestling unwieldy sacks, back towards the relative safety of the garrison perimeters. Metres before they reached the road, without warning British artillery guns started bombing the enemy around, Jail Hill. Being in enemy territory, the advantage of the bombings turned quite the contrary for the two. Shells started dropping around them like a gigantic hailstorm of metal. Mongseng decided it would be best to make a dash for their side of the war zone, as with indiscriminate bombing there was no way to judge where the next one would fall.

Just as he was about to relay his decision to Raan, he heard the whooshing sound of an artillery shell and dove for cover. He crouched behind a rock with his hands folded over his head waiting for the deafening boom. Instead, he heard the quaking voice of Raan mumbling something. Craning his neck over the rock he looked up and saw Raan trembling in the same spot where they had parted. Fortunately, the thirty-pounder bomb landed on rain-soaked clay earth that cradled the detonating pin instead of pushing it in. Raan touched his throbbing heart and kept reciting verses from a pocket book of *Hanuman Chalisha* that he always carried, and thanked the bachelor monkey god, whose verses he was reciting, for protecting his life.

Mongseng realized he couldn't trust Raan to hear bombs whizzing down from the sky, a sound that was only a step away from silence. He collected the fitful Raan and, without exchanging any words, they crossed over towards the garrison. But when trouble comes, it often arrives along with its twin brother. A sentry at the frontline confronted them with his rifle on the ready, "Stop!"

"Friends. Friends." Mongseng replied, trying to look as friendly as he could. With no moon, the stars were not enough to reflect back his friendly face or his nakedness to the sentry. Just being visible would have been enough of a password for the sentry to let them in. The story of a naked headhunter fighting for their side had spread amongst the garrison defenders like sunlight permeating through a dark forest – everyone knew about Mongseng. But in the moonless sky he was a mere silhouette.

Tightening his grip around the cold metal of his rifle the sentry repeated, "Password?"

The password was 'Lilly Little'. A phonetic tongue twister, deliberately contrived so that if a Japanese soldier tried to infiltrate into the Garrison in the guise of an Indian or British soldier, even if they found out the password, they wouldn't be able to pronounce it correctly, giving them away. The tongue twister added an extra layer of security. A layer of security that for Mongseng with a similar tongue of a Japanese, even he found the password difficult to pronounce. Raan already with a quivering tongue because of his near encounter with death was still trying to get a grip on himself and couldn't utter a single word. Friendly territory seemed even more threatening for them.

Mongseng contemplated if he should knock out the sentry or try and find another unguarded path to sneak in. As he thought over his options, a bomb exploded nearby and lit up the surrounding. The flash of light from the explosion illuminated Mongseng's face and the sentry instantly recognised him and let them through.

Raan had enough adventure he could handle for a day. Without any hunger left for more, he was glad to head back straight to their bunker. Once safely inside, Raan, fidgety from his foray into enemy territory began fussing around, preparing onions and corned beef, Mongseng went and sat in a corner.

"Tam." Mongseng, usually the silent warrior, called out and startled Tom. Even Raan looked up from the pot he was stirring.

"Yes, Mongseng. What is it?"

"I think about war." He began, leaning over an ammunition box, resting his chin on his palm.

"Okay. What about it?" Tom turned to face him, offering the warrior his full attention.

"Why you fight?"

"Why? To defeat the enemy of course." Tom eyed Mongseng, wondering if he had had enough and was planning to leave.

"What do after defeat enemy?"

"We all go home."

"No take heads? No take land?"

"Of course not! We don't take heads Mongseng. You can have them all! And this land is ours, not theirs to give. Once we, errr, defeat them, I guess the enemy will go back to their country too."

"Country?"

"Big land, where there are many villages and many homes; where they are from."

"If they have big land, why fight to take small land?"

"Hmm…"

Before Tom could think of an appropriate answer, Mongseng continued, "Ho! If no take head, no take land, what use fight?"

"Well, like I said, Mongseng, to defeat the enemy."

Raan noticed Tom's cheeks were glowing as red as ember, he looked down and gave the dish he was cooking an extra stir.

"What use of defeat?"

"We win. They lose. We stop their march into our country."

"What use is win? Win no make good crop. Win not fill tummy. Stop fight now, peace come…now, happily."

Tom turned to Raan, "Is dinner ready? I sure am hungry." Tom turned his back to Mongseng and busied himself shuffling papers. Inside, Mongseng felt perplexed to find out that Tom, like the enemy, had no good reason to fight. While Raan served, Mongseng decided to give his *dao* a quick sharpening with a rock. As two senseless sides kept fighting, he was happy to collect some of those senseless heads.

THIRTEEN

SANDRA WAS ON AN UNDULATING MEADOW THAT EXTENDED AS FAR as the eye could see. Completely relaxed, she lay amid a bed of wild flowers in every colour of Mother Earth's palate. A bright red little beauty caught her eye. She drew it closer to breath in its aroma. But instead of sweetness, the flower smelt metallic, something very unbecoming for such a beautiful blossom. Suddenly the red petals melted away in her hand, leaving her palm filled with blood. As she moved to shake it away Sandra found herself sitting up in bed. Yet another morning wake up call to the smell of metallic dry blood. A nauseating feeling of rotting flesh engulfed her. Breathing in the damp, putrid air filled with the odour of decomposing flesh felt as if it would rot away her insides.

But Sandra had no time to mourn for her self, let alone the dead. This morning, like all mornings that week, she willed her senses to cope with the surrounding stench and carnage. The trenches of the Advance Dressing Station were narrow. Some of the middle channels had to be left without cover to let in more air. That morning, just when Sandra wondered how she could take any more, the Japanese started shelling. One of the dressing station's trenches, open to the air, took a direct hit from a seventy-five-millimetre shell, turning a trench dedicated to recovery into a readymade grave for its five patients.

Walking past the newly-formed grave, Sandra felt lucky, and for those now entombed, she hoped they died instantly from the explosion, not by suffocating under the resulting mound of earth. With no time to ponder, Doctor Young requested Sandra's help with a shrapnel victim. The torn metal had almost severed the soldier's pelvis from the rest of the body and he had lost a lot of blood. The wounded Indian soldier was hallucinating and crying for his mother. Being the only female in the unit, Doctor Young thought maybe Sandra could bring him some comfort. It worked. In his semi-crazed state the soldier saw his sixty-year-old mother in thirty-two-year-old Sandra. He held her hands and clasped them to his cheeks. Pacified, salty water silently poured over her wrists. Below, the man's intestines lay exposed, attended to by Doctor Young who was valiantly trying to tuck the innards back in.

As soon as the soldier stopped struggling, Doctor Young stitched up the shrapnel laceration. He didn't have enough gauges to wrap up the wound and hold it in place. Sandra had a scarf wrapped around her neck, which she offered to Doctor Young. It was a scarf her mother had given on the day she was admitted into boarding school. Since that day Sandra had used that scarf more to find love and comfort, rather than simple warmth. Since the day she moved from their bungalow to the barrack on Hospital Hill, she had her mother's scarf around her neck every moment of her waking hours. Now she hoped the scarf would not only hold the wounded soldier's stitches but would also help to heal.

Since the fighting intensified, Sandra had come to dread the moments whenever she saw an occupied stretcher coming towards the ADS. With trepidation she always looked at the occupants, hoping that the wounds were not too bad, and that there was no one she knew on it. Especially, of course, her husband. Tom had been coming to visit her almost daily. And with every visit, increasingly he spoke of Mongseng. It was beyond doubt that Tom was fond of him but, after her first impressions, Sandra was growing a little wary of that fellow. Her distrust for Mongseng didn't stem so much from his behaviour, but rather one of her recent recurring nightmares. It came to her as she was drifting to sleep, and then again in the morning, waking her up prematurely. The dream started off like a routine day. She was preparing a patient, cutting the shirt off his bloodied arms to bare it for urgent amputation. Then Doctor Young came in, picked up a sharp and glittering blade and with a seriousness of purpose moved closer to the patient and turned his back on Sandra. But instead of amputating the shredded hand, he would saw off the patient's head. Once surgery was complete Doctor Young turned around with a broad grin across his face and Sandra realized that it was Mongseng in the surgeon's robe.

Sandra wanted to support her husband, and to believe in Mongseng's seemingly friendly gestures. But somehow the frequency of the nightmare kept her suspicious of him, thinking it was some sort of a sign. That day, Mongseng came visiting with Tom. Sandra was pleasantly surprised to see that the warrior now sported a flap of deerskin, covering his genitalia, perhaps his small contribution to the observance of modern-day etiquettes. Though he was oblivious of her embarrassment, Mongseng had come to think of Sandra as an exceptionally red-faced woman. That day Mongseng noticed that Sandra wasn't glowing red, instead she looked pale and welcomed him with a weary, yet striking smile.

Gently, with as much affection as a couple of words could carry, Mongseng asked, "You…fine?"

"Oh, yes, Mongseng… Hello, I am fine." And with a self-conscious glance at her husband, the colour rising in her cheeks, added, "Thank you for asking."

Seeing the colour back in her face, Mongseng felt glad. Around his neck Mongseng wore a couple of necklaces to ward off evil spirits; black beads and cowries, tied into a string woven out of Himalayan bear fur. He slid his *dao* out from his cowrie belt. The action made Sandra take two steps back and Tom's hand moved to the butt of his revolver. Watching on, a recuperating patient who had heard of Mongseng's exploits covered his face in a feeble attempt to shield his head from the wrath of Mongseng's fabled blade. Feeling a little humiliated for the mistrust, Mongseng hid his tinge of bitter sadness, letting it slip beneath his tattooed face. With his *dao* Mongseng sliced through the bear fur holding the necklaces together. He took one from the bunch and offered it to Sandra, "For good luck."

With trembling hands Sandra accepted the gift from the benevolent savage. Her hands shook not out of fear but for the collective embarrassment she felt for their mistrust. He, who could sense a lot more than most human beings, had read Sandra's emotions fully. As she accepted the gift, Mongseng nodded his approval. As the two exchanged smiles, Tom rubbed his palm on the butt of his revolver as if there was an itch that he badly needed to scratch.

Sandra wore that necklace all day and before going to bed placed it carefully over one of the few vanity items still in her possession – her piece of mirror. It was a broken piece that Raan scavenged for her from the rubble of the District Collector's bungalow. It was a tiny piece that could accommodate to show her only portions of her face at a time.

Being the only woman in Doctor Young's team, she had been given a bunker to herself. And like all women, Sandra had the innate ability to turn the small unlikely space into a home. Within a few days she had put destructive battlefield elements to a more constructive use. With Raan's help she used the planks of wood from an empty box of artillery shells as a base for her bedroll – a far cry from the teak wood and cane bed she shared with her husband at the Tamulguri Tea Estate. Another metal 303 ammunition box had become her bedside table. On it, a used artillery shell had become a holder for a few knick-knacks including her comb, hair clips and lipstick. Though of late she hadn't been wearing her red lipstick at all. There was far too much red around her already.

Sandra filled her bunker also with a few familiar objects from their bungalow to make her feel at home inside the bunker. On the wall opposite her bed hung from a protruding root was a picture from the days when she and Tom had first started dating. It showed a shy couple, glowing with anticipation standing among undulating tea bushes. The photo had been taken with the Conway camera that her father had gifted her on her fifteenth birthday. Back then she had wanted to become a photographer; to capture people's emotions, their blood, sweat and tears. Now it seemed that to look through the lens was so easy, rather than the blood, sweat and tears which she now had to deal with directly. Amidst her items of comfort, her most valued object was missing, her camera. Sandra loved capturing life and the moment she heard the approach of the Japanese, she sent her camera to Shillong to be kept safe with a friend. She took pictures to capture beauty. She was no optimist to believe that she would be able to find beauty in hatred.

When life was only about living and appreciating the beauty that abounded around her, she took pictures of people and nature abundant with the vigour of life. Once she finished a roll she had to send it to Calcutta for developing. Along with the roll she would also send a list of instructions about what she wanted done with her favourites in the roll. After a long wait they returned from Calcutta, all developed and some framed. Then to her pleasant surprise she would realize that some of the spontaneous ones that she took to finish the roll came out even better than the ones she composed intentionally. Those superior pictures she had to be content slotting inside inferior frames purchased locally in Tezpur.

After moving to Kohima, whenever she had to finish a roll, she went after Raan. Raan dreaded those days, as he had to be watchful all the time, lest he was frozen in photographic images forever caught at a wrong moment. Yet his apprehensions disappeared when he received his copies of the photographs. He took them to his room and pasted them on the walls around his room. Whenever there were pictures taken of him not cooking or cleaning and he reckoned he was looking like a Hindi movie hero, he posted them to his mother who was actively looking for a bride for him. She didn't approve of her son becoming a cook. She felt her son had chosen a profession fit only for women. She considered a man's job was outside the kitchen.

As a child Raan never saw a division of labour in his household. His mother always wore the pants or *dhoti* in his parents' relationship. She was as good at cooking as she was at growing what she cooked in their *bigha* of ancestral land her husband inherited. Her husband thought he contributed enough towards the family by inheriting that plot of land. Rest of his days he spent at the village *theka,* the local bar, where he exchanged some of the fruits of his wife's hard labour for bottles of local brew. His father not being able to stand firm on his feet as a role model, Raan didn't grow up with a bias towards any profession as being exclusively for men or women.

If his mother found out now that he wielded a gun along with a ladle, she would be proud. A cook would find a few proposals for marriage. But an army cook would double the number of parents offering their eligible daughters' hand in matrimony. Unfortunately, before he managed to take leave and go home to visit the houses of prospective brides and be treated like royalty for once in his life, the Japanese came visiting. He hoped to come out of the battle alive and find himself a pretty wife.

That night the shelling was sporadic, and Sandra's nightmare did not revisit. In the morning, as she woke up she silently thanked Mongseng, thoughts interrupted by a burst of gunfire. Brought back to reality, instead of panic, Sandra decided to maintain her calm. Quickly and quietly she made tea and sipped it from the white enamel cup into which she dunked some dry, rationed biscuits. Again Sandra smiled at Mongseng's kind gesture. Tom rarely gave her gifts; never made much out of occasions. He never remembered her birthday or their anniversary, unless Sandra reminded him.

That day her mood in the ADS recovery trenches was infectious. She spread her cheerfulness like a bunch of sweet-smelling jasmines wrapped around the bun of a fisher woman – the fragrance spreading like a breath of fresh air to prevail over the stench. Despite the gloom, for a moment patients, attendants and doctors alike, forgot their pain, dread and questionable future, and smiled in the present, happy to be alive. Fear stayed out till it gathered enough momentum to barge in again.

FOURTEEN

THOUGH HUNDREDS WERE ALREADY DEAD IN THE GARRISON, amidst fifteen men, Bahadur was the first to go. To be the first dead amongst fifteen, everyone mourned his death. However, they couldn't mourn him for long. By the evening of Bahadur's death, he was a dry marigold garlanded, cobwebbed photograph, relegated to dusty walls of the men's memories.

By morning, Chetri's prediction that sooner or later they would come face-to-face with the enemy came true. It turned out that the tennis court was the place to be. No longer sitting in the backbenches waiting to be called, the fighting came to their doorstep; now they were in the playground and the match had begun. From where they were, the enemy no longer looked miniature.

In the bunker behind them, Raan was entertaining his own thoughts. Alerted to the growing proximity of the enemy, he checked and re-checked his rifle to see it was loaded. Then he flicked the safety clip off and on. Next he counted his bullet clips. Ten. Certainly that didn't seem enough! Opening a box of ammunition he crammed his pockets with more clips, each clip holding five bullets. Raan's nervousness was not doing any favours for Tom. Faking his own calm he asked, "Planning to shoot all the Japs by yourself, are you, dear chap?"

Snapped out of his fearful trance, while evading Tom's question, Raan feebly asked, "Tea *Sahib*?"

Tom didn't respond. In his mind he couldn't avoid the inevitable question: should they have stayed where they were? If so, perhaps that soldier who's name still eluded him, would be alive and they wouldn't be sitting targets. Relocating again was not an option. He hoped that the frontline around them was strong. Just one hundred yards below, a road now separated them from a big contingent of holed up Japanese soldiers, now fully entrenched in the old Naga village. On their side next to the road, the District Commissioner's bungalow stood – or what remained standing of it. Once, the Commissioner's bungalow had been the most beautifully kept house in Kohima. It was a point of envy for Sandra when they visited the house for lunch or dinner parties. Now all that remained of that pride of the town were a few burnt pillars surrounded by twisted corrugated sheets and the debris of what once comprised the walls and interior décor of the house.

As he peered out of the bunker, next to the rubble of the bungalow Mongseng could see the enemy burrowed in. But now he saw things more clearly. He saw no difference between the Japanese army or the British-Indian army. Only clothes, or lack thereof, and skin colour, offered distinguishing features between the warring parties. His eagle eyes observed the same fear in the enemy, as he could see in the eyes of his hosts.

The road between the garrison and the Japanese positions, which acted as no man's land, had already been breached. The enemy now occupied some trenches dug for the defenders. Mongseng watched as Japanese runners sprinted from one burrow to the next. They were so close that the simultaneous click of a hundred bayonets being fixed to rifles was unmistakable. Mongseng let loose a deep-throated cry. The onslaught had begun.

Chetri removed a spent magazine from his Sten gun and jammed in a fully loaded one as he ordered his men to fix bayonets and ready their loaded 303s. Just below them, with shrill war cries and shots ringing the Japanese were already out of the trenches and upon the first line of defence. Guns blared, and bayonets sliced and pierced through flesh. The attackers shot and were shot down. The defenders shot and were shot where they were holed in. With no protection to shield their advance, the Japanese seemed to fall down in rows, a stack of crumbling cards under a desperate rain of British bullets.

Tom was nowhere to be seen, leaving Chetri and his men to hold their nerve and make their own decisions. Biding their time, Chetri and his men watched as some of the enemy fired and charged at full speed before coming to a literal dead stop. Others managed to reach defenders trenches before bayonets skewered them. Still others were shot in mid-air, falling into the trenches with their hearts and guns still pumping. Bullets and cries engulfed the air. It was an entangling broth of carnage boiling in front of them. As the perimeter was being breached and the front trenches swarmed over by attackers, Chetri ordered his men to open fire. Now, with only metres between them, the Japanese were plump targets. The living jumped over the dead and the fallen, to fall ahead of those already dead or fluttering on the ground with the last breath of life struggling to stay within. Of the countless attackers, the numbers still standing slowly dwindled, and yet the Japanese commanders kept sending their men, to be shot down or blown to bits by grenades or mortars.

As wave after wave kept surging, Chetri and his men kept

firing, kept killing or maiming, taking it in turns to stop and reload their machines. For Chetri's men, while one fired, the other reloaded. Each clip held five bullets, so they loaded a maximum of ten bullets in the rifle magazine and one more in the chamber. Eleven bullets a round didn't seem like enough to stem the relentless surge of hundreds. Chetri's and his men's shoulders ached from the constant kick of their guns. Their wrists strained from the action of bolting their rifles. All eyes burned from the acrid air and constant need to focus. Their throats and noses were clogged with pewter fumes of brass, lead and gunpowder. Their ears were deafened. Yet they kept firing. Until Chetri's Sten gun jammed at the same time that three more guns under Chetri's command fell silent. The unforgiving opportunistic tide of attackers flooded in. Chetri and his men readied their bayonets and fell back in the trench, poking madly at whoever jumped in.

There was a momentary laps in their defence and Bikash was gone. Unlike Bahadur's death, to mourn Bikash, a flicker of an eyelid, the skip of a heartbeat, was all Chatri and his remaining three men could offer. The four shot and skewered. Between the moving Japanese wall, Chetri spotted one of his novice soldiers from the other trench running towards them. He seemed a personification of the garrison – bloodied, battered and badly bruised. He ran wide-eyed and open mouthed towards them. But the tsunami was too close behind. Chetri saw a bayonet rip through his ribcage and retract. He fell to the ground as his slayer charged forward trampling him under. Chetri sent a bullet. The slayer became the slain and dropped inches ahead of the novice.

From Tom's bunker he couldn't be sure what had happened. But there was no time to ponder or grieve. It was the inevitable moment Raan had been dreading. To survive he had to kill. His heart skipped a beat the moment Tom gave the order to fire. He realized in that startled moment that he had squeezed the trigger and one of the charging Japanese soldier lay dead. He didn't feel guilty for taking a life. His hand automatically cocked the rifle again and pressed the trigger and another Japanese dropped dead. As long as he didn't aim too high or too low there were enough Japanese to find his bullets.

While Tom and Raan were trying to flatten the incoming tide, Mongseng stayed with them and pierced and chopped those that managed to make it through the volley of shots. The perfect ally, Mongseng filled in where guns didn't finish the job. Mongseng's right hand held firm to his *dao*, while the flat edge of the spear grasped in his left hand pierced the throat of an attacker, slicing off his head, only to swing the spear's cone-edge and jab another foe through the heart. Mongseng's *dao* and spear moved as swiftly as bullets, as he made his way around the bunker, picking out any approaching enemy while keeping clear of crossfire. The shrill cries of his war dance kept Mongseng's bunkmates company, encouraging them and keeping them focused.

Mongseng continued even when Tom and Raan's guns started malfunctioning, over-heated by the relentless bullets. As fast as they came, he kept stacking a wall of bodies in front of the bunker. A puddle of blood collected on the floor, as well as severed torsos, limbs and heads. The quenched earth, which had drunk enough already from the early monsoon, refused to swallow what it didn't ask for. Even Raan, the former vegetarian, was smeared in blood and guts, and in the frenzy of battle didn't care whether he stood on water, blood or human parts. Only a long while after his bunkmates' guns had gone silent did Mongseng slow down. Even he was no inexhaustible killing machine. His arms began to ache, and just when it seemed that he could wield his *dao* no more, a barrage of shots from overhead began to pluck away at the overwhelming opponents. Twenty yards above them, three Bren guns had come to their rescue. As the automated killing machines demonstrated their effect, all the remaining soldiers needed to do was to keep their heads low and watch the Japanese drop. At the same time, heavy British artillery guns positioned at Jotsoma, a kilometre down the road, started pounding the Naga village. Mortars from Garrison Hill joined in and started pounding the area near the Deputy Commissioner's Bungalow, which was overrun by Japanese. The attackers had to scatter. The Japanese commanders realizing the futility of a daytime attack had to call off their offence.

In Chetri's trench, only he and one other survived. As the gunfire ceased, both living and dead lay entangled in the trenches. The living were immobilized by both grief and the inert bodies of the enemy that had flung themselves inside their bunkers. Pegged where he lay, Chetri began to shiver as the warm blood around him and in him, slowly turned cold. His adrenalin burned up, Chetri was taken over by futility, fear and disgust. Shutting his eyes and letting his mind drift off, Chetri tried to compose himself. He reminded himself why he was where he was. Long ago, to rid himself of a similarly helpless feeling, Chetri had enlisted into the army. But now the weight of the dead felt worse than those ropes that robbers once used to bind Chetri down. The battle felt worse than those robbers that had taken away his life with his parents in Bahadurpur. Yet, after robbing and humiliation, the determination which had grown strong roots by now helped battle against the helplessness he felt. Anger, an emotion he seldom experienced, added to give him such strength that he at last freed his hands and flung off the limp ragdoll bodies trapping him.

In death, friends and foe, British, Japanese, Nepalese, Indian, now mingled together, lying strewn around like pieces of driftwood on a riverbank after a furious deluge.

Chetri and his single surviving man staggered to Tom's bunker. The act of freeing himself and his man from the dead had drained the last of his energy. He peered in to find the three in Tom's bunker alive but worse for wear, and keen to be moving out. At the sight of each other, all five men, bloodied and torn from battle showed their relief, but no words or questions were spoken. Right now, for the moment, all the five men wanted to do was to distance themselves from the dead. Looking for an empty bunker further up the hill, the five men set out with Mongseng at the lead. While each of them carried only the basic necessities – guns, ammunition, *dao,* spear, grenades, Raan found the strength to lug along his kitchen equipment.

Destiny was done testing them for the day. They soon found two unoccupied trenches and lay their beaten bodies and shattered minds down on the bare earth to rest.

FIFTEEN

NO MATTER HOW BAD AN EVENT, A LITTLE REST HAS THE TENDENCY to wipe the slate clean. During sleep the soul is in charge, positive and pro-life by nature. Until the waking consciousness stirs, and the mind takes over.

As dawn scattered its light, Mongseng peered out of the trench through an opening under the tin roof. The reserves around Garrison Hill were in position around the perimeter – a motley crew of soldiers from different battalions. It was like filling the holes of a leaking bucket with whatever material could be found – clay, putty, metal or rubber. Only time would tell if each material holds up or gives way for the Japanese to seep in.

Tom stirred awake. Raan followed soon after. Long awake and seeking amusement, Mongseng watched as Raan shifted into autopilot, rolling up the small piece of tarp he had slept on, pushing it in one smooth motion into a corner. Then he lit the kerosene stove onto which he placed the single pan of the makeshift kitchen and poured in some water from a tarp sack. After placing a piece of metal on top, Raan poured more water into a nearby mug and, taking in a 360-degree view like an owl scanning its hunting ground, cautiously moved out of the bunker. But in this instance Raan was no hunter, feeling more like easy prey. Taking it one step at a time, he made sure he trod out auspiciously, putting his right foot first.

Behind a nearby tree stump Raan performed his morning ablutions in an empty milk powder can, put the lid back on and gently flicked the can across enemy lines and walked away. The can landed on its side and rolled downhill. At the bottom was a bunker occupied by three Japanese soldiers. The can landed inside the bunker on a stone, flicking open the lid and splashing its content on the unsuspecting enemy. The three occupants bailed out of the bunker and ran across, towards the road. Unfortunately for the escaping Japanese soldiers, a Bren gun had been positioned in the Club House the previous evening and they fell straight in line of the gun. It mowed down the three fleeing soldiers. Unknown to Raan, the can turned out to be his own lethal brand of grenade. The sound of gunfire made Raan crawl back to the bunker. Now fully awake, he snapped out of auto mode and made everyone some tea.

"Good morning, Mon Ji, tea?" For the first time that morning Raan acknowledged Mongseng, who was observing him all along.

Raan had started calling Mongseng by a shortened version of his name out of friendship, but there was also another reason. Raan preferred the first half of Mongseng's name to the latter half. He reckoned if he called him 'Seng', it would sound very close to the Bengali surname, Sen. But because Subhas Chandra Bose, a Bengali, and commander of the Indian National Army was fighting alongside their enemies, Raan didn't feel any camaraderie towards the Bengali community. Helping the Japanese as guides in Kohima, the INA believed in achieving Indian independence from the British through armed struggle. Raan knew that the INA was opposed to the political stance of the Indian National Congress led by Mahatma Gandhi, the gentle soul who was trying to free India from colonial rule through non-violent means.

"*Ho.*" Mongseng replied in Nagamese instead of '*Haan*' in Hindi, feeling his share of hostility towards Raan for using the same mug to pour tea out of, in which he carried water for his morning ablutions.

"While you are at it, do make me a cup too." Tom called out from his corner, preoccupied with thoughts returning from the previous day.

As was his habit, Tom finished his tea and busied himself with a map. Raan, keeping his mind busy, focused on the morning preparation of breakfast. Mongseng, having no duties to attend to immediately, became busy observing the city of insects living in the bunker's mud walls. Different creatures went about their business, unbothered by each other, or the presence of three men, each busy with its own activity. For a moment Mongseng envied them roaming around carefree, despite the battle going on over ground. He remembered his carefree life as a child. How insects and animals were a part of his games. He and Sangkok used to catch dragonflies, tie a string around their middle and hold on the other end and make them fly. Right now he felt trapped, tied down like those dragonflies.

Mongseng's thoughts moved to his lovely wife Meailing. What would she think of his new habits – wearing deerskin, speaking English? He knew she would understand. She was one person to whom he could open his heart and she would read every beat of it clearly. He had stayed away from her too long. He never knew he could miss her as madly as he did.

After they had married, the only time they spent apart was when he went on hunting and battle expeditions. But those separations were for a day or two at the most.

Moreover, Mongseng was starting to grow tired of Tom. He had no problem with Raan, but Tom was like two people in one. Never was the person in front of Mongseng who he actually was. In any given situation, Mongseng observed that Tom reacted in ways that appeared totally different from how he really felt. Mongseng's mind and emotions were as clear as a mountain spring, but he found Tom very opaque. Whenever Tom interacted with him he always had on a different face. He knew very well that Tom could never accept Mongseng for himself. He expected Mongseng to come into his world, to work towards his needs, without any reciprocatory steps.

Tom reminded Mongseng of the other person that he knew with the same skin tone. The padre also didn't accept him and his fellow villagers for who they truly were. Instead, these men wanted them to conform to new ways. The white men brought along their homes from a distant land to Mongseng's land, yet expected that Mongseng and his villagers would confirm to the rules of those distant foreign lands. Mongseng wondered if Tom and the padre would ever really be happy surrounded by people who were different from them. Even if he learnt new ways, spoke a new language, ate their food in their ways, he would still never look like them. He knew ultimately their feeling of superiority stemmed from them being a few shades lighter in colour. Would they then want to peel away a layer of skin from him? After all, the difference was only skin deep. He had seen the sliced sections of the necks of many of his hunted heads. Within, all looked the same.

Bursts of rifle fire nearby shook Mongseng back to the present. Raan was busy giving finishing touches to breakfast. It was a can of beans, watered down, plus some edible leaves Mongseng had foraged to add bulk to the dish to be shared by three men. The first plate with a little extra helping he offered to Tom. Raan knew that if Tom gave even a slight positive nod, the breakfast was cooked well. Tom took in a scoop and frowned. At that moment the blast of a distant mortar shell shook Raan. As well as *his Sahib's* disapproval, he didn't need that extra shock. At that moment, while everyone else in the garrison was missing peace, Raan was missing the Kohima farmer's market. And his spice rack.

After breakfast Raan attended to his and Tom's utensils. By now Mongseng knew that Raan preferred him to take care of washing his own cups and plates. He was happy to oblige, after all that was the least he could do to thank Raan for cooking him such exotic dishes. Back home, dish cleaning wasn't an activity he or Meailing took part in. They ate off banana or teak leaf plates and these disposables were cleared along with any remaining food morsels by the pigs that lived in the sty on the ground floor of their bamboo stilt hut. Back home their earthen cooking pots and bamboo cups were rubbed with ash from the hearth and rinsed clean at the nearby stream. These dishes too were disposable. If the bamboo cups became beyond the cleansing power of ash, they became fuel for the fire and Mongseng chopped some mature bamboo to forge out new cups. Stained or broken pots too, returned to earth, the same place from where new vessels emerged, shaped by the village potter's skilful hands over his wooden wheel. Nothing was wasted; nothing was taken forever from Mother Nature. What Nature gave, eventually went back to her.

After breakfast Tom returned to his map. He looked through the shrinking defence perimeter of the Kohima Garrison. With a red-inked fountain pen he had marked the original area of Kohima that was occupied by the defenders of the Garrison. Now portions of the red area were marked over by black lines to denote the defence positions that were run over by the Japanese. The map now looked like a misshapen red *chapati* with burnt edges rolled and cooked by a rookie. At the length of an arm from the misshapen *chapati* lay Dimapur. Tom wondered if he would be able to traverse that distance ever again and walk away alive from the battlefield.

Chetri appeared in the bunker. "Good morning, *Sahab*." He greeted Tom, curt and a little uncomfortable.

"Morning, morning, Chetri. Anything to report?" Tom put his captain's hat on.

"I hear this morning they are closing in from Jail Hill." Chetri replied. A piece of news he had picked up from the reliable Gorkha grape vine.

"Hmm.... How are your men? How is morale?" asked Tom, as usual, out of habit.

"*Hajur,* sir, I have only one man left. He is happy to be alive." Chetri corrected him, no hint of apology or contempt in his voice.

"Oh, oh, oh, yes, yes, of course..." Tom lost his composure for a moment, "Go have a cup of tea." Tom gestured towards Raan.

"Thank you, *Sahab*." Chetri responded with a salute and turned towards Raan, only too happy to wind up his brief report. He actually hadn't come to report. Chetri had felt lost in his bunker, trying to bring up conversation with his only remaining man, Bheema. Neither wanted to talk about what they went through in the battlefield. Talking about their lives back in their respective villages in Nepal seemed futile. Both were at a loss for words.

A couple of hundred yards away, in the advance dressing station, Sandra was winding up. It had become too risky for the stretcher-bearers to collect and bring in the wounded during the day. The omnipresent Japanese snipers were ever-ready to take the life of anyone caught out in the open. Sandra hadn't slept a wink through the night, attending to the wounded of the previous day. When the sun was still low, Sandra moved out of the ADS and crawled towards her bunker. She was still close enough to hear the moans of the wounded, yet far enough to shut out their pain for a while. Again her nurse's uniform was red and crisp with dry blood. She removed the dress and put it in a corner where it stood like a headless, limbless mannequin. With what little water she had Sandra tried to remove the dirt, blood and grime of war from her own arms and face. Lying on her bed, images of the wounded, their agony-ridden faces, came to haunt her. The previous day's attack had redoubled the injured. She put her hand on Mongseng's gift, the beaded necklace, but even it couldn't comfort her – too small a talisman to offer warmth against this monstrous winter of human hatred.

She had taken up nursing to heal the wounded. Now she felt all she was managing to do was hurt herself. That annoyed her. She swung out of bed and decided to make a cup of tea to distract her mind from the negative thoughts. But it was hard to find a distraction amidst the gloom. She stared at the piece of ginger she had put in to the bubbling water and it made her feel as if she was that floating piece amidst the turmoil.

Back amongst the men, Bheema, alone in his trench became jittery from the enemy mortar blasts. By now Japanese mortar attacks had become routine during daylight hours, when they were too exposed to launch infantry raids. Looking for his *Subader*, Bheema entered Tom's bunker. Thankfully the delivery runners from DIS had managed a provisions run between a lull in the shelling. Chetri and Bheema stayed for lunch. Food was still an activity that punctuated the day, and separated their minds from battle. Chetri and Bheema had the same ration as was supplied in Tom's bunker, but something in Raan's hands made all the difference. Mongseng found delight in observing Raan prepare his meals, and on that day, Chetri and Bheema sat back and watched too. The audience offered Raan a little further inspiration.

In Tom's bunker they ate well, compared to the front trenchers who could concentrate on nothing but survival. They didn't have the luxury to eat cooked food, but had to sustain themselves on bully beef and biscuits. While one or more soldiers watched out for Japanese intruders or snipers, others gobbled straight from the cans, lest it became their last supper.

By 6 pm it was dusk, the light in the sky fast disappearing from golden to grey, towards black. As anxiously anticipated, the cacophony of bombs and bullets, accompanied by the moans of wounded friend and foe began. It was a night repeated, with the intensity cranked up a notch. With the perimeters of the garrison shrinking, there wasn't much difference between front line and inner zones. Tom and his remaining men stood their ground, albeit on feeble feet. Mongseng disappeared for a while and returned with a bloodied *dao*. Tom knew what it meant and asked with a gesture of his hand, how many? Mongseng raised three fingers. From the frontline's dogged defence, Chetri and Bheema helped a wounded soldier. Propped up between their shoulders, they carried him to the ADS. There they spotted Sandra who could hardly acknowledge them, before disappearing into a sea of the severely wounded. Dutifully, they returned to their position to withstand the night.

Meanwhile, near the rubble of the Commissioner's Bungalow and Tennis Court the combat was intensifying. At some stage of the evening, the A Company of West Kent, left with less than half their men, was relieved by the B Company, and moved behind to Kuki Piquet. All around, the Japanese swarmed the area. A Scottish private, small in stature but giant in spirit, tried to hold off the surge. Part of a Bren gun unit, he relentlessly kept shooting while the others refilled the Bren's spent magazines. A spare barrel was kept at the ready to replace the current one when it became smouldering hot. But like moths to a flame, the Japs kept coming. With no care for his life, the Scotsman stood up to get a good field of fire. While other members of his unit dropped dead around him he shouted for more ammunition, single-handedly keeping the enemy at bay.

Returning with ammunition, the private's mate found him slumped over his weapon, and looked up as a Japanese bayonet flashed at him. But the West Kenter's time wasn't up. As the bayonet caught his belt's webbing the soldier pulled the Bren from under his dead mate's body and emptied the magazine into his attacker. And reloading the Bren, took the place of the dead Scottish private.

As the night went on, so did the Japanese surge. Only in the last hour of darkness did the Japanese attack ease, just as the West Kent Bren gunner was running low on ammunition. Exhausted, his eyes reluctantly closed, and he came around maybe minutes or maybe an hour later. Assuming he was dead, a Japanese officer had entered the trench. Suddenly wide-awake, but unable to reach for his gun, he charged at the Japanese officer making a move for his sword. But before he had it from the scabbard, the adrenaline-charged soldier kicked the Jap's hand and lunged at his neck, locking it with his right arm and breaking it. As the body slumped to the ground, he removed the officer's sword and drove it into him, just to make sure.

Peering out of the trench the Scotsman saw the Japanese had saturated the area, now occupying trenches of dead garrison defenders. The area east of the Tennis Court and under the Commissioner's Bungalow now belonged to the Japanese infantry. Behind the scene, garrison defenders still held the high ground around the Clubhouse. Picking up the Bren and last bandolier of ammunition, the soldier jumped from the trench and ran for his life uphill towards his comrades, making it in record time. Miraculously, he had lived through the night. A night ricocheting with a question mark – who will be so lucky to see another morning?

SIXTEEN

IT WAS THE 12TH OF APRIL, 1944. THE GARRISON HAD BEEN holding on to hope of relief for a week. But with dawn came the Japanese, attacking two platoons of Rajputs on FSD hill. Luckily Rajput eyes and guns spotted them in time, welcoming the Japs with a hailstorm of lead. With no cover, the enemy withdrew to take shelter beyond the thirty or so bodies newly strewn at the bottom of the hill.

Over the last week, the garrison perimeter had shrunk to an area no larger than four football fields. During the day routine Japanese shelling continued, every explosive finding a target, killing or injuring the rapidly dwindling defenders. At the ADS Sandra had no time to rest. Yet, with medical supplies running low, too often now the only help Doctor Young and his team could offer the injured were words.

As predictable as night following day, as darkness fell the Japanese let fire its barrage of artillery and mortars followed by a wild infantry charge. North of the Tennis Court a few defender's trenches were overrun. One trench held a box of grenades that the retreating West Kent Company couldn't lug back up hill. Having seen their explosive effects, the Japanese infantrymen, who weren't used to grenades with pins, lobbed the whole box towards the withdrawing company, with the safety pins intact. Returning the favour, the retreating soldiers sent back the grenades with the safety pins removed. Within an hour of losing their trenches, the West Kent Company reclaimed their position.

The next day repeated itself. The Japanese 31st Division kept pushing; the motley crew of garrison defenders dug in their heels and refused to budge. Heavy losses befell both sides.

On the morning of the 15th of April, with the routine early morning Japanese barrage and incursion attempt over, Mongseng noticed a gigantic eggshell dangling from the stump of a burnt tree near the ruins of the Commissioner's Bungalow. By now Mongseng knew what aeroplanes were. But he wasn't quite convinced that parachutes weren't the soft-shelled eggs of those manmade birds. To him the airdrops carried out at night looked like metal birds laying eggs mid-flight.

In the tree behind the misshapen eggshell Mongseng observed some movement, as if a giant chick was trying to hatch, and decided to investigate. On the other side of the dangling balloon, three Japanese soldiers were desperately trying to dislodge the parachute from the stump. Through a torn slit one of them noticed Mongseng approaching. By now his skills were well known in the Japanese camp. Behind the parachute the three soldiers froze. With his curiosity piqued, Mongseng's interest got the better of him. Except for his eyes focused on the huge dangling eggshell, he didn't have his other senses tuned in. Examining the fabric the curious warrior gave it a tug and the caught fragment came loose. The parachute fell over him.

Springing to action, the three frozen Japs pounced on the enveloped warrior, pinning him down, wrapping him tightly in the thin cloth. Once contained, they dragged Mongseng to their commander's post in a partially destroyed hut in the Naga Village. Just finishing breakfast with a glass of sake, the commander was annoyed that little moment of quiet was interrupted. His mood, however, turned quickly when his soldiers unwrapped the package. Disoriented and breathless, two soldiers held Mongseng by his shoulders and made him stand up, while another soldier cut a length of string from the parachute and tied Mongseng's hands. But the soldier made the same mistake as Tom's Gorkhas who captured him at Aradura Spur. The knot was too simple; a mistake that would cost the enemy dearly.

Returning via the hidden stream where he had joined Raan to fetch water. Mongseng hid the four heads, and returned to Tom's trench with a bloodied *dao* in his scabbard and a bottle of sake. He offered the bottle to Tom who poured some into his canteen and passed it on to Raan. Knowing Mongseng won't have any, Raan poured a generous tot into a pan and left the rest for Chetri and Bheema. Not much of a drinker, Raan immediately felt tipsy. Losing the inhibition that he usually felt under in his *Sahib's* presence, Raan broke into a Hindi song from the hit movie *Zindagi*. Tom let him be, while Mongseng tried to keep rhythm tapping his fingers on the *dao*'s scabbard.

Hearing Raan, Chetri joined in from the adjacent bunker. In welcome camaraderie, the nearby West Kent soldiers broke into 'Onward Christian Soldiers'. Catching on, it seemed the whole garrison lit up and melodies started to flow until orders came in to quieten down. That evening the Japanese shelling was unusually heavy.

The next morning Tom peered out to assess the night's ferocity and was greeted by the sight of blood and rotting bodies, rank in the damp air, heavy with smoke from the smouldering fires of mutilated tree trunks and exploded shells. Nearby he sensed the swarms of maggots picking over the decaying corpses. All the while, pregnant flies injected their eggs into the recent dead so they would hatch and join the existing army of maggots when the flesh rots.

These sights, smells and sounds took over Tom's mornings. It became a day out of many such foregoing days when Tom tried to look at the morning with what little enthusiasm he could gather and moments later felt tired. Like on so many previous occasions, it was another tired morning that couldn't tell how different it was from an exhausted, spent evening.

Now fully awake from the little nap he could scrape way from the night, Tom was confused. Had it been ten days or was it a month since the Japanese had encircled them? Lines of communication between the garrison posts still moved in some directions, but Tom had shut himself off as much as he could from the larger war and was focused on dogged survival. He had known that he would lose men. All leaders did. What was most important, after all, was the leader's protection. Leaders were a central point, a focal point for the men. The situation of battle was so much worse for every man involved. The notion of war had taken on a new meaning.

Just then Mongseng greeted someone, "Oye!"

From the joy that the word without meaning emitted, Tom knew it must be someone well acquainted, probably Chetri.

"Tom *Sahab,* there might be troops coming through from Dimapur. The siege might end any day now." He was brisk, saluted Tom, passed on the morsel of hope and returned to his post. Having just one man with him, Chetri couldn't leave his post for long.

As the rising sun brought better visibility to the day, the

enemy shelled the Garrison, and the Second British Division from Jotsoma responded by shelling Japanese positions. It was a morning like many others – hopeless.

Tom saw Raan napping. He would have liked a cup of tea. But seeing Raan sleeping blissfully, he didn't want to wake him. As his Captain and employer, the protection Tom couldn't offer to his vulnerable cook was being offered by sleep.

Looking out of the bunker, the first sight that caught Tom's eyes was the leg of a buried corpse, stiff and slowly rising out of its shallow grave. Rigor mortis had set in and it's stiffened appendage poked out of the soil as if the dead soldier was marching on back to the battlefield. With half the garrison defenders dead, any help on the battlefield would be welcome, Tom thought – the dead giving hope to the living.

The dead soldiers in the garrison took with them more than double the number of Japanese, but that didn't seem to lessen the teeming Japanese numbers across the Imphal road.

Doing the calculation in his head, more subtraction than addition or multiplication, Tom turned around and spotted Mongseng washing his face with half a cup of water. He looked fresh; Tom wondered if Mongseng had been stealing naps while on guard duty. A tired mind in Tom tried to be equal with Mongseng by declaring that he was a cheat. What Tom wasn't privy to was that Mongseng who had grown up in the midst of battles, knew more than anyone else how to live a normal life in the midst of true, continual life threat. Even under these circumstances, while sticking with his men, he was accustomed to extract the maximum replenishment out of relatively little sleep. Even for days on end. To add to that, most in the garrison now sported a beard or stubble, Mongseng almost looked clean-shaven. Courtesy of his mongoloid genes he hardly had any facial hair. Compared to the unruly growth of others, his face looked fresh. Mongseng wore no clothes to pick up dirt or tear and become a rag on him. The loincloth made of deerskin that he had started wearing around his groin somehow made his appearance more handsome. Less confronting. A little less wild, if you managed to ignore the tattoos. Dirt mixed with his tattoos now, only to form new shades of the manly form that was his body.

Tom suddenly felt conscious of his raggedness. Being Mongseng's officer he should have looked superior in character and clothes. He could try to micro-manage his outer character, but he couldn't hide his shabby clothes. His boots that once shone like a mirror were now caged under layers of muck. For over a week he hadn't changed his clothes. They had taken on the look of Rip Van Winkle after he woke from twenty years of sleep. His khaki shirt's left pocket ripped and only a couple of threads held it from totally severing its ties from the shirt. His once khaki pants were of no particular colour. Three remaining belt loops on his trouser helped the belt to stay in place, holding up the pants to his reducing waistline. Around the knees, dry, sticky mud held his pant legs together more than threads. Then, with no more time or silence to contemplate his attire, the volley of fires began. They had shifted three posts, but always the war came. It was there. They were in it. Would relief get here, or would they all die today? Should he get Sandra?

Raan jumped up from the corner where he was napping, took hold of his gun and the watch began. The Japanese attacked the frontline. Mongseng concentrated on a frontline trench that looked vulnerable. There were only two soldiers in the trench and one of them was sick. The sick soldier couldn't stand on his two feet. His mate manned both their rifles. The sick soldier was loading them for him standing with the support of the front wall. They were successfully thwarting the Japanese attackers coming at them. Looking ahead, Mongseng could see a degree of fierceness lacking in the Japanese attack. He detected fear in their eyes. A few were turning back realising the futility of their attack, only to be sent back by their commanders whose tired brains and starved guts lacked any better ideas.

Once the sun shone down fiercely, revealing their stupidity, the attacks ceased. The morning was then followed by a monotonous afternoon.

Going by the Japanese clockwork offence of previous days, the garrison knew there would be no more attacks for a while. The Japanese kept their attack to twice daily – once in the morning at first light, before the sun showed up, and then again in the evening. As the sun went down and darkness descended, the immanent threat materialized. Tom, Raan and Mongseng waited it out. That night the Japanese assault didn't last long. It seemed even the Japanese were playing a waiting game. Their attack was just a feeble attempt; nothing was achieved except losing some more men to the determined shrinking defence. That day, the shrunk perimeter of the Garrison Defence was not crushed further.

For the first time since the siege began, Mongseng opted to take a nap before the other two. Neither Raan nor Tom could object, but Raan decided Tom should sleep too. He couldn't see his *Sahib* standing as equal with him.

"You rest *Sahib.* No point both of us losing sleep. Looks like the Nippons will not disturb us any more tonight."

Exhausted, there was only one conclusion, to let Raan stand guard, "Okay, Raan. Thanks, old chap. But of course, if you need to, wake me up, and umm, also wake him…" Tom drifted off, pointing towards Mongseng.

For Raan, every sound was the enemy. Every shadow became a sneaking Japanese. Fear kept him company. Then shivering took over. Fear and cold made sure Raan stayed awake and alert. A respite in the shelling and shooting in days gave the other two tired bodies peace that made them turn their naps into long slumber. Some time before dawn, Mongseng woke up. Everything was silent, except for a lone crow. It sounded desperately sad, and Mongseng realized what his ears were missing. He had to get away from this racket of metal and gunpowder. These were the sounds of the hatred of men. Mongseng listened to the crow and felt the tide of change approaching.

To play spoilsport on Mongseng's hope, the shelling began. By now Mongseng had calculated that the shells came in lots of sevens. The first one landed amongst the rubble of the District Commissioner's Bungalow. Mongseng calculated, the rest of the six shells would gradually work up their way but not quite reach the Tennis Court. This batch was meant for the frontline defenders. He kept his head out and watched the bombardment. Only when the next instalment of seven start falling, he would need to be careful.

The crow was long gone. The last of the first instalment of mortar shells shook Tom and Raan awake. Tom sombrely put on his uniform over his nightclothes. If a shell did make them its target this day, he wasn't going to be caught dead in his pyjamas. After the end of the first instalment, there was a momentary truce with peace, a deafening silence took over and the ground under their feet stopped trembling. A deceiving hope rose in Raan that maybe the enemy would run out of shells for another barrage and they would be spared. Without knowing, there was truth in his hope. Since the Japanese 31 Division didn't have a supply line from Burma, they were rapidly running short of supplies in ammunition for their big artillery guns and mortars. They had to ration their shelling to a strict quota.

Shattering hope, the first of the second instalment of shells came down a few yards from them with an ear-splitting boom. Mongseng signalled and all three fell into their bunker as deep as they could, their bodies crumpled against the damp mud floor. Mongseng felt an acute sting on his back. He rolled over to check out the source of the sting and figured that he had blocked the entrance to the nest of a spider wasp and she had given him a tap with her sting to move out of the way. Mongseng rubbed his pimple of a wound and smiled. He watched her fly away. He wondered how many live spiders would she find around the battleground.

To Tom and Raan's relief the last of the shells landed safely without paralysing their destinies. Then as if in response, a barrage of artillery from the 2nd British Division from Dimapur road landed on the enemy. The friendly fire seemed closing in. Just as the dust began to settle, Mongseng spotted movement at the frontline. Through a haze of smoke he could see human figures approaching up hill. The ones in front didn't seem to be pointing guns in their direction. While the ones behind looked to be pointing guns towards the enemy. All three readied their weapons. As an extra measure, rifle in one hand, Raan picked up a grenade in his other. He would pull the pin with his teeth and roll the grenade down the slope and start firing as soon as Tom gave the orders. Raan tried to hold his nerve. As the figures came closer, a drop of sweat ran down Raan's cheek. Tom's palms felt sticky. Mongseng shuffled his weapons, waiting for the Japanese to close in for combat. Then Tom shouted, "Fire!"

But, instantaneously, Mongseng shouted, "Noooo!"

Raan's lobbing arm stopped mid-air, clutching the grenade's leaver tightly. He looked at Mongseng, surprised. Deflecting Tom's angry stare, Mongseng pointed towards the figures, "Friend." He said, firmly jabbing a tattooed finger.

The first soldier who emerged, Tom spotted that he did have a beard unusually thick and long for any Japanese to possess and instead of a helmet the soldier had a turban on his head. And when the whole contingent of them came clear of the smoke, he saw the majority of them wore a beard. Most of them sporting a beard took away the odds of genetics making an exception amongst the supposed Japanese soldiers. From their beards Tom's gaze went to their crisp, spotless uniforms. He realized those soldiers didn't belong to either side. Because amongst the seizing army or the besieged, all they were left with on their bodies in the name of uniforms were pieces of rags. On closer inspection Tom figured they were, in fact, wearing Indo-British uniforms.

It was the 18th of April 1944; sixteen days after the first guns were fired. Finally, some hope trickled through the Japanese siege. The spotless soldiers were a company of the 1st Punjab Regiment, who managed to break through the Japanese barricade. Flooded in relief, for Raan it turned into a horror of sorts. He had pulled the pin of the grenade early, but had thrown it and still had the grenade in his grip. As a Sikh officer approached he looked around frantically.

"What do you think you are doing?" Tom hissed, slightly embarrassed.

"Sahib, can't find the safety pin." Raan whispered out of the Punjab Officer's earshot.

"What safety pin?"

"Grenade pin." Raan answered sincerely.

The Sikh officer peered into the trench to see an Indian and British soldier scampering on the floor, and a semi-naked savage in the corner, grinning at him. It was clear they had been touched by war, a bunch of crazies. Just then a haggard Chetri approached with a fresh grin on his face. The Sikh officer returned Chetri's salute. Tom gestured to Chetri to join Raan's search and gave the Sikh officer a firm salute. He was finally managing to get his salute perfect.

Interrupting Raan, Chetri asked, "What are we look for?" As Raan explained, Chetri shook his head sending a smirk in Mongseng's direction, and bent over to search.

Following on from his salute, Tom extended his hand for a firm handshake, "So glad to see you chaps! Don't know how much longer we could have held on."

"Yes, Captain. Our company managed to break through. But the road is not yet clear of the Nippons. The Second British Division's artillery is currently pounding them. It should be clear soon."

Tom gave out a long sigh and nodded. The Sikh officer signalled his men to march forward. Giving Tom a sympathetic salute, he joined his men. After waiting for rescue for so many days, now when it seemed a real possibility, Tom couldn't bring himself to believe it. Being on shaky ground for so long, he couldn't hold on to any firm hope.

With the safety pin firmly locked back on the grenade Raan busied himself with preparations for breakfast. Mongseng's attention was diverted to the threat across the fragile, dog-eared perimeter. Allowing himself no rest, he kept watch.

After breakfast, Tom felt he should go to garrison headquarters to know for sure if there was confirmed news of relief. Since he moved his men near the tennis court, whatever information came in about the developments in the battle was through Chetri's Gorkha grapevine. The urge to go and access news from the horse's mouth himself won over the urge to keep his whereabouts secret from the garrison commander.

Tom put on his tin helmet and ventured out of the bunker and immediately heard gunshots. He knew those rounds were routine, not directed at any particular target, just harassing fire. Once the smoke from bombings disappeared and the dust settled the Japanese always fired a few rounds to keep the garrison defenders in place. As long as Tom kept mostly to the ground he would be safe.

With Tom away, and with the arrival of the Sikh regiment, the threat of war seemed easing. Raan was willing to relax. He agreed to play a board game Mongseng had taught him a few days earlier and keep his mind off the battlefield. A while into the game, they got into an argument, as instead of cowrie shells with which the game was supposed to be played, they were playing with pebbles, which made keeping score confusing. As their argument heated up, the game's equipment went flying out of the bunker.

Tom was just returning and, a few metres from the bunker, he felt a cracking noise on his helmet. He froze, thinking a sniper finally found him. What a rotten luck, he had to be shot down now when rescue was so close, so imminent. He lay flat on the ground waiting for the pain to set in. Moments crawled by like a snail, yet nothing happened. He felt his head around with his hand under the helmet, no blood. He removed his helmet and checked it, no hole. Suddenly life returned to him like a body of water gushing through a broken embankment. He rushed into his bunker and hugged and greeted Raan and Mongseng like long lost friends.

"Oh…there is wonderful news my men! We have to hold on for a while longer before we are free! The 1st Punjab Company is too small to relieve us all in the Garrison. It won't be long before we are back in control of the road to Dimapur. Not long my dears, not long before we get out of this hell!" Tom relayed the news with flourish.

Mongseng understood the gist of Tom's recitation and nodded cheerfully. He had never been worried about roadblocks. If he had wanted to leave, no Japanese blockade could have stopped him. But to Raan the piece of news was like a situation with their game of pebbles. It was not yet clear to him if the situation was looking up or down. Unknown to Raan or to Tom, a little pebble from their game that Raan had flung out had hit Tom's helmet and it changed Tom's outlook on the situation.

The Garrison defence perimeter was shrunk into a tight spot; so tight it was hard to tell where their defence stood and where the enemy lines began. It was a dance of death that even death would wish for an end.

Thus would go another day and night, to be followed by another anxious sunrise that would toil through a laborious day, a day that would happily relinquish its load of misery on to the night. After repeated days and nights, a repeat of life and death, and of setbacks and small victories; a repeat of gained grounds and lost positions; inches and feet gained by the Japanese 31st Division, their bellies empty and spirits lean; inches and feet lost and regained by the mixed bag of Indo-British soldiers, fighting with stubbornness and hope that they would soon be freed, either by reinforcements that would break through the Japanese grip, or by death – finally a conclusion was crawling towards them.

SEVENTEEN

THE NIGHT WENT ON LIKE ERRATIC SLEEP, TOSSING BETWEEN CALM and confusion. Now in reply to a shell that would land on the garrison, there were three shells landing across. It was a clear indication that the garrison's defences were receiving fortification from beyond those holding it under siege. There was no infantry attack from the Japanese that night. In small groups, the large Japanese Division lay scattered munching on rice they managed to grab from the enemy; their spirits, as fragmented as the non-sticky rice their palate had to adjust to.

Mongseng had been taking a nap upright, resting his head on his folded arm over the ledge. His arm hurt. He opened his eyes expecting to see the dull day under a dull yellow-grey sky. Instead, a flesh of pink – a long streak of soft pink, surprised him. He forgot the pain in his arm. Amidst the charred remains of a cherry tree, a young new branch carried happiness and joy in pink blossoms. Sticking up like a middle finger amidst the gloom to the warring parties and telling them that it will survive no matter what they threw at it. Mongseng knew instinctively what it portrayed – it was the harbinger of good news to come.

When he looked around, the rest of the surrounding was as bleak as the previous day. The surrounding made the cherry blossoms look like cheerful fools amidst the gloom – innocent and ignorant. Chetri waved at Mongseng from across the blossoms, from his bunker and quickly put his hand down. Mongseng responded with a quick wave. A sniper hiding behind the rubble of the District Commissioners bungalow reciprocated their gesture with a single bullet.

The bullet was for Mongseng. The sniper might have had better luck if he had targeted Chetri. When the sniper pressed the trigger releasing the hammer which struck the bullet's cartridge igniting the gunpowder inside the shell, a sound much subdued and created a fraction of a second before the sound created by the exiting bullet – that sound Mongseng picked up and ducked. That split second was all he needed to make the bullet useless. The bullet went and lodged behind Mongseng with a dull thud, harmlessly lost in a heap of earth. Mongseng moved a couple of feet away from where he was, towards the edge of his bunker and peeped out and caught Chetri's peeping eyes. Mongseng pointed where the sniper was and Chetri replied to the sniper's greeting in the same language, which however found its target.

Just as the sniper plummeted backwards with a hole in his head, Mongseng had another rush of adrenalin when he sensed a presence behind him. Then as quickly he found out that the presence was non-other, but Raan. Raan, who too was taking a nap, was woken by Chetri's gun. He came and stood behind Mongseng staring at the cherry blossoms across Mongseng's shoulder. Their eyes met. Mongseng's momentary tense face relaxed and Raan's serious wonderment softened into a questioning nod. A runner approached them as Tom was waking up. But before he could be ready to receive the news from the runner, the runner had already passed on the news to Raan and hurried off to the next bunker. Tom looked on at the reducing back of the runner with a frown.

"*Saaahhib*!" Raan turned to Tom and wailed, his face lighting up like a *Diwali* sparkle.

Tom responded with a stern, "What?" annoyed at Raan for shrieking out like a child.

"We are saved, *Sahib*! We are saved!" Raan jumped around like a child possessed.

Tom looked for hope in Raan's excitement, but hope that had been such a slippery object in the last few days, Tom needed to be sure, he probed Raan further, "What do you mean? Can you be more specific? And stop jumping around and behave like a soldier."

Raan never quite graduated from a cook into a soldier; nevertheless he obeyed his *Sahib*'s order and stood in attention and replied calmly, "*Sahib,* the One hundred Sixty One Brigade is breaking through the Japanese ball...kaid...block, as we speak..." But he couldn't contain his excitement for too long. As he uttered those words, his controlled, serious expression couldn't hold back his excitement and the captured emotions were let loose again, "*Sahib,* the siege is broken, *Sahib!* The siege is broken!"

Tom couldn't decide what he should believe. To gather himself he grabbed Raan's shoulder and stopped him from bouncing around, "Are you sure the messenger said that? Did he come from Garrison Hill?"

"*Aare*...yes *Sahib,* yes! He even showing me latter signed by Commander Richards *Sahib.*"

Tom wanted to cry, but that would be unbecoming of an officer in front of his batman. His heart began thumping vigorously; his arms and legs began tingling. Momentarily, anger creeped in that he couldn't be free to express himself. But his ragged uniform contained it all. He was a mixed bag of emotions fighting with one another. He hugged Raan and immediately let go. Raan not knowing how to react towards his *Sahib*'s sudden warmth, looked away. The war kept him away from everything; he had postponed his life to serve his *Sahib.* And that half-hearted hug from his *Sahib* was enough for Raan to think it was all worth it.

While they were busy dealing with their emotions from the news of relief, Mongseng's keen ears picked up a rumbling noise. It was different from any noise he had heard on the battleground before. It was not the noise made by metal birds, it wasn't sky fires dropping either. He followed in the direction of the noise, crouching, careful not to catch the attention of any snipers lurking in the shadows. The sound took him to the northern perimeter of the Garrison defence, just below the hill on the Dimapur road. He craned his neck and stood on toes to get a better view. Then in the curve on the road, in the distance, he saw a strange creature crawling into view. It looked so strange that he involuntarily leaped backwards. He crept behind a rock and took another look at the beast. It seemed like a huge black beetle with a long snout. Besides it, on either side, walked soldiers. He could make out that they were mostly the colour of Tom and a sprinkling of soldiers, the colour of Raan. From that sight he came to two conclusions. Firstly, that the beast did not eat humans as there were men walking besides it. And his second conclusion was that the beast must be friendly, fighting for Tom's side, as the soldiers marching along were the colour of friends.

From the ridge above he looked on curiously at the beetle crawling towards him. First there were those flying metal birds that dropped food for them. Now he wondered what these metal beetles will do for them. As if in reply the leading beetle sent out a fiery ball from its elephantine snout towards an enemy position in the ruins where once the Commissioner's Bungalow stood. With a deafening boom the fiery ball landed on a bunker occupied by the enemy. It sent bodies and fragments flying out. The enemy remaining in the nearby bunkers scattered away towards the Naga Village.

Mongseng returned to the bunker and announced, "Right, right!" to none of the two occupants in particular. "Raan right." He specified to Tom's querying face.

Before Tom could question him further, they saw soldiers from the 1st Royal Berkshire Regiment pouring into the Garrison's perimeters. Those soldiers coming through, breaking the Japanese siege of sixteen days, seemed as if they were merging into a confluence of rivers – a muddy, weather beaten river being met by the clean, fresh new waters of a mountain river. The new arrivals spread out, relieving soldiers from the bunkers in the Garrison's perimeter and working their way up. Tom heaved a sigh of relief. The one-way road to hell now suddenly was a two-way road and in no time they would be hopping on to the other lane to turn their backs on hell.

It didn't seem real. It felt as if the battlefield was playing a practical joke by showing a beautiful dream in the middle of the day. From the folds of a dog-eared novel, Tom took out his regimental badge and stripes and put them back on over the same tattered shirt he had been wearing for the past two weeks. It made the badge and stripes glitter. He scraped a fistful of soil from a wall of the bunker and rubbed it over his Assam Rifles emblem to match it with his well-worn shirt so that no one doubts that he had taken the badge off. He didn't rub any dirt over his captain's stripes and left them as is, for he was not supposed to be wearing them on the battlefield anyway. Though he was not out of the battlefield, he was eager to regain his lost self and one way he felt he could do it was by putting his stripes back on.

By the time a Platoon Commander came along with his men to relieve them, Tom became the officer he was. He washed the grime off his face as best as he could. His voice was back to being firm and business like. Gone was the tone of despair. He exchanged his knowledge about the enemy with the relieving platoon commander, "You have to watch out for their snipers. They have been keeping us at our toes… those Japs come after you in clockwork precision, once before sunrise, once after sunset… between that the bloody snipers keep us busy…yes, they are tenacious…" So on Tom went on and the new officer solemnly listened on.

And in the other corner of the bunker, amidst banter and casual exchange of family history, culture, to likes and dislikes of food, movies and popular songs on the radio, Raan passed on his and Mongseng's bits of information about the Japanese to the soldiers accompanying the officer of the Royal Berkshire Regiment. Raan and Mongseng's knowledge, though it was acquired within just about sixteen days, was equivalent to years of fighting. Because what Raan passed on was first hand information of two men who had no previous knowledge about the Japanese or had any preconceived biases against them. Their experience was raw, unstained. What they saw was what they passed on to the eager ears.

This battle in Kohima had very few parallels of such intensity, such close quarter fighting elsewhere. Nowhere else during the Second World War had such a small bunch of soldiers held off an entire enemy division.

When Raan moved into a bunker for the first time with Tom, he wasn't very impressed by it and was never keen on staying in one for too long. That urge was not just exacerbated by the war, the barebones living added to it. Yet when the time came to leave the bunker, leave all the horrors behind, he felt the bunker was a treasure chest of memories that he had to disown and walk away. He was parting with a portion of his life that made him more than just a cook. A couple of weeks packed in a lifetime of new experiences in them made him feel as if he had lived in the bunker for years. He touched the walls as if he was patting a favourite cow from his mother's stable. Tom instructed Raan on what he needed to be packed and left to meet Sandra. Raan took his time to pack his and Tom's rucksacks. Mongseng stepped out of the bunker with his personal belongings, which took him less than a minute to gather. Besides material objects, Raan was also gathering his memories to take along.

A part of everyone – Tom, Sandra, Chetri, Mongseng, would stay behind on the battlefield.

Tom left early because Sandra would be one of the first to be evacuated as the hospital staffs were leaving with the wounded in the first convoy of trucks that were bringing in fresh reinforcements of soldiers from Dimapur and were returning with the besieged from the Kohima Garrison.

Raan, overwhelmed with the past and overjoyed with the prospect the future promised, forgot the present and stepped out of the bunker casually to join the procession of tired defenders making a beeline to leave the garrison. There were a few soldiers between him and Mongseng. Mongseng heard a shot wringing through the valley. Something told Mongseng that the shot was personal; it was close, too close. He saw Raan waver, as he was about to join the haphazard queue. Mongseng ran towards Raan.

A couple of days earlier, a shell had landed on soft earth unexploded and saved the soft-hearted Raan from an untimely death. This time it was a bullet, a solid lead piece that didn't have a choice to veer away from its set trajectory. Its destiny to pierce through Raan's heart was already written by the Japanese sniper when he pressed the trigger. Mongseng looked around helpless, holding Raan's lifeless body cradled in his arms. Chetri came running and engulfed Mongseng and Raan's limp head. The face that was always bright, always welcoming when Chetri saw him, was now a question mark. Raan's eyes and mouth were wide open. The expression on the lifeless face seemed to question Chetri, why me? Why did I have to fall when everyone else was going home? Chetri, the pure blood Gorkha, broke down.

Blood and tears mixed in with Mongseng's tattoos. Mongseng trembled inside. His grief was deep. Raan was someone he had considered a brother, a younger brother whom he had to protect. Two weeks in confined, life threatening shared space had created a bond as thick as blood. And now the blood dripping from Raan over his arm and mixing into the muddy earth was taking away that bond, drop by drop. Every drop dripping out of Raan infuriated Mongseng. For him, to kill a retreating warrior from a battlefield was backstabbing.

In a daze, Mongseng's eyes looked only for one object. They wanted to find his brother's killer. His vision pierced through the groups of retreating soldiers and scanned the rubbled landscape beyond the garrison perimeters. He saw nothing moving, except what little was assisted to move by a mild breeze. A few dry, dead leaves rolled around on the ravaged earth. The collar of a dead soldier's shirt fluttered as if it was trying hard to fly away from its dead, stiff, owner. A piece of paper, probably a love letter written by a dead lover to his dearest, floated around as light as the dead soldier's soul.

Then the scanning eyes spotted a movement that couldn't have been caused by the mild breeze – a sheet of tin shifted in the Commissioner's rubble. Mongseng's eagle vision caught a pair of fearful eyes darting around in the darkness. He let Raan's head drop into Chetri's arms. With one swift movement he raised and along with him his spear, which simultaneously flew out cutting through the damp, death-soaked air of the Kohima Garrison, flying across the hazy sun and pierced through the tin sheet, that had moved independent of the breeze. The spear pierced into a skull in which resided the pair of fearful eyes that had met Mongseng's. A pair of eyes that were minutes ago taking aim to send that bullet into Mongseng's none blood related brother, to spill his blood and rip him away from the procession escaping the life devouring conflict.

A hundred witnesses that saw Mongseng's last kill in the battlefield thanked him silently. He picked up Raan from Chetri's cuddling arms and moved away from the thankful eyes whose lives he might have saved just as they were, like Raan, stepping out from the cage of death that was the garrison of Kohima, which had been under siege from the 5th of April 1944 till that day of the 18th of April 1944. Thirteen unlucky or lucky days of captivity, depending on who was walking out and who stayed buried or cremated within the garrison.

Mongseng walked towards the Advance Dressing Station

with Raan's lifeless body straddled over his back. Chetri followed behind. Bheema, his remaining soldier joined the procession of evacuees. As the pair climbed the incline towards ADS, they saw Tom heading in their direction. Tom spotted the familiar duo walking towards him and wasn't sure what Mongseng was lugging on his back. As they came closer, he vaguely guessed what Mongseng might be carrying. He went towards them with hastened steps. He reached them with questions, "What happened to Raan? Is he, is he...?"

Tom couldn't dare to finish his question. He hugged the dead body. The body that would have skipped a heartbeat, had Tom hugged it so warmly when it had a beating heart. Sudden remorse engulfed Tom. Regret encircled him for not showing his warmth when Raan was alive and so deserving. He regretted not going through with his hug in the morning when Raan had relayed the news of the breaking of the siege to him. He remembered the disappointment he saw in Raan's eyes then, when Tom had stiffened away. Tom finally let go of his Captainship and sobbed. With death Raan broke the barrier between *Sahib* and servant. Between white master and brown batman.

"*Saahab,* you must control yourself." Chetri consoled, wiping a tear from his own undisciplined eyes.

Chetri's words pricked Tom like needles. He swung around, "What for? Why? What's this bloody war given us? What have I been able to do staying under control? I...I...should have..."

His words exhausted, he breathed heavily and came around to his senses. Looking up at Chetri, he asked, "Was it a sniper?"

Chetri merely nodded his head and then added, "Mongseng got the sniper, proper. He threw his spear and split his head." Chetri almost took delight in passing him that information.

Mongseng broke in, "No more. No more die. Enough dead. Come, we go, no more see enemy, no more kill enemy, no more we die. Come."

Tom and Chetri followed his lead. Mongseng took them to the Dimapur road, but instead of following behind the evacuating soldiers, he crossed over and went down the slope. Tom and Chetri didn't question where he was leading them, something told them it was not for them, Mongseng was walking for the dead man straddled across his back. They stumbled through rocks and loose soil, then through bushes and shrubs. At length they reached a stream, out of sight from the evacuating soldiers or enemy. Mongseng laid Raan on the bank of the stream and drank some water bending down on his arms, drinking like a tiger. Tom scooped some with his helmet. Chetri drank by scooping some in his cupped palms.

Once his thirst was quenched, wiping his mouth and pointing at Raan's still body, Mongseng declared, "We find cave or tree hole and put him there. Give his death respect."

"We don't give respect to the dead by putting them in a tree burrow, Mongseng." Chetri dismissed his suggestion.

"How you know how his clan respect the dead?" Mongseng queried.

"Because he is Hindu, I know."

"What Hindu?"

"You pray stone, river, fire. We also pray same and have Gods for each."

"Oh. You Hindu like him?"

"Yes, he me same, same. We both are Hindu..." After a pause Chetri added, "He was."

"How you Hindu pay respect to dead?"

"We burn their body."

"Oh." Mongseng frowned, "Then we pay respect to Raan, we also burn him."

"Here?" Tom, who was till now a bystander to their conversation, echoed Chetri's question.

"Yes, you wait. I go, come get wood." Mongseng had already disappeared into the thicket before either of them could add anything further on the matter.

Mongseng made six trips to haul enough dry wood for Chetri to prepare a comfortable bed for Raan. They placed him on the pier and piled some more wood on top. Then Chetri went to the stream and scooped some water into his helmet and went around Raan's funeral pier sprinkling water on it with his right hand fingers while reciting Sanskrit *slokas*. The *slokas* he knew, he was not sure if they were appropriate for a funeral, yet he felt he had to recite something for the safe passage of the soul of his departed friend. While Chetri recited the *slokas*, Mongseng made a torch to light the pier by tying clumps of dry grass and moss around a sturdy pine brunch. He smeared the torch with some pine resin so that it burnt well and sustained the flame. He watched Chetri and hoped that he wouldn't sprinkle too much water on the funeral pier and make it damp.

Chetri let the none-Hindu, none-blood-related, none-culturally affiliated brother of Raan, to light the pier. A breeze blowing through the valley ignited the fire and took Raan along with it on to his next journey. Within a couple of hours the pier was reduced to smouldering pieces of red charcoal. The three men paid their last respects in their own ways – two moving their right hands across their bodies forming different religious symbols and recited hymns and *mantras*, and the other made sounds so deep from his body that it resonated the very sounds of the stream they were standing by and the wind blowing through. Chetri took his water canteen and filled some smouldering ash into it with a stick. The rituals complete, they hiked down towards the curving Dimapur road and came out ten miles from Tennis Court.

The ten miles they travelled from the battlefield, cradled amidst the womb of the forest, seemed like they had crossed seven seas and reached a place where there was no battle going on behind their backs. It was a thoroughfare of friendly soldiers. There were soldiers guarding the road, there were stalls setup by soldiers with water and food, there were truckloads of fresh soldiers and supplies passing by, on their way from Dimapur to the garrison and the returning trucks carrying the battle worn soldiers from the garrison to Dimapur. The relieving troops saw the garrison defenders as heroes, but they found it hard to place their perception of heroes upon that ragtag bunch of unwashed, unshaven soldiers in tattered, soiled clothes. Hence, the new soldiers coming in the trucks from Dimapur cheered and greeted the defenders returning to Dimapur with shouts and smiles that were mixed with pride and pity.

Tom waved down a truck returning to Dimapur and the three climbed aboard. Mongseng rode on a motorized vehicle for the first time. He would have savoured the experience a lot more did he have his friend Raan by his side; sitting, not as ash strung across his shoulder inside a water canteen to quench the thirst of loss for his family. In the ten-mile walk through the forest, Mongseng was debating in his mind whether to return to Poilung or be in the foreign world a while longer. Raan's blood and Tom's tears sipping into Mongseng's skin, acted like glue pulling him along deeper into the foreign world.

The dead go away, leaving a perceived burden of responsibility on the living.

EIGHTEEN

CHETRI HELD THE LADDER WHILE HIS ELDEST SON BALANCED on it and hammered the last nail. On his ancestral house in Bahadurpur, the silver corrugated iron roof shone. For Chetri, the hammering of the roof was in so many ways significant. Many years ago sheets of tin had led him from these tranquil surroundings and eventually into the middle of hell. The rhythm and crack of the hammer reminded him of the bolting of a 303 rifle while loading a bullet into the chamber. An otherwise talkative man, Chetri turned quiet whenever someone asked him about the war. Soon after the war, he had retired from his commission with the Assam Rifles. Being ex-army, he was entitled to a gun, but the only metal or wood implement he ever picked up again was his plough. The only things he killed were weeds around his favourite fruit trees, and mosquitos in the monsoon. His children came to know of the war only through second-hand sources. A doting husband and father, he never raised his voice or hand. Although, once when he heard his son read his history lesson aloud, he flew into a rage. When his son mentioned the Great War of 1914, Chetri shouted, "No war is great! Wars only kill! Never, never again will you ever call it the Great War! Understood?!"

The chirping of birds and the clicking of beetles restored Chetri to the present. He had returned with his wife, Chandrika and eldest child from Assam to settle for life in his ancestral village of Bahadurpur. Their daughter was born in the first spring they spent in Bahadurpur as husband and wife. Chetri locked up Kohima into the deep recesses of his mind. He never talked about it to anyone.

Since two years, Sandra's Conway was gathering dust in a corner of the attic in their tea estate bungalow. After the war she could never find beauty through its lenses. In the trees around the bungalow a great multitude of songbirds were tweeting. Sandra wasn't swimming in their river of music. She was focused on something less melodious. She was supervising three housemaids who were by her side, each with a dusting cloth, broom and a bucket of water to make the sitting and dining rooms spick and span for a visit by a neighbouring tea estate manager and his wife. It were the small details Sandra was focused on. Bits that an Indian house cleaner considered a part of furniture, when left to clean unsupervised. To her European eyes, those specks of dust stood out like festering wounds.

Clearing away dirt from nooks and crannies in teak wood sofa sets, clearing streaks of dust accumulated under photo frames on the shelf over the fireplace, which their friends from the battlefield had sent. Getting her silver cutlery polished and shone till they glittered like stars. Scrubbing dirt, tidying minor mess was a way to clear her mind. It was sort of a hobby she picked up on weekends, a habit that developed after her return from Kohima. Cleaning kept her mind busy; she hoped it would wipe clean the memories that kept her awake at night. The scar of war was a stubborn wound that only an ointment of time would eventually heal.

However, those thoughts of gloom came to Sandra only over the weekends when she was away from work. On weekdays, after work, she was too tired to need any cajoling to fall asleep at night. After they returned to Tamulguri estate, she did what she thought she would never do. With help from doctor Robin she opened a hospital in the tea estate. It was the first hospital to be opened in Assam exclusively for the tea labourers. But she stopped being hands on as a nurse and became a trainer and inventory manager. She began training tea garden girls to become nurses, girls who didn't want to follow their parents into the hereditary profession of tea plucking. To Tom's annoyance, when they went for walks around the estate, labourers came running to talk to her while merely acknowledging his presence with a customary *saalam*. He was their manager; she was their guardian angel who was showing them a life beyond their generational confinement of tea estates.

Tom juggled the fresh news in the *Assam Tribune* and the stale news of a few old copies of the Indian *Statesman*, reclining himself in his favourite rocking chair, under the shade of a *bakul* tree. The daily *Assam Tribune* reached him every afternoon. It had to travel about one hundred and eighty kilometres from Guwahati, first by train, then by foot, then to reach Tamulguri Tea Estate by cycle. Twice a week, along with the *Assam Tribune*, the Indian *Statesman* also appeared. The *Statesman* was a daily too, but it had to travel almost a thousand kilometres from Calcutta, so half a week's papers came bundled up twice weekly.

That day, the *Assam Tribune* and three Indian *Statesman* had arrived together. The afternoon delivery was perfect for Tom, arriving at his office as he was just winding up for home. The delivery boy made it a point to be on time to save himself the trouble of cycling the extra two kilometres, to the *Sahab*'s bungalow. Although Tom lived in a nook of the world which not many people knew about, he liked to be informed. While immersed in worldly news, his driver scrubbed at the car, trying to bring it back to ship shape. For work he had his horses, but when Tom went to the club with Sandra he liked to travel in his Morris in style. In the two years since their return from the army, Tom had changed many drivers, but none could restore his Morris to her past glory. The present driver, even after hours of hard work to make her seem the ride of a *maharaja* on the exterior, couldn't make the engine return to its past glory. He switched on the ignition and the engine missed a stroke and let out a loud boom. The noise sent Tom flying out of his rocking chair, sending news from far and near all over the garden as he took cover behind the *bakul* tree's trunk.

Sandra tried forgetting the horrors by taking up the task to train people to heal. Tom tried forgetting the images from the battlefield by filling his head with news from the present. But every creak, every tic-tac out of the unexpected took him back into the battle field.

NINETEEN

FROM THE RAT HOLE IN KOHIMA, MONGSENG HAD MOVED INTO A tent in Dimapur. He wasn't too impressed with it. With all the wild animals that lived in and around the impenetrable jungle of Poilung, he didn't think a house made out of cloth would last very long in his village. His little cloth house was one amongst a row of such cloth houses next to a house where Tom and Sandra stayed along with other white men. That house was solid and big. Mongseng was impressed. It was so big; there was not a single plot of flat ground in Poilung big enough to fit that house. After their move, he hardly saw Tom. Sandra did come often to see him.

Seeing his curiosity about the Officers, Transit bungalow, Sandra took him around on a tour of it one day when all the officers, including Tom, were out for a briefing. Even before they entered the house Mongseng had a little accident. He banged his head on a transparent wall while trying to peer inside. He was surprised how sunlight could go in through the wall but his head couldn't. The tour of the house took them over half an hour. He didn't think a house could have so many rooms. In spite of so many sunny rooms inside the house, he was a little surprised why he had to stay in the little cloth house. Why his meals were brought in to his room and he was never invited to come in and share the meal Tom and Sandra had with the other white men in the gigantic dining room? It couldn't be that there was not enough space. The dining table around which the white people ate their meal was so long that at one sitting it could accommodate half the people of Poilung.

One afternoon after lunch when he was bantering around with a few batmen occupying his neighbouring tents, he was called into the officers' bungalow. It was a while after his tour of the big house that Tom eagerly invited Mongseng in to introduce him to a friend who had come visiting. Mongseng thought it was nice of Tom to introduce him to his friend.

"Come, Mongseng, come. Meet Captain Andrew. He is a good friend of mine just returned from fighting the Japs in Imphal."

"Hello, Mongseng, how do you do?" The captain called out in a patronising tone, as if he was speaking to a two-year-old.

Mongseng merely nodded in a friendly way and went and sat on the chair opposite the guest and his two hosts. The furniture in the common sitting room of the officers' bungalow was so arranged that all the sofas were on one side, next to the airy and bright floor-to-ceiling glass windows, except one single sofa placed against the opposite wall. That was the chair Tom insisted that Mongseng should sit on. The light coming through the windows made him dazzle in all his glory. His features, his tattoos stood out brightly in the light of the afternoon's slanting sun, making him a perfect specimen for display.

"So, Mongseng, I have heard a lot about you. I hear you were very helpful to Tom in the Battle of Kohima."

"Yes, we fight good, together."

"What are your plans now?"

"I don no. Maybe stay little more. After, go back my village."

Andrew turned towards Tom, "Oh, aren't you going to give him a job, my dear fellow?"

"Ah, he does do a few things around but his skills are nowhere near what I would expect from a batman or peon."

"I am sure he can be useful around your tea estate, when you wind up here. He looks capable."

Tom lowered his voice and answered, "Ah, you have to understand, Andrew. He comes straight from the jungle; I can't expect to teach him many tricks. I guess as long as he keeps us entertained, wouldn't that be enough of a job getting out of him?" As Tom and Andrew shared a chuckle, Sandra shifted uncomfortably in her seat.

While Tom assumed his whisper didn't travel to Mongseng, he forgot that Mongseng's sharp ears could travel to his whispers.

Mongseng had the answer to why his instinct had been agitated and telling him to leave all the while he stayed with them. He followed Tom and Sandra into their world pulled first by Raan's death; the emotions attached to his death seemed to have disappeared from Tom the moment the flask containing his ash was sent away to Raan's family. Later, only curiosity kept Mongseng hooked. To Tom, Mongseng had become nothing more than a museum piece. An antique he could take out of his display case from the backyard to show off to his guests. Mongseng calmly sat through the disgrace. He had seen enough of how they lived. He had no intention of letting anyone dictate how he lived. That very evening he merged into the shadows of the night and disappeared.

When you lived as one with Nature, everyone and everything shares similar qualities – birds, animals and men. Mongseng's natural homing ability directed him from the army camp in Dimapur. First he headed to Kohima. He was pleased to see what just a few months of peace did to Kohima. Once humans were done with their act of hatred, Nature had taken over the bomb ploughed battlefields and again covered her with an abundance of bushy green. The raped landscape was slowly transforming back to virgin green.

The bow-shaped branch of the rhododendron tree pointed Mongseng towards the cave in Aradura Spur. As he removed the rock concealing the long and narrow cave, he was worried that somebody might have stolen his prized possessions, as there was no stench. As his eyes adjusted to the darkness, there they were sitting for him glowing white. All the heads now looked the same, there was no way to distinguish them as Japanese or Naga or British; they were reduced to mere skulls. He smiled. His worry of taking home too many Japanese heads was gone.

Mongseng went and collected rattan vines and wove baskets out of them and packed the skulls into the baskets. With two sturdy bow-shaped branches he built a sledge and piled the baskets on. Keen to get home, he was aware of his precious yet unconventional cargo, so walked at night and slept during the day. Also, he did not want to bump into other Naga warriors who might fancy the heads for themselves.

It took ten moons to reach Poilung. At seeing Mongseng the whole village knew no bounds to their joy, except a few whose interests didn't tally with his return. One of those few was Sangting. When there was no news of Mongseng for months, Padre assumed his hurdle in the village was removed forever. Since the deadline of a year to collect the most number of heads between the two brothers was almost over, Padre had hastened the process and instated Sangting as the new *Wangba*. When Mongseng arrived, the village was overjoyed to see him – trailed by his bounty of forty-five heads. Meailing, who had thought her husband might never return, was overjoyed, especially when she spotted the mountain of heads. He had left Poilung a little meek. She was proud to see her husband return as a tiger again. In a tight embrace they melted into each other, the sound of their heartbeats syncing together. In their happiness, time stood still.

Without delay, a feast was organized along with singing and dancing to celebrate Mongseng's return and honour his hunting expedition. That night, songs were sung praising his bravery, dancers mimicked his hunting prowess. It was a celebration organised to such a scale that a festivity as grand was never seen before in Poilung. It was befitting the bounty of heads. On one single occasion that big a bounty of forty-five heads had never been collected in Poilung even by their whole troop of warriors, let alone by a single warrior. Everyone came dressed in their best beads, tusks, fur, feathers and skins. Even the youngest of children were washed and dressed for the occasion. The merriment continued throughout the day and night, and it spilled into the next day that became days and turned into a weeklong celebration. The smell of spilled rice beer prevailed over the air of Poilung for months.

Once every man returned to his senses, and the women were done cooking, cleaning, singing, dancing and resting, the village gathered together for the ceremony to crown the new *Wangba*. There was no protest or contest to instate Mongseng as the new *Wangba* of Poilung. Saningla, the oldest queen mother, brought the crown. It was woven from the finest cane, covered with black bear fur and decorated with *mithun* horns on each side, wild boar tusks in the front and a circle of hornbill feathers adorning its back. As she raised the crown towards Mongseng's head, he smiled and stopped her from putting the crown on him. Instead, he took it from her hands and re-crowned Sangting who had just stood up from the *Wangba's* wooden throne to relinquish his claim. A collective hush rose amongst the crowd. But none dared to raise their voice against the decision of the slayer of fifty-five heads.

The sixteen days of slaughter that Mongseng witnessed in Kohima made him realize one thing – absolute power was evil. Whenever the Japanese or the British had an upper hand in the battle, both sides behaved in similar manner. By crowning Sangting as the *Wangba,* Mongseng took away the jealousy Sangting felt towards him. Relinquishing the *Wangba's* post restored brotherly love. Mongseng became the elder brother that Sangting revered and look up to in the daily matters of governing Poilung. By refusing the throne Mongseng received a higher place in the villagers' eyes. He became a higher appellate authority over and above the *Wangba,* not by vote but by choice.

Sitting on the fence Mongseng had a bird's eye view of Poilung; from there he could see everything and maintain the balance.

EPILOGUE

ANGSEN RECEIVED A CALL IN THE TEACHERS' COMMON ROOM during a break from lecturing students of History. He had to go to Poilung a second time within the month his grandfather had summoned him first. This time he had to go to attend his grandfather's funeral.

It was an apt time of the year. Mongseng lived till the ripe age of ninety-three and passed away when the paddy fields were ripe with golden husked red sticky rice. The village organized a grand feast to send Mongseng off, cooked with the fresh harvest.

Mongseng was a Nature worshipper and till his last breath, he stayed true to his beliefs and tradition.

When Angsen saw him in a coffin inside a church, he knew his grandfather wouldn't want to go on his next journey that way. Angsen wanted to give him a burial befitting the life his grandfather lived. But by now, traditional burials had become extinct. Being a history teacher, Angsen felt guilty that he taught his students the history of the world, yet he didn't know much about his family's past, and dead traditions. With a heavy heart he agreed to bury his grandfather with Christian rituals. The rituals that tried to conquer Mongseng all his life, won at his death.

After the surviving members of the family returned from his service, Angsen's grandmother, Meailing, anticipated the question on his mind.

Smiling, she said, "It was time that changed our Konyak ways, not the Padre. Once you take off a man's head, he looks and becomes the same as any other man."

With that comment she pointed towards the moss-covered skulls on display at the morung. His grandfather's collection from the Second World War was displayed alongside his local collection of heads. Angsen knew his grandfather's bounty of Japanese heads was forty-five, and he had killed ten before he went to fight in the Second World War. In his grandfather's collection of heads from the locality Angsen counted eleven.

Seeing his surprise, his grandma winked at him with a childish grin and continued grinding betel nut in her ancient mortar – 'thuk...thuk...thuk...' the valley reverberated with its sound.

ACKNOWLEDGEMENTS

THIS BOOK IS MORE COLOURFUL BECAUSE, IN 2014, THE *WANGBA* (village chief) of Hamphui and his fellow village elder-men – Nagaland's last surviving headhunters – opened their hearts and homes to me and offered insights not formerly on record. It was also a pleasure to meet P. Atuo Mezhur, trustee of the Kohima War Cemetery and managing director of Mezhur High School, who provided valuable insights into the role of the Nagas in the 1944 Battle of Kohima. My gratitude also to Susan Bayer (Ma Anand Nirmala) for reading through the initial draft; and Manimugdha S. Sharma, editor at the *Times of India*, for aiding the factual accuracy of the book. To my editors at Pan Macmillan India, Dr Prasun Chatterjee, Teesta Guha Sarkar and Isha Banerji, thank you for allowing the book to evolve to its final form. To my mother, Joya Chaliha Bardalaye, my love and gratitude for always allowing me to be curious. And my deepest love and gratitude to my wife, Dr Susie Colles, for being the first pair of eyes to see my work and direct and redirect my pen until finally the words become fluid.